THE
HALF
BROTHER

THE HALF BROTHER

CHRISTINE KEIGHERY

Published in 2023 by Ultimo Press,
an imprint of Hardie Grant Publishing

Ultimo Press
Gadigal Country
7, 45 Jones Street
Ultimo, NSW 2007
ultimopress.com.au

Ultimo Press (London)
5th & 6th Floors
52–54 Southwark Street
London SE1 1UN

    ultimopress

 A catalogue record for this
work is available from the
National Library of Australia

The Half Brother
ISBN 978 1 76115 150 7 (paperback)

Cover design Christabella Designs
Cover images Sky by oleshko andrey / Shutterstock; man by Cloudi / Shutterstock; both women by Cloudi / Shutterstock; house by stevecoleimages / Getty Images
Typesetting Kirby Jones | 11.5/18.5pt Sabon LT Std
Copyeditor Dianne Blacklock
Proofreader Pamela Dunne

10 9 8 7 6 5 4 3 2 1

Printed in Australia by Griffin Press, an Accredited ISO AS/NZS 14001 Environmental Management System printer.

 The paper this book is printed on is certified against the Forest Stewardship Council® Standards. Griffin Press holds chain of custody certification SCS-COC-001185. FSC® promotes environmentally responsible, socially beneficial and economically viable management of the world's forests.

Ultimo Press acknowledges the Traditional Owners of the Country on which we work, the Gadigal People of the Eora Nation and the Wurundjeri People of the Kulin Nation, and recognises their continuing connection to the land, waters and culture. We pay our respects to their Elders past and present.

To Helen Louise Keighery.
Sisters forever.

PART ONE

SEDUCTION

CHAPTER ONE

Hannah canvassed the room, aware of the irony of her students' rapt attention. She was teaching 'The Love Song of J. Alfred Prufrock'. It was the poem that best suited the intimacy of a tutorial. The passion, the fire with which she recited – it had all been genuine once. She had been so young when she first ingested the old man. Now the performance was skin deep. Change volumes and tempo, cue to stay still and cue to move. Every year, it was the same. And every year the tutorial room, with its grey plastic chairs and muted yellow tables, came alive.

There was a pause after she finished. One of the students clapped. Bethany of the smooth, olive skin. Half her head was shaved, the other half shoulder-length hair, dark and shiny. A tattoo snaked down her neck. Hannah couldn't place it exactly, but it was obviously some kind of mythical beast. It would be an interesting piece to sport in later years when the scales would be rendered authentic by the aging process.

Another student joined in the applause. Ethan? Ewan?

He was really putting his back into it. He was likely one of those who'd arrived fresh and enthusiastic from his gap year, having done Thailand and Vietnam. He caught Hannah's eye and held her gaze. He broke away first, but it was enough to suggest that his view of her extended beyond the teacher–student model.

He was handsome too, in a generic slim, sensitive way. His beard was slogging it out with some degree of success. The aesthetics were pleasing until a smile revealed crooked teeth that any good parent would have dealt with in adolescence. Her own had been on to it, of course. No Fidler daughter was going to reach adulthood with crooked teeth. The old steel-trap braces had played havoc with her confidence, but she was grateful now.

The two-person ovation looked set to take hold, then petered out. Students recorded essay questions on various devices. His name was definitely Ethan. Hannah confirmed it from a printed essay on the table in front of him. 'The Stanislavski Method'. So one of his other majors was drama. Hannah would have guessed right had she been inclined to guess.

'Where are you off to?' Ethan asked, staying back after the others.

'My office,' Hannah replied, slipping her laptop into its case.

'Can I walk with you? Maybe discuss the poem?'

She nodded. For a moment, she was tempted to give him her laptop to carry. Those impulses, the testing of the waters, were coming frequently of late. Probably had something to do with flipping over to the wrong side of forty. She predicted he would be surprised, but he would take it. She resisted.

The air outside was bracing. Wind whistled between the two buildings.

'You're an inspiring lecturer,' he said, parallel talk making him brave. 'You care.'

It was actually quite disarming, the way he said it. Hannah was almost convinced he was right. They wound around a corner. Rex's office was on the fifth floor of the Language and Literature building. He could be looking down at them right now. Perhaps he could see them through the leaves of the fern on his desk in front of the bay window? Hannah breathed in the idea, feeling it expand in her chest.

Ethan was talking. There was some cliché about passion being infectious. He was drinking her in as he spoke. She was conscious of her lean, muscular body, fit from all those circuit sessions. It was subtle but still evident under her grey cashmere jumper and black linen trousers. She felt the faint swish of her sandy hair against the small of her back.

If Rex was looking down, would he see her through Ethan's eyes? Maybe it would stir something in him? Hannah willed Ethan to keep his head level so Rex wouldn't get a glimpse of his teeth.

'My mum works in a supermarket. She's been there for years, says she likes the security of it. I reckon it's more important to find something you're truly into.'

Was he comparing Hannah to his mother? It didn't really matter anymore. The bubble had burst.

'What would you like to do after you finish your course?' Hannah asked like a proper lecturer, not a forty-one-year-old temptress. She didn't add 'when you grow up', though it was on the tip of her tongue.

'I want to be a triple threat. Write, act and direct,' he said, and though he was trying for a casual drawl, his enthusiasm practically barked. 'When you do it all, you kind of get artistic control, you know? Like, other people might be better actors or directors. But you're the only person who can make it happen the way it was born in your mind. Most likely it would be theatre, but it could be movies. Just not your commercial, bullshit ones.'

It was definitely enough for today. Hannah took her leave.

•

'Jesus, Rex, you scared me.'

He was at her office door with his lurking face on. Looking scruffier than usual. His white shirt was untucked on one side above his camel chinos. There was strain on the middle buttons from his paunch. His salt and pepper hair was fluffed up. Hannah suspected he'd been napping in his office, on his deluxe chair in front of the bay window. Eyes closed and Ethan-oblivious.

There was about the same age gap between Hannah and Rex as there was between her and Ethan.

'Ooh, you spook too easily, Han.' His smile showed teeth. Rex had lovely teeth. 'I've just been enjoying watching you work.'

She hadn't seen him much during the week. He'd been on a bit of a bender. Not the extreme kind – he'd come home every night in a good enough state to brush those lovely teeth. But mostly Hannah had been asleep.

'Are you making your way to the Burrow tonight?' he asked.

He wasn't being cruel. Rex didn't do cruel. It was just a little inside joke about Hannah's family. Her mum and dad lived in Burwood, and their lives were burrow-like. Their three-bedroom brick veneer was the same house (with moderate updates) that Hannah and her younger sister, Stef, had grown up in. They rarely saw the need to come into town.

Hannah had escaped, literally and figuratively. But Stef lived just a few blocks from their parents with her two kids. Though she'd tried to tuck herself cosily inside the suburban archetype, Stef's burrow-building hadn't proved quite as airtight. Hannah had tried to tell her sister that high school sweethearts rarely made it long term. That was before Stef dressed up in white lace and tulle and took on Liam's surname as though the two of them could merge entirely. They must have bored each other to death towards the end. There would hardly have been an uncharted corner in their minds for the other to discover.

Still, despite the implosion of their nuclear family (one boy, one girl), Stef had stayed in the area. She worked on the floor of some furniture barn where the couches were modular and the coffee tables looked like spaceships. Stef relied on their parents to help with the kids. The social fabric of her Burwood existence hadn't completely collapsed.

'Dinner at Mum and Dad's every second Friday,' Hannah reminded Rex. 'Like clockwork.'

Rex's mother was dead. He spoke to his father on the phone sporadically. He sat on the office chair next to Hannah's and spun it like he was young and spinning an office chair was still thrilling.

'I'm not going to make it tonight, Han,' he said, stopping the spinning and looking into her eyes. His own were clear blue, rimmed with red. Hannah wanted to kiss them. 'I've got PhD students who need some time.'

She nodded. She and Rex weren't co-dependent. They assessed and reassessed their relationship on the basis of ongoing merit instead of hurtling on conventionally. Rex was not duty-bound to go with her tonight, even if it was her mother's birthday. If there was a small feeling of annoyance creeping up Hannah's spine, she recognised it as a default setting. An indoctrination she could easily reason away. And he was genuine about his students in a way Hannah could only aspire to.

'I've got something for your mum though,' he said. He stood up to get his briefcase from the hallway. There was a lot of foot traffic from students and maintenance people today, but Rex didn't believe in theft. Or at least he regarded it as a freak circumstance. He chose not to dwell on it when their townhouse was robbed. Hannah handled the insurance claim.

Rex retrieved the briefcase, fished out something and gave it to Hannah. It was an old book, covered in red leather with little tears and rips along its spine. *The Christopher Robin Verse Book*. The frontispiece had been signed by the illustrator: E. H. Shepard, 1 October, 1963. Rex knew about Marg's obsession with A. A. Milne. Hannah and Stef had been raised on his books. Rex was a good listener. When he was present.

Hannah rolled her eyes and shook her head. Having no sons of her own, Marg was predisposed to cherishing her daughters' partners. She was going to be swept off her feet by this, even in Rex's absence.

'You piece of work,' she said with a grin. 'I only got her a lipstick.'

CHAPTER TWO

Stef let the engine idle as she watched Liam, her ex-husband. He walked through the side gate and lifted the brick, but of course the key wasn't there. The kids dropped their school bags and climbed onto the play equipment in the backyard. Heath stood on a plastic swing, lifting one leg to create a challenge as he lurched forward. Rosie slumped on the other swing. She was wearing a pink fluorescent skirt Stef hadn't seen before. Tacky.

Even from a distance, Stef could see Rosie was distressed. Her guess was that Lara had been excluding her again. It seemed that her best friend's star was ascending in the last weeks of primary school while Rosie's was plummeting. Stef hadn't quite pegged it, but it definitely had a lot to do with who was going where for high school. A couple of weeks back, Lara had invited some kids over to her place for a 'gathering'. Rosie wasn't one of them.

But a guess was just a guess. It was exhausting, especially after a demanding day. Her bosses really leaned on her expertise to keep them up to pace with what was happening in their category at the Furniture Gallery. Being the only one who could make the displays look professional as well as advising customers was a big responsibility, especially on top of pretty much all the ordering.

But a lot could change in Rosie's world in a week with her dad and Prue. Stef would just have to catch up. Again.

A flush of guilt rose through her. Maybe she shouldn't have taken the key. In theory, the kids had their own, but they were frequently missing in action. The spare key was backup. But Stef didn't want Liam to have access to it, just like that. He'd been in the house before, without the kids. Stef could tell. He'd been snooping too. The pile of bills on the spike in the kitchen had changed order. He'd put butter in the pantry again, like he did when they were together. She'd had to make it clear after that – no more waiting for the kids inside. It was her house now. The theory was their lives should be separate.

Liam undid his zip and pissed against the lemon tree.

Stef switched off the ignition and got out. She paused on the front porch then walked down the hallway, opening the glass sliding door to the backyard.

Heath leaped off the swing and into her arms. Stef kissed him, pushing his cheeks together. He let her. She wondered whether it was a sign of regression, being the child of a fractured family.

Rosie stood up, watching. A girl island. That's what Hannah had called her once, nailing Rosie's demeanour with words Stef could never think up in a million years.

'How are you, honey?' Stef asked.

'Hungry,' Rosie replied. Even that was reluctant. She kicked at a tuft of grass.

'What happened to the spare key?' Liam asked.

Heath scooted between them into the house, already pushing the 'on' button of the PlayStation. Rosie disappeared down the hallway to her bedroom. Liam paused for a moment then moved to follow the kids inside. Stef stepped sideways to block him.

'Oh, don't be ridiculous,' he said. He moved past her into the kitchen. All the walls, bar one, were duck-egg blue. Liam hadn't finished that job. Surprise, surprise.

'What do you need to tell me?' Stef countered.

Liam rolled his eyes. 'It's the Book Week Parade on Monday. Come as your favourite character. The kids tell me you haven't organised their costumes yet? I could get Prue to do it, I suppose.'

'I'm not sure Barbie and Ken are what they're looking for,' Stef said.

Liam tried for a scoff, but she could see the corners of his mouth turn upwards.

'Heath has catch-up homework. Rosie has been a pain in the arse.'

'Why?'

'I think it might be genetic.'

Stef took a deep breath and counted to ten like her counsellor taught her.

'You gotta get me a key, Stef. It just makes sense,' Liam said softly. Ever the reasonable parent. 'Mind if I get a beer?'

It wasn't a request. He was opening the fridge door before she could answer. She poured herself a glass of white. The longer he stayed, the less clarity she could muster.

'Just one drink,' she told him. 'I'm taking the kids out.'

Liam folded some newspaper and put it under the table's rickety leg before he even put the beer down. When he sat, it was in his old chair.

'Ah. Friday night, Marg and Jim's. Jeez – it's Marg's birthday, isn't it?'

The sun was setting. Stef had put a lot of work into the backyard since he'd gone but ghosts of their old life together lived between the shadows. The stringybark tree had been cut down but the willow bottlebrush planted in its place still looked like a stand-in. Shards of light came through the hole in the paling fence. Reminders of how bad their relationship had become towards the end. The incremental slow slide followed by the grand shove.

Thank God no one knew. There was a moment when Stef had been bursting, about to pour it all out to Hannah. But then big sis had gone all fount of wisdom about how she and Liam were stuck in a holding pattern because they'd been together since they were teenagers. Pretty rich for Hannah to assume she knew it all when it came to relationships. She'd started her first serious one with Rex at bloody thirty-eight. And despite Hannah trying to sell it as 'evolved', it seemed pretty much all on his terms.

As a teen, Stef had envied her friends with older siblings. The luckiest ones had brothers. Older brothers who could help make sense of the rules of their species. Sisters could be okay too, as long as they actually had a clue. Her own always had her head stuck in a book. Smart at school, dumb at life. Hannah could stick her fount of wisdom.

There was no way she'd share the ugliness of her marriage breakdown with her parents either. Marg and Jim had no yardstick for marital strife. The worst Stef had ever witnessed between them was a gruff word here and there. Small annoyances that were resolved quickly and in full.

So she'd managed to keep the details to herself.

Stef noticed a silhouette at the opening between the hallway and the lounge. It had the beginnings of breasts. It was Rosie.

'Are we going to Gran and Pop's?' she asked.

In relative terms, her tone was eager. Stef exchanged a collusive glance with Liam. Rosie was hanging on to childhood, but look away and it might be gone forever.

Stef had a sudden sense of Rosie being held above stormy waters by the strong arms of her grandparents. They were there, always. With practical help. With pick-ups and dinners and baths and pep talks. They were the port in the storm.

'Prue got this skirt for me, Mum,' Rosie said.

'It's lovely,' Stef lied.

'Prue's a loser. I hate it.'

Rosie walked over and sat on Stef's knee. She lifted a sneakered foot onto her father's lap.

Stef could see Liam mulling it over, deciding not to reprimand Rosie's rudeness when she was on the cusp of a week with her mother. He was choosing his battles. It was a skill he could have developed earlier.

Both of them could have.

'Are Hannah and Rex going to Marg's birthday dinner?' Liam asked.

Christ, was there a whine in his voice? They were her parents, after all. You didn't get shared custody of parents. He was lucky they didn't know the half of what went on. They loved Liam, but in the end, blood was thicker than water.

'Hannah's coming. Not sure about Rex.'

'How are the Intellectual Giants?' Liam asked, taking the last swig of his beer.

When they were married, Stef and Liam often used that term to refer to Hannah and Rex. Having had shitty parents himself, Liam wouldn't hear a bad word about Marg and Jim, but Hannah and Rex were fair game. It was sport, mimicking the way they talked about lit-er-a-ture. Taking the piss out of the wanky statements about their unconventional relationship.

Now though, Liam's reference made Stef squirm. 'Hannah and Rex are fine.'

She got up from the table. How big did the hint need to be?

Bigger obviously, since Liam was behind her, taking a second beer from the fridge while she reached for the sauv blanc. She remembered him kissing the back of her neck in that other lifetime.

'I beat the game! I beat the game! I beat the game!' Heath did his victory dance across the lounge room carpet. Both arms up, skinny hips thrusting. He danced over to Stef, pushing his head into her belly for the victory hug.

'I'm going to tell Pop,' Heath ranted. 'He'll probably make me a ...' He paused, his mind ticking through the options. 'He'll make me a SWORD,' Heath said and at the mention of a weapon, even a toy one, neither parent dared to breathe.

But it was so gorgeous how he laughed.

She had to be careful with Heath around. If she got lost in his laughter, she might lose her grip on how she should feel about his father. Stef squinted so she could make out the hole in the back fence in the twilight.

Liam reached out. He touched Stef's cheek.

'You gotta get me a key,' he said again.

CHAPTER THREE

As she navigated the Friday evening traffic, Hannah felt the restlessness that visiting her old neighbourhood always brought. The Indian restaurant she passed offered a perfect example of her discomfort. Australian-flag bunting hung from the awning like an apology for being anything other than white middle class. Open gratitude for being tolerated. It was freaking tragic.

Everything around the hilly suburb was controlled. In her teens, the lack of public transport had felt like a conspiracy to keep her there. Trapped in the endless, facile dramas of her peers. The break-ups and make-ups she was supposed to care about, as though there was nothing outside their bubble, no wider world to explore except in a day trip.

Stef's teen years had been the opposite. Boys adored her. She was soft-edged while Hannah was sharp angles. Of course, Hannah had envied her ease, her curves. But Stef had bought the whole, insular package. When she and Liam got married, they didn't even consider other places to live.

Hannah had always fantasised about something else. Now she had it. A townhouse in Carlton. Job as a lecturer. Travel. Rex.

There had been a twenty-year reunion a few years back. Hannah couldn't quite believe how many of her old PLC and Scotch College acquaintances had either stayed put or gravitated back to the area. Though it certainly seemed there was a defensive edge to their collective choice.

'It's a good safe place to raise kids,' Leah Graves had told her, apropos of nothing. Her assertion seemed to attract a herd of ex-classmates to bleat their agreement.

'I understand what you mean,' Hannah had offered. 'Though of course, having children isn't a given.'

Leah, two down and one on the way, had looked at Hannah as though she was nuts. The others had backed away slowly.

Since she was running ten minutes late to pick up Stef and the kids, Hannah texted from the car. When she pulled up out the front, Rosie emerged from the house first.

Even in the semi-darkness, she looked different. Stef was an open book, so Hannah would know if Rosie had got her period. But the realisation that it wasn't far off was jarring. Little Rosie, their prickly tween.

'Hey, you,' Hannah greeted, giving her niece a quick hug as she slid into the passenger seat. 'You don't think your mum might want to sit in the front?'

'Mum won't care,' Rosie said firmly as Stef and Heath got in the back.

Hannah turned to her sister. Stef's eye roll said *don't ask*. She looked knackered. And like she'd stacked on weight, even just in the last fortnight. Working retail in that furniture barn place would be sedentary as well as banal. Stef wasn't one to exercise regularly. She loved her food too. The combination was showing – Stef looked set to burst out of her leopard-print wrap dress.

'I just beat my game, Han!' Heath announced. 'It took me two weeks. I'm a legend.'

Hannah wasn't big on kids, but God this one was cute. He was always bursting with the latest news. It was Heath's particular gift that the content never mattered as much as the delivery. Hannah high-fived him.

'Whatever,' Rosie mumbled.

•

The wrought-iron gates were open and the porch light on, timed for their arrival. The Fidlers had an aversion to showiness. The security surveillance sign on their neighbour's stucco fence was showy, in Marg and Jim's shared opinion. And pretty much all of their opinions were shared. It was also counterproductive – an indication there was something worth robbing.

As soon as Marg opened the door, Rosie barged through. 'Gran, can you take up my new school dress? Lara put a chalk mark on the right length,' she said, holding up foot traffic as she produced her PLC uniform for next year. Of course she was going to PLC, because Hannah and Stef went to PLC. That's what you did. Even if it meant the grandparents had to pay the fees.

'Well, hello to you too, Rosie,' Marg said, bypassing Hannah to give Stef a motherly, in-the-know wink that suggested the chalk mark might magically go south.

'I beat the game, Gran!' Heath cried, scooting around legs and under the school dress. 'I only had it for two weeks and—'

'Oh my God, loser. Can you shut up about that stupid game for one second?' Rosie's shrill voice flew into the house, luring Jim up the hallway to rescue his grandson.

Jim planted kisses on the tops of heads, starting with Hannah.

'Now Heath, matey,' he said, 'is this the game where you only had two more villains to defeat before you saved the world?'

Hannah watched their backs as they walked down the hallway and outside towards the shed, deep in discussion.

She kissed her mother's powdered cheek.

The hall was lined with photos. Marg and Jim had always been scrupulously even-handed. A baby photo of Hannah was paired with one of Stef. Hannah in her academic garb was followed by Stef's crowning glory – motherhood. Stef with Rosie as a toddler, Heath as a baby, with Liam's hand supporting baby Heath's head. But the portrait of Stef and Liam with the kids had been relegated to the second shelf of the bookcase in the lounge.

Further down, in a bold move of mixing up chronology, there was one of the Fidler family. Hannah must have been about six and Stef four. Hannah was a mini Marg, pale and fine-featured. Stef had her dad's colouring – olive skin and brown eyes.

'So, what happened to Rex?' Marg asked. 'I made his favourite slow-cooked lamb casserole. And a pavlova for dessert.'

'Yum, I'm starving,' Stef said.

'Hmm, my darling, I don't think so,' Marg responded, looking Stef up and down before walking towards the kitchen.

'Hmm, my darling, I don't think so,' Hannah whisper-echoed.

Stef rolled her eyes. 'Your turn will come,' she said and Hannah chuckled, because of course that was true. Little barbs designed to encourage self-improvement from Marg were as reliable as their dad's head kisses.

'Rex had two PhD students who needed extra time with him tonight, Mum,' Hannah replied, following her into the kitchen. 'Exams are coming up.'

Marg nodded. 'So what will Rex eat?'

Hannah glanced back. Stef and Rosie had already bagsed seats on the nearside of the table. This meant that Hannah would be relegated to the far side, heavy curtains weighing against her back whenever she moved. It was a familiar game of musical chairs and Hannah had lost.

'Yes, what will Rex eat?' Stef asked pointedly, leaning back on her chair. Hannah gave her the finger.

'Rex can cook, Mum. He doesn't need me to do it for him.'

'Easy, tiger,' Jim said, checking the scores of a footy game on the muted TV screen before switching it off. 'That kind of thing could be contagious.'

'Well, Rex is terribly dedicated, isn't he?' Marg replied, emerging from the kitchen with a casserole dish in one hand, rice in the other. The placemats were already down to protect the table. After they'd gone home, Marg would reset the table for tomorrow's breakfast. And so on, ad infinitum.

'Yeah, Rex is dedicated, Mum,' Hannah said, 'but he's also sorry he couldn't make it. He asked me to give this to you.'

Marg remained standing. She stroked the cover of the old book reverentially, then held it up for everyone to see.

'*The Christopher Robin Verse Book*,' Rosie said. 'We've read loads of those poems. Like "Halfway Down", right? And that guy also wrote *Winnie-the-Pooh*.'

'I wanna go to the Book Parade as Winnie the Pooh,' Heath said. 'How cool would that be?'

'If you go as Winnie the Pooh, I will literally kill you,' Rosie said. 'But wow, that book looks ancient.'

As everyone helped themselves to casserole, Marg opened the cover.

'Why are you making that face, Gran?' Heath asked.

Hannah, partially draped by floral curtains, looked over at her mother. Marg's hazel eyes looked strangely empty. As though her mind was suddenly somewhere else.

Her dad stood. He put his hand on Marg's shoulder and she started coming back to them. 'Honey, are you all right?' he asked. He helped lower Marg into her chair. Then he poured her a glass of water from the carafe on the table and handed it to her.

Marg took a sip. She wiped her mouth with a napkin. Slowly her eyes went back to normal. The feeling in the room didn't.

'I'm fine, love,' she said. 'But please, can you turn off the radiator? It's too hot in here.'

•

Jim and Marg walked them to the car as usual. They checked Heath's seatbelt and doled out plastic containers of leftovers, one for each daughter. Marg gave the largest one to Hannah with an offer to email her the recipe. She asked Stef if she'd like them to mind the kids over the weekend so she could squeeze in a hit of tennis or at least a long walk.

Things were back to normal.

Hannah pulled out and they travelled a couple of hundred metres before she stopped so Heath could retrieve a toy from the floor.

She adjusted the rear-view mirror. 'Look, Stef,' she said.

They watched as their parents held hands to cross the road.

'What? What is it?' Heath asked, his little neck swivelling. 'Oh, I know what you're looking at. Gran and Pop are holding hands.' He leaned forward. 'Like you and Dad used to do,' he offered.

'Yeah right, loser,' Rosie scoffed. 'Mum and Dad were the perfect, lovey-dovey couple. That's why they got divorced.'

Hannah could practically feel the arrow piercing Stef's heart. Rosie could be so brutal.

'Hang on, Rosie,' she said, 'there were loads of times your mum and dad were happy together.'

No matter how much her sister pissed her off sometimes, Hannah couldn't bear it when anyone hurt her.

Stef smiled weakly. Squeezed Hannah's leg.

'Whatever,' Rosie yawned.

'Hey, Han,' Stef said, already unhooking her bra as Hannah pulled up outside her house. 'Wanna have a sleepover?'

CHAPTER FOUR

S tef tried to stay in the moment and be with her daughter
wholly. To connect. Every now and then, a squeal from
Heath's room as Hannah read him a bedtime story would
distract her.

It wasn't that she didn't want to be there, in Rosie's room,
hearing her sombre confidences. And it was good not to be split
down the middle for a change, with either no kids while Liam
and Prue had them, or both kids together. It was rare to get
time to put Rosie to bed alone.

It was hard to focus properly though, as Rosie told her
about Lara's brand-new phone, not old and second-hand like
hers. Why she needed one herself. Et cetera. Rosie's sarcastic
comment about Liam and her being lovey-dovey ate away at
her. If their marriage had ultimately failed, did that mean it had
always been a failure? Or could she hold on to small credits
for the times she and Liam adored each other? In Rosie's eyes,
obviously not.

Stef flushed. Tuned back in enough to discover Rosie had
moved on from the phone and was now complaining about
being excluded from another gathering of the kids who were

going to the local high school. Stef itched to tell her that none of that would matter in six months. That she'd see the kids from primary school here and there, but in fact, primary school was such a small chapter of her life and soon this whole being excluded thing wouldn't matter.

But you had to pick your moments with Rosie. She could lose it. Which would mean Stef would have to calm her down. Which would mean a delay in getting to drink wine in the lounge with Hannah and find out what she'd made of the strange moment with their mother earlier. So she stroked Rosie's hair as she listened. And drifted.

'So, Mum, do you think Gran will actually take up the dress to where Lara marked it? I think she might cheat.'

'Sweetheart,' Stef said, 'maybe you could ask Esther over for a play since she's going to PLC too. You could keep each other company, at least at the beginning.'

Rosie drew in a breath. Stef could see her own nose on her child's face. It was a nice nose, smallish and subtle. It was something she'd always liked about her appearance, and she'd managed to pass it on. A small victory.

'Everything's going to change next year, isn't it, Mum?' Rosie asked. 'Again.'

Stef wasn't going to cry. 'A lot of things change, Rosie,' she said. 'Sometimes for the better.'

Rosie bit her lip. 'If it comes back wrong, we can fix it without Gran knowing,' she decided.

It took Stef a moment to realise Rosie was talking about the dress.

•

'Jesus, that kid's a treat,' Hannah said as they met up back in the lounge room. Stef handed her a glass of red. 'Heath has that figurine Dad's in the middle of making for him on his pillow. The thing hasn't even got a face yet, but you can tell it's pure love.'

Stef smiled. 'He'd be in that shed every day if he could. He wants it to look like some anime character he's obsessed with. Can't you just visualise the two of them, working away?'

Some feeling wafted through Hannah as she visualised Heath and their dad pottering in the shed together. A tenderness that seemed to hollow out her insides. She filled it with a slug of shiraz.

'It must be nice for him to have a boy around, finally,' she said. 'He was probably desperate to have a son, even though he'd never admit it. The poor guy had to make do with me.'

Stef grinned. 'Are you going to stay the night?'

'Sure,' Hannah said. 'I'll just let Rex know.' As she picked up her mobile to text, Hannah noticed the time. It was eleven fifteen. His reply came back almost immediately.

Ok x

You could be completely tanked and still manage that reply. You could still be at the pub, having traversed the few hundred metres to get there from the uni.

Or you could be at someone else's house. And if that were the case, it would go undetected. There would be no enquiry from Hannah.

'Mum's little dizzy spell was weird,' Stef said. 'Her eyes looked really strange. It was kind of scary, don't you think? I got the feeling it wasn't physical so much as, I don't know ... emotional.'

Stef was a good host. Hannah was relieved to see her glass filled almost to the brim this time. God, the couch was comfy. There was a softness to Stef. Always had been. She looked like a young Nigella Lawson. For a moment, Hannah considered letting things go a bit, putting on a couple of kilos.

'I actually wondered whether it had something to do with the book Rex gave her,' Stef continued.

Hannah pulled herself back to the conversation. She shook her head. Hannah, first born, was methodical. Where Stef just floated around ideas, rarely homing in properly. Even now, Hannah suspected that being inside her sister's head would be like a Caribbean cruise. If there was a causal link between the book and their mum's episode, Hannah would have figured it out.

'I don't see how it could have anything to do with the book, Steffie,' she said, 'but I agree it wasn't entirely physical either. Maybe you don't remember. Dad and I probably shielded you from it, but Mum had those ... turns when we were growing up. Sometimes they lasted for days. She'd just sort of retreat into herself. I remember going into their room and she'd be in bed, eyes open but not really seeing.'

Stef nodded but Hannah could tell the memory was vague for her. Stef, who always had attention from so many sources simultaneously, could cruise through periods of their mum's withdrawal. For Hannah, though, those times were frightening.

'Actually, I know what you might remember,' Hannah said, shifting position, almost splashing wine onto the couch. 'Those were the only times Dad was allowed in the kitchen. We'd have boiled eggs for dinner. Baked beans on toast. Or he'd make fish fingers and you'd have a meltdown?'

Hannah could see that sparked something. Stef didn't baulk at many foods, but she'd always hated fish fingers.

'It didn't happen often,' Hannah continued, 'but sometimes Mum kind of checked out. It used to spook me so much, but then she'd come back and things would be fine again.'

'Actually, I do remember,' Stef said. 'I'd go into Mum and Dad's bedroom to complain, because Mum knew I couldn't eat those things. And she just ...'

Hannah watched her sister remember. She wondered if everyone could read her so easily, or if it was just because they'd grown up together.

'She ... gave me this blank look, like she didn't know who I was. It freaked me out so much I forced down the fish fingers.'

'Yeah,' Hannah said. 'It wasn't just the once though. Dad used to reassure us that Mum just needed a rest. He advised us to leave her alone, that she'd be back with us when she was ready. And I know we haven't seen it for years, but perhaps Mum still needs that time every now and again. Sort of a mental health break she eventually emerges from at her own pace, and tonight was just a snapshot. It's not like Dad would tell us. He'd think it disloyal to mention.'

Stef's nod conceded the point. 'Still,' she said, 'it was definitely rare while we were growing up. Sometimes you have to go AWOL to save yourself. I get that now. As a mother.'

There were times Hannah had to draw reserves of patience from deep inside. People with children could be so simplistic. Approximating Marg's episode as parental burnout was so obvious, so lazy. Did it follow then that only women with children could experience malaise?

If she was more sober, Hannah might have argued the point. 'Steffie?' she said instead. 'I need to go to bed.'

CHAPTER FIVE

Hannah woke to an energetic Heath clambering over her with pointy knees and one hand (complete with figurine) raised in the air. He positioned himself between the sisters so that he was high on a pillow, looking down. Stef tried to pull the cover over her head.

'Come on, buddy. I'll make you breakfast,' Hannah whispered. As Heath crossed his arms, the faceless figurine found itself in a headlock. An impish smile crossed his face.

'No offence, Hannah, but I'll wait for Mum,' he said, tugging the covers off his mother mercilessly.

'Sorry, Stef. I tried to buy you a moment, but the child is incorrigible,' she said.

'Incorrigible!' Heath repeated. 'I am in-corrig-ible.'

It was another thing Heath did that was so endearing. Hannah had a sneaking suspicion that she may have triggered a new word crush for her nephew. It was the sound of it he liked obviously, since he hadn't asked for the meaning. It made Hannah think of all the word crushes she'd had as a child. Crushes she still developed from time to time.

Stef sat up, her head resting on her elbow. In her nighty, in the midmorning sunlight that streaked through the bedroom window, she looked tired and pudgy.

'Come on, guys. I'll make pancakes,' Stef said, up and pulling on a dressing-gown.

Hannah was figuring out how to say no to a fatty brunch when her phone pinged with a message from Rex.

Hannah Fidler, you are cordially invited to a seafood feast with Albie and Sonia. Venue: our place. Kick-off: 12 pm.

•

There was a lightness to Hannah's being as she opened her front door. A sense of relief that she'd avoided yet again being consumed by Burwood. But it was more than that. Waking up to Heath had put a spring in her step.

Hannah hung her bag on a peg in the hallway. She gazed down her sleek, minimalist hall with its blond floorboards. Midway, the sun streamed in through the skylight. At the end of the hallway was the kitchen, the stainless-steel bench and white stools she and Rex had picked the week they'd bought the house. The courtyard was cement slabs and shiny black pebbles. Six yuccas lined the sides, three to each, evenly spaced. It was the antithesis of Stef's jungle.

Yes, there had been an undeniable flutter as she drove home. A small feeling of irritation, or something resembling it, as she understood that Rex would be hosting the lunch with or without her. Hannah had looked at the feeling; there wasn't any point refusing to acknowledge feelings when they popped up. But here was the thing – it was important to then relegate them to their proper status. The day – Heath, the sunshine, coming home – had a certain buoyancy. Hannah wasn't about to let that sink under any reactive, emotional stone.

Rex emerged from the kitchen. He stood in the beam of the skylight, holding his head and arms up to the rays as though he was being taken by aliens. It was an old joke, unsurprising. Yet it signalled his mindset as clearly as a grin. Hannah stepped into the beam of light with him. Immediately, his arms circled her waist. Rex's kiss was more than hello but just less than full strength. A promising kiss. Most likely he'd flirted wildly last night but not followed through. That seemed to be the case more and more these days.

'Hannah Banana, good to see you,' Albie said as she walked into the kitchen. Rex must have spent hundreds on the seafood array on the bench. He did that kind of thing off the cuff. He'd shown Hannah, by example, how to let go.

Albie poured a glass of Veuve Clicquot and handed it to her. He was one of Rex's oldest pals, a slightly jaded legal aid lawyer with a wicked sense of humour. He was short and squat, and wore black, heavy-framed glasses and a Friar Tuck circle of grey hair. Hannah had liked him from the start. Not so much his new (internet) partner, Sonia, who'd struck Hannah as a combination of boring and neurotic the few times they'd met.

Today though, Hannah was going to grant her a clean slate.

'We were just talking about Felix,' Rex said.

'As you know, Hannah, he's a good kid,' Albie said. 'Handsome, intelligent and infinitely charismatic, just like his father. And he's doing fine at uni. But I think he might be going too hard on the party drugs. You should see him on Sunday mornings after a festival gig. Well – afternoons is more apt.'

'You *think* he's going too hard on party drugs?' Sonia replied. 'Really, Alberto?'

'Well, yes,' Albie said. 'It seems pretty standard in his social group, but only one or two times a month.'

'That doesn't mean you should condone it,' Sonia objected and now Hannah wasn't so sure about the clean-slate approach.

'As long as he's safe,' Hannah said. 'I know a lot of my students go to those festivals and I'm pretty sure most of them take something to elevate the experience. I'm totally on board with pill-testing at festivals. It would save lives for sure.'

'It would normalise drug use,' Sonia said. 'And, with respect, having students who are doing drugs can hardly be compared with knowing your own child is' – Sonia tilted her head and frowned – 'elevating their experience,' she continued. 'I can tell you, my Emily doesn't touch drugs.'

'But can you, Sonia?' Albie asked. 'Perhaps she just tells you what you want to hear? At least Felix is honest with me.'

'Actually, I do know, Alberto,' Sonia said, and yes it was his full name, but nobody ever called him that. 'For goodness sake, you're a lawyer. Those drugs are against the law. It's a pretty simple equation, isn't it?'

33

'If you're Dr Phil,' Hannah said. Perhaps it was a bit of a low blow, but Rex turned around and she knew it was to thwart a laugh. Albie cleared his throat for the same reason.

'Can I help you in the kitchen, Rex?' Sonia asked. 'I guess we should get things started.'

CHAPTER SIX

Albie and Sonia were barely out the door when Rex slipped his arms around Hannah's waist.

His kiss was lusty this time. She suspected it was fuelled by comparison. Sonia had been dull, her views facile. She was humourless. Hannah was expansive and funny.

Hannah pulled him into their bedroom and towards their bed, crisp with hotel-quality sheets. His eyes burned through her. His mouth smiled.

She slowed them down. Undressing in front of him, watching Rex watch her, Hannah felt beautiful. This was the man, the only man who'd ever made her feel that. Her small breasts were beautiful. Her boyish slimness, too. Tonight though, there was more to it. Something almost tribal or spiritual.

He rose from the bed as though he couldn't wait anymore. Couldn't deal with the intensity without touching her. He reached for her. He did not reach into the drawer for a condom. She did not remind him.

•

Hannah drifted into the outskirts of sleep, her thigh touching Rex's. Something new had happened between them tonight. A depth that needed no classification. The kernel of that thought followed Hannah into her dreams.

She was at some kind of small-town, beachside summer carnival. Rex had won a plush toy and given it to her. An octopus. Hannah loved the ridiculousness of it. The stuffing that felt like straw and the stick-on eyes with loose pupils that moved as she threw it up in the air. When it fell to the ground, Hannah saw him. The beautiful, white-haired urchin boy was crouching underneath a caravan, hugging himself. He looked lost and lonely, but Hannah knew instantly and thoroughly that he was meant to be theirs. She walked over to him, offering the octopus. He took it. And beamed.

•

Hannah woke to a new mobile ringtone she suspected Heath of loading on her phone. *Boing. Boing.* Rex's name appeared onscreen. She flung a hand over to his side of the bed. It was empty.

'Rex. Where are you?'

'I'm on my way to Brunetti's and will return with sweet morsels. Decide whether you'd like the New York cheesecake or the Sacher Torte. Both mini, of course, since we must be conscious of maintaining our gorgeous figures.'

Hannah smiled a drowsy smile. Rex's paunch had been growing steadily. Luckily, her own body responded to the discipline of the gym. She would allow herself this splurge.

It could be atoned for by a workout this afternoon. Besides, after last night, she felt softer somehow, and it wasn't all that bad.

'While you decide that important matter, I'm at the chemist right now. The pharmacist needs to talk to you, okay?'

Something did a duck-dive in Hannah's gut.

'Am I speaking with Hannah Fidler?' The voice was female.

'Yes.'

'I have Rex Carlisle with me. He would like to purchase Postinor-1, a tablet to be used for emergency contraception. Do you give your consent for us to provide this to Mr Carlisle?'

'Yes.'

There was more. How to use the pill. How effective it was, the possible side effects. But it all came through muffled and disjointed because her phone was face down on the mattress.

●

Rex carried everything in on a tray. Coffee, mini-cheesecakes and tortes, the Sunday paper. And a silver blister pack with the pill, unpacked from its box and all ready for consumption.

He'd been clear about it from the start. If she wanted children, Rex wasn't the man for her. He'd been there, wasn't going back. His adult son lived in the US. Their relationship had only recently started to develop now that Leo was independent. The mother had poisoned the father–son relationship simply because she couldn't own Rex outright. Couldn't manipulate him into the narrow confines of a nuclear family.

Rex had been pleased that Hannah was so unequivocal. She had no desire to have children. At thirty-eight there was no ticking biological clock. She was an academic. Unlike her sister, Hannah didn't need the validation of breeding.

It had never been a problem. That time last year when the condom broke, Hannah hadn't hesitated to take the morning-after pill. There was certainly no ethical dilemma. But even now, it wasn't that.

There was no clarity or precedent to her thoughts. No framework with which to share them with Rex. Just a mental image of the boy from her dream.

Rex put the tray on the dresser. He slid in behind Hannah and stroked her hair.

'Han. You okay?'

'I'm having … I'm experiencing some doubt about taking the pill,' she said. She heard the mewing in her voice. Foreign. She wasn't herself.

So then, who was she?

'Han, this is just a precaution. There's not much chance anyway. I'm fifty-six. You're forty-one. And we have an agreement.'

Rex kept stroking her hair, but the pressure changed. It was lighter. As though he was halfway out of there.

The Great Debater, Mr Magnanimous, was not going to discuss this.

The rage Hannah suppressed was sudden and appalling. She loved this man. She hated him. She shrugged as if it were of no matter. Put the pill in her mouth and swallowed it with a swig of lukewarm latte.

CHAPTER SEVEN

'Is that all you got? Just a text from Dad?' Stef asked from the passenger seat.

She suspected that he had told Hannah more. Especially if it was bad news. As the eldest, less emotional one, Hannah would have been called upon to reframe the information before passing it to her younger sister. Stef just hoped it wasn't cancer or MS or anything terminal. She'd even started the bargaining process with a blurry god figure and given him the go ahead to make it a curable illness.

But Hannah shook her head. She handed Stef her phone. The message was identical.

Please come tonight at 7 pm. No partners or children. There's something we need to discuss. Dad x

Stef breathed in. 'Do you think one of them is sick?' The words tumbled over themselves, only just making it out of her mouth.

'I don't know, Steffie.'

The streetlights blurred.

'When Dad dropped the kids off on Thursday, they told me they'd had fish fingers for dinner,' Stef said.

Hannah pulled over to the side of the road. 'Jesus,' she said. 'Did they say whether Mum was there?'

'Apparently she was having a rest,' Stef said. 'But, Han, there's more,' and even as it leaked out of her, she realised how hard she'd worked to minimise the information. 'Heath insists there's a bed in Dad's shed.'

Stef saw the indentation as Hannah bit the inside of her lip.

'I guess that means no one's sick,' she said eventually, and Stef already knew this in her heart, but Hannah made it real. If this was about an illness, their parents would be supporting each other, not choosing separate beds. Between them, drifting like dust motes, were guesses. Neither of them spoke.

Before she knocked at the door, though, Hannah put her arm around Stef's shoulders and squeezed. 'Whatever it is, be strong, kiddo,' she said.

•

There were no cooking smells. Marg's lipstick, burnt orange, matched her linen dress. She led her daughters down the hallway and into the lounge without speaking. A plate of cheese and biscuits and a bottle of white wine were arranged on the coffee table.

Jim sat at the edge of the couch, a Scotch and dry balanced on the armrest. A small act of defiance in a house where coasters were requisite. Stef immediately sat beside him, leaned into him. A kiss landed on her head like a shock absorber.

Hannah sat opposite Marg. Her mother breathed in. Her eyes were focused on a spot above Jim's head.

'When I was seventeen, I had a child.' Her voice sounded mechanical. The voice of someone who'd recited a painful sentence enough times to deaden the emotion upon delivery.

Both daughters, in their own way, experienced the world shifting. The axis off kilter. Stef felt herself leaning – a subconscious attempt to steer their lives away from the impact of Marg's words. But there was no going around this. The hit that landed on Stef's chest was sharp and immediate. Marg looked up briefly to check no one had keeled over. When she continued, it was pressing on a bruise.

'It was nineteen sixty-three. A pregnancy outside of marriage brought terrible shame. My parents sent me to a convent outside Ballarat where I saw out my pregnancy. In the meantime, they arranged an adoption. My son was …'

There was a catch in Marg's throat. She paused. Hung her head. When she looked up and over to the couch, Stef could see the veil lift, shame and pain written all over her face. Their dad sighed.

'I had two days with my baby.' Marg's voice, when she continued, was a ghost of itself. An imposter without tone or intonation. 'Then he was adopted out. I had no further contact with him. I believed that was for the best. I was told to forget. To move on.'

Stef could feel her dad's heart thumping against her back.

'His name is Alex, and he has contacted me through the adoption agency,' Marg said.

Her dad sighed and rubbed his eyes. 'Your mother is flying to Adelaide to meet him next week,' he said. He didn't look at any of them. Just got up and lumbered out the back door towards the shed.

•

In all her childhood years, Stef had never knocked on the shed door before entering. Now though, it seemed necessary.

'Come,' her dad said.

The lumpy single mattress that had been pulled out for mass kid sleepovers decades ago was laid out on the floor at the far side of the shed. Folds of a too-big sheet criss-crossed over it. There was no cover on the lone pillow. Marg, most definitely, had not been here.

Stef's eyes welled. Through her tears, she witnessed her giant bear of a father, his back against the wall. Stef sat down next to him. She wished she'd urged Hannah to follow him instead. She would have had she not been so terrified to be alone with her robot mother. Hannah could have handled this without crumbling.

'I thought we told each other everything,' Stef's dad said into the ether. 'Whenever Margie got the blues she insisted it was part of her make-up, her cycle. And I was too stupid to press her. She said I should leave her be and she'd come out the other end. She never once suggested there was something particular

42

that caused it. But if I looked after you and Hannah and gave her a rest, she would emerge when she was ready.'

Jim stood. He picked up a chisel from the tool display on the shed wall and a piece of balsa wood from the scrap basket and put them on the work bench, studying them as though he'd had a plan that now escaped him. When he put them back in their allocated spots, it seemed a kind of surrender.

'Marg was my only,' he said.

•

Hannah sat on her parents' bed. The sheets were snow white with hospital corners. Four cushions were placed on the diagonal – two red, two cream. The bedspread incorporated the red and cream theme.

Marg knelt to retrieve a wooden chest that was hidden away at the back of the closet. She sat next to Hannah, her posture still straight but with a slight rounding of the shoulders Hannah hadn't picked up on before. As Marg opened the chest, Hannah saw Rex's A. A. Milne gift on top. Rage swept through her body again, without a label Hannah could cling on to for understanding.

It should have been Stef, more empathetic, in here with their mother.

'I don't generally believe things happen for a reason,' Marg said. 'But he – Alex – contacted me out of the blue and then … the book.'

'The inscription,' Hannah said, quelling the storm inside with sheer will, 'was it his birthdate?'

43

Marg nodded. Stef had been right about the book triggering Marg's odd episode. Maybe Stef had an instinct that Hannah lacked. Maybe Stef had a lot that Hannah lacked.

'Those times you went underground, the days you spent in bed with the curtains drawn ...'

'His birthday, Hannah. And some other times here and there when the burden of not knowing my son, not knowing where he was or how he was or what kind of people he was growing up with, got too much. The rest of the time I tried to be there for you and Stef entirely.'

There was a taste of reprimand and Hannah was a little chastened. But there was so much to ask and she wasn't sure she wanted to know the answers.

Marg lifted the A. A. Milne gently and put it on the bed between them. Then she brought out a plastic hospital bracelet. Blue for boys, with a clear sleeve.

'Baby Ingles'. Marg's maiden name.

'We wanted to keep him,' Marg said. Hannah bristled at the 'we'.

Marg turned the bracelet over and over again. 'I loved Antonio. He loved me. He told me that he would figure out the finances, that I should just focus on staying well and delivering our baby. We thought we would be a family. But our parents had planned otherwise. By the time I went into labour, Antonio was on a boat back to Italy.'

Marg sighed. 'I never heard from him again. But I should have fought for my baby.'

I should have fought for my baby too, Hannah thought, *my change-of-mind child*. Of course it was ridiculous. There probably had never even been a baby. And if there ever was one, there would be no Rex.

'I'm sorry you're going through this,' Hannah said. Stef would have embraced Marg but Hannah couldn't. As her mother put things back in the chest, Hannah saw a handwritten letter in neat cursive script.

'Is it from … Alex?' she asked.

Marg nodded but closed the lid without offering to show her.

'Hannah, I'm going to need you to lead the family while I'm away. Look after Stef, of course, but Jim too. He's thrown, and since I'm the one who's done the tossing, I can't seem to help him.'

'All those years and you didn't even mention this?' Hannah replied, hoping it sounded more in wonder than in judgement, though she wasn't sure where it emanated from. Her parents were so close. Surely this was a betrayal?

'I didn't tell anyone. Ever,' Marg said. For a moment, there was pure loneliness sitting in a burnt orange dress and matching lipstick.

Hannah watched her put the wooden chest back in the closet. This time she left it on the top shelf, exposed.

'Someday, someday soon, you'll meet your brother,' she said.

CHAPTER EIGHT

Stef had butterflies. A big brother. She'd dreamed of such a thing in her adolescence. Some of her friends at PLC had them. Alison Carter's had been nerdy and sweet. Keisha Friedman's had been a giant spunk. Rhett Friedman – even his name was romantic. Flirting with him had been great practice. Jules Morrow was sullen and brooding and so, so interesting ...

Anyway, the point was, whoever Alex turned out to be, Stef was going to welcome him with open arms.

The Thai banquet she was preparing in her parents' kitchen would be self-serve. Stef was happy to do masses of prep so that she could be properly present when their mum – and their brother! – arrived straight from the airport. In a way it was a shame that their dad decided to go and stay up north with Uncle Bill. But in another way, it saved a layer of angst. Just before he left, he'd confided that he felt impossibly awkward about being the only one in the family who had no blood connection with Alex. He would come back after they'd all got to know each other a little. After 'the dust had settled'.

And one stress head was enough. Hannah had been fixated on how quiet their mum was about what had been happening in

Adelaide this past week. But Hannah didn't have a maternal bone in her body. She probably couldn't relate to how overwhelming the experience would be for their mother. If it had been Rosie or Heath ripped away from Stef and returned fifty-six years later, she would totally have gone missing in action. Stef absolutely respected that their mum needed time and space to process everything.

From her Adelaide calls, Stef thought Marg's tone seemed way more … evolved, more emotional. Sure, she only gave basic information about Alex, but that was most likely because she wanted to get to know him properly, to let their relationship take form before trying to communicate what he was like. And every time Marg had signed off, she'd told Stef she loved her. That kind of stuff was usually their dad's domain. In fact, Stef would go so far as to predict their mum was going through some kind of spiritual awakening. All the details about Alex would follow in due course.

Honestly, Stef could feel the stirrings of her own spiritual awakening too. And she knew she might be getting carried away since she hadn't even met Alex yet, but it had always felt like there was something missing in the Fidler family. The something had turned out to be someone.

And now, a key was turning in the front door.

Stef looked in the mirror on the mantelpiece to bouff her hair one more time and started up the hallway.

●

Hannah pulled into the driveway of her parents' house and veered right to the pebbled surface so she wouldn't get parked in. She turned off the ignition and sat in the darkness to collect her thoughts.

Their mother had been seriously evasive in her communications. Despite using Alex's name to kick off practically every sentence in the phone calls from Adelaide, all Marg had really told her and Stef about were straight facts.

- Alex had been married for five years earlier on but was now divorced.
- Alex had no children.
- Alex was the sole heir to an impressive property called Hughesdale in the Adelaide Foothills. (Hannah had googled it. It was impressive.)
- Alex didn't work as such, but managed a business portfolio handed down through the generations. (Confirmed. Google. Carpenter Enterprises.)
- Alex had completed two master's degrees in Marg-couldn't-recall-exactly-what.
- Alex was handsome. (Hannah had googled images, but the few on the internet were grainy.)
- Alex was well-dressed.
- Alex spoke beautifully.

In response to questions about what Alex was actually like though, what kind of a connection Marg and he were forging, their mother had been unusually taciturn. When Hannah asked questions in that direction, Marg would insist that she didn't want to put Alex in a box.

Alex was 'complex'. Marg 'couldn't even begin to describe him'. A fact that seemed unusually evasive given she tended to have a lot to say about the way her daughters operated. Surely she would have a more comprehensive sense of Alex by now. She hadn't even spoken much about what they were doing in Adelaide except for letting it slip that she was staying in a hotel rather than at his grand mansion. When she called, there were more questions about work and Rex than normal. It seemed like deflection. Hannah got it, to a certain extent. It was a huge deal to meet your fifty-six-year-old son. But anticipating meeting an older brother wasn't exactly a small thing either.

Apparently, Hannah and Stef would have to figure Alex out – form a relationship with him – in their own ways.

Hannah wished their dad was going to be here too. It would be quite natural for him, the only one who didn't share DNA with Alex, to create some boundaries. But going to stay with Uncle Bill was a form of self-preservation. Jim would come back when he was ready.

Right now, in the moments leading up to the very first meeting, Hannah would have liked to be calm and self-assured and not dealing with a clusterfuck of thoughts. It didn't seem that Alex would have a financial agenda for seeking out his birth mother after all these years, but there could be a million other issues at play. Hannah understood that family reunions could be fraught. There was no doubt that Stef was going to throw herself at the guy without an ounce of scrutiny. But Hannah would be both welcoming and reserved. Also, she really was going to get out of the car and go inside for a wine with Stef any second and ask her to please, take it slowly. She would, if she could move.

Perhaps Hannah had been sitting there, in the driveway of her parents' house for quite some time, because the clock on the dash read 7.30 pm when a taxi pulled up.

Hannah watched their silhouettes. Her mother. Her tall brother. As the porch light came on, she could see he had a hand on the small of Marg's back. She could see Stef greeting them, barely letting them set foot inside before throwing her arms around the tall silhouette.

Fight or flight. Hannah did get out of the car. She straightened her pinafore and strode to the porch.

They were still in the hallway. Alex had his back to Hannah as Stef hugged him, sobbing. Marg reached out and held Hannah's hand.

Finally, Stef released him and he turned in Hannah's direction.

'It's good to meet you,' Alex said, and it was ridiculous because she wasn't a bleeding heart like Stef, but Hannah also had to choke down a sob.

Alex was the spitting image of her. Older, yes. And perhaps more distinguished with his greying hair. But Alex was tall and slim and angled, with the same chiselled cheekbones. His pinstripe navy linen suit was one Hannah would have worn herself.

'You look like me,' Hannah said. The understatement hung in the air between them. They gazed at it.

And soon, all four of them were laughing.

CHAPTER NINE

Stef was determined not to make another comment about how much Hannah and Alex looked alike. But she couldn't help switching focus from one to the other as they sat opposite Stef and their mother at the dining table. Tall and slim – check. Hazel eyes – check. Impossible cheekbones – check.

'I hope you don't mind that I didn't want to introduce myself over the phone,' Alex said.

Marg was right. Alex was beautifully spoken. His voice wasn't super deep, but it had a musical timbre.

'I was nervous about the first impression I might make,' he continued. 'It's a tiny bit difficult to know where to begin in such a situation.'

Hannah chuckled, and Stef nearly felt pissed off with her sister's rudeness before realising that Alex was deliberately understating the oddness of the situation. God, she hoped she wouldn't get left behind in this new family order.

'I like the photo gallery in the hallway,' Alex continued. 'It gives me a little insight into your lives. Your ... family.'

'It's pretty much a crash course on the Fidlers,' Hannah agreed. 'Photoshopped to omit the warts of course.'

Stef would not have been able to make up the line that made Alex smile.

'Of course, Hannah,' he bantered, 'it's like the opposite of the Crown Jewels. Nobody wants to see the Family Warts, even if they do differentiate from the generic.'

Stef cleared her throat. She needed to speak soon or she might disappear. 'So, Mum and Alex, maybe you can give us an idea what you guys got to know about each other in Adelaide?'

Stef noticed that her mum was focusing on Alex. And did he just give a small nod of consent? Marg wasn't the kind of woman who needed approval before speaking. Stef erased the thought.

'Alex has really made something of his life,' Marg said. 'He sits on many boards, some of them philanthropic. He manages Hughesdale too, and it's a lot of work restoring it to—'

'Unfortunately it's all a little dull,' Alex interrupted. 'Clearly, I was given a silver spoon. Perhaps I wasn't born with it, but it found its way into my mouth.'

There was an awkward silence as Stef helped herself to another serve of Pad Thai. She was eating too much. She probably seemed greedy. She handed around the platter. It was a relief when Alex took another serve.

'This truly is amazing, Stef,' he said then, taking a mouthful. 'The whole spread is amazing.' He motioned above the dishes on the table. 'Yum Talay, Tom Kha Kai – such delicate flavours. It's evident you made it all from scratch. I've tried and I can do a reasonable job, but I could definitely learn from you.'

'Stef is the sister with the culinary expertise,' Hannah said, and now Stef didn't feel quite so overwhelmed by Alex and Hannah's likeness.

'Why thank you, Han,' Stef said. 'What about you, Alex? Do you have any siblings?'

Alex put down his fork. He dabbed the corners of his mouth with a napkin and rested his chin in his hands.

'My mother …' Alex blinked several times and tapped his fingers on the table in a way that made Stef already wish she hadn't asked the question. 'My mother,' he repeated, 'adopted Ricky and me in the same year. First, she got me at two weeks old, then Ricky at a few months. The story goes that we were chosen, two for one, by Gillian because we had similar colouring. Which of course all seems ludicrous now. But in nineteen sixty-three, adoption was virtually a baby smorgasbord.'

Beside Stef, her mother seemed to shrink.

'I'm sorry, Margaret,' Alex said, tapping on the table, index finger to little finger and back again. 'I think perhaps I said that all wrong.'

Marg tried to reassert proper posture.

'Please don't apologise, Alex,' she said. And the others waited for more, but it seemed like Marg's words had dried up.

•

The image conjured up by Alex's baby smorgasbord comment was vivid. In her mind's eye, Hannah saw a row of abandoned babies. Her own imagined boy peeked through the slats of the very last cot. He reached out to be picked up and then disappeared.

Hannah's new brother sat right next to her. And maybe there was a touch of Narcissus in there, but Alex was a magnet of the best kind. Smart and intense. Stef probably wouldn't have noticed the changes in his body language when she asked about siblings, but Hannah was perceptive. The rapid blinking, the table-tapping. Of course, everyone wanted to get to know each other, but they should probably let things unfold rather than rushing at him with their questions.

'Maybe we should take a step back?' she suggested. 'Get to know each other organically?'

Alex turned to her and tipped a non-existent hat.

'Good idea, Han,' Stef said. Hannah could tell that, underneath the table, she and Marg were holding hands. 'We have all the time in the world, don't we? Where are you staying?'

'I'm staying the night here, if that's still okay with you, Margaret?' Alex replied.

She nodded. 'Of course it is,' she said. 'I set up Hannah's old room before I left for Adelaide.'

'Thank you, Margaret,' Alex said, and it seemed to Hannah that a tenderness had crept into his voice in lieu of the disallowed apology from his baby smorgasbord comment. She could take at least a little credit for that. 'Tomorrow I'll get a hotel in town. I have a couple of weeks before I need to be back in Adelaide.'

'Do you think you could come to my place for dinner tomorrow night?' Stef asked. 'We're just around the corner. And the kids, Rosie and Heath, they're desperate to meet their uncle.'

Hannah's heart felt weirdly flighty. Rosie ... desperate to meet Alex? She didn't think so. And wasn't the 'uncle' thing a bit too ... familiar, for the stage they were at?

But Alex didn't skip a beat. 'Yes, thank you. Maybe we could cook together, Stef?' he suggested, and it made Hannah's throat close over.

Tonight, Alex would be sleeping in her old room. The ghosts of her teen angst might seep into his consciousness. Hannah had never been any boy's number one choice.

Stef's room (now a sewing room and not an option) would have told an entirely different story. Stef had been the number one choice for so many hopefuls she probably didn't even remember their names.

For a moment Hannah wished she'd asked Alex to stay with her and Rex on his first night, where the reflections of her life were so much more flattering. She brushed the thought away. He seemed observant.

Alex would figure it out.

CHAPTER TEN

Stef had cleaned the house and done the grocery shopping. All the ingredients for tonight's Greek dinner were on the bench ready to go. Rosie and Heath would both be happy with moussaka, and the salad ingredients were fresh and fragrant.

The doorbell rang right on 4 pm. Alex handed Stef a bunch of yellow tulips and two bottles of shiraz. He kissed her on the cheek. There was an awkward moment when she stayed put because she thought he was going to kiss her other cheek. She thought of how she'd thrown her arms around him as soon as they'd met last night. Tonight, she would let things unfold organically. She would not mention his resemblance to Hannah.

'I knew you'd have a flair for decor, Stef,' Alex said as they walked into the lounge. The afternoon sun streamed in from the garden jungle.

'I've actually done ... well, mostly done, two-thirds of an interior decorating degree,' Stef offered.

'Aha,' Alex said. 'Margaret told me. But I think you might also be one of the rare ones with an innate sense of how to make a place feel like home without it being homely. Perhaps your degree is icing on the cake.'

Stef's heart billowed as she arranged the tulips in a vase. They splayed perfectly, as though demonstrating Alex's point. It looked as though they'd always belonged on the washed back green bureau near the glass doors.

'Is it too early to open you?' Stef asked one of the bottles of shiraz.

Her brother (her big brother!) grinned. 'Special occasion,' he said. 'The rules don't apply.'

Alex found wineglasses in the top right-hand kitchen cupboard without asking. Stef handed him an apron to protect his white shirt and he didn't baulk.

'How about I talk you through the moussaka-making while I do the salad?' Stef asked. 'I'm expecting Liam – my ex – to bring the kids back at six.' She paused for a moment. 'Did Marg also tell you about Liam? About our semiconscious uncoupling?' she asked.

Alex's smile told her he got it straightaway. 'A little,' he answered, 'but of course I know nothing. Nobody knows what goes on inside a marriage. Especially a marriage breakdown. Except for the participants.'

'It's nicer when you cut the eggplant really fine,' Stef advised. 'You were married too, right?'

Without further instruction, Alex seasoned each thin slice of eggplant before putting it in the pan. 'Yes. Cara and I were about five years in when the marriage became … untenable. We both simply knew it couldn't continue. That it was time to move on.'

Stef made herself keep chopping rhythmically. Apart from the timeline, Alex could have been narrating her own story with Liam. But she wasn't going to catapult herself in there. She was going to let things unfold. It was enough, at the moment, to realise that Alex had at least an inkling of how things felt from the inside of an ill-fated marriage.

'There were … misunderstandings. We couldn't …'

Their conversation was interrupted by the opening of the front door. Three sets of footsteps echoed down the hallway. Liam did a double-take as he entered the kitchen.

'You must be Alex,' he said, reaching out for a handshake. 'Good to meet you, mate.'

Alex wiped his hands on Liam's old apron before responding. Stef looked at the clock on the stove. It was 4.30 pm.

'Jeez, you look like Hannah,' Liam said. 'On the red already? Well, I guess you two have a lot of time to make up.' He got a beer out of the fridge, opened it, took a swig, and clinked it against Alex's glass in one continuous movement.

Heath sock-skidded into the kitchen and wrapped his arms around some denim legs. When he looked up, he saw they didn't belong to his dad. His laugh couldn't have been freer, more delightful.

'You're such a loser, Heath,' Rosie said from the doorframe.

Heath switched to his dad's legs.

'Rosie, come and meet your uncle,' Stef encouraged.

Rosie gave a bored wave. 'How long will dinner be?'

'It's moussaka, Rosie!' Heath said, eyeing the half-prepared dish on the bench.

'Der,' said Rosie, already turning to leave.

'Rosie is filled with excitement to meet you, Alex,' Liam joked. 'But I wouldn't take it personally.' He turned to Stef. 'Your daughter called Prue a waste of space this morning,' he said with an exaggerated grimace. 'Prue is not impressed.'

'Is that why you're an hour and a half early?' Stef asked pointedly.

Liam ignored the question. Pointedly.

'You're tall,' Heath said to Alex. 'Can we measure you and mark it on the laundry wall? Everyone's there. Even Gran and Pop. But last time we measured, Pop had shrunk. Weird, huh? Rosie and I just get bigger.'

'You're getting bigger every day,' said Stef, ruffling her son's hair. 'Can you go and get your school stuff ready for tomorrow?'

Heath gave his mum a belated hug and left the kitchen.

Liam went to open the fridge door again. Stef nudged it closed before he could reach inside.

'So, Alex,' Liam said, 'I hope you got to catch up a bit with Marg in Adelaide? She's a good egg. So's Jim. Salt of the earth, though I hear he's decided to do a runner until everyone settles a bit. The daughters though ...' He hung an arm over Stef's shoulder. She stepped sideways and it fell. 'The daughters are a bit tricky,' he smirked as though Stef's sideways shuffle had illustrated his point.

In the ensuing silence, Stef topped up her and Alex's glasses.

'Guess it's all a bit full on at the moment,' Liam said. 'A bit of a crash course in the Fidler family?'

'There's no need for a crash course,' Alex replied. 'Time stretches ahead of us as well as behind. I'm in for the long haul.'

'Ah, that's the spirit,' Liam said, leaving his empty beer bottle on the bench. 'Then I guess I'll be seeing you around.'

As he nodded, Alex transferred the bottle to the recycling bin.

•

The wine was something else. It complemented the moussaka and Heath's chatter over dinner. And mitigated the effect of Rosie thumping her knee on the underside of the table. Stef insisted Alex hang with the kids in the lounge while she cleared up. She could hear them from the kitchen.

'I have fifteen, no, sixteen PlayStation games,' Heath told Alex as Stef stacked the dishwasher. 'Two of them, no three actually, have scratches so they get stuck. But it's not so bad. I just make it part of the game.'

'Good story, Heath,' said Rosie.

'Do you have a better story, Rosie?' Alex asked.

Stef paused before stacking the next plate. It was probably good that Rosie was being challenged. She really gave Heath a hard time.

Stef closed the dishwasher and picked up wine bottle number two. Honestly, it just got smoother with every sip. On impulse, she googled the label on her phone. Mount Edelstone

Shiraz, 2015. Two hundred and twenty dollars per bottle. No wonder it was good. Alex was a class act.

●

'I don't like him,' Rosie said as Stef leaned down to kiss her goodnight.

She was tired and it was a work day tomorrow, and Rosie and Heath had both insisted she put them to bed like she always did after they'd done a stint with Liam and Prue. She probably couldn't have expected Alex just to wait in the lounge room until she was done, but it was still disappointing that he had taken an Uber back to his hotel. She wanted to keep talking to him without the kids around. Or Liam, for that matter. She wanted to know more. More about his life. His upbringing. And his marriage, definitely that. She wanted him to know her, too. To share confidences deep into the night.

Alex was right, though. What had he said to Liam? That time stretched ahead of them as well as behind? That was almost, well, it seemed like poetry. Not that Stef was really the one to judge – she was no Hannah. Alex was spending the next evening with her, and they'd probably get around to poetry, what with Rex and Hannah being all into literature. Alex was going to be in high demand, tugged in all directions – Marg, Hannah, herself.

'Mum,' Rosie said, eyes narrowed, 'Alex is weird.'

'Oh for Christ's sake, Rosie. You've only just met him,' Stef snapped.

Rosie jerked the covers over her head. But she must have made an opening tunnel for her mouth because what she said next was clear. Rosie was determined to have the last word, like her father.

'Weirdo.'

CHAPTER ELEVEN

Hannah was doing a speed-reading of *Waiting for Godot*. She'd taught it many times before, but she wanted to check an integral quote before giving the afternoon lecture. The image of birthing astride a grave never failed to blow her away. Hannah was lost in the visceral effect when her phone rang.

'Something very special is happening to our family, Han,' Stef gushed. 'I know it's meant that Dad's gone away and Mum's gone quiet. It might take a little while for things to really gel. But Han, Alex was really there last night. I feel like I'm starting to get to know him. He even talked a little about his marriage and I reckon we would have unpacked that more except Rosie was being a bit of a twat and insisted I put her and Heath to bed with all the rituals. He left then and that's probably a good thing because I'm already a bit hungover and it would have been worse at work today. I have a really good feeling about this, Han. Can you even believe we're finally getting our own—'

Customer service to Dining. Customer Service to Dining.

Stef waited out the announcement before continuing. She was probably in some kind of kitchenette at that furniture barn with Tetley teabags and Nescafé sachets.

'Our own brother?' Stef continued. 'And Alex just has something too, don't you think? Some element we were missing as a family before and we didn't even know it. He's so … accomplished. He helped me cook dinner, but it wasn't like he needed instructions. The guy knows his way around a kitchen. And you know what he brought over last night?'

'A sacrificial virgin?' Hannah joked, but honestly, Stef's enthusiasm was a tad contagious. 'A goat?'

'Haha,' Stef said. 'Really expensive wine. Two bottles – two hundred and twenty dollars a pop.'

Hannah pulled her chair towards her desk and typed the Beckett quote into Google Images, searching for something she could pop into her PowerPoint presentation.

'I don't think he's after our immense fortune at least, Stef,' she said.

'Me neither. You know, Alex was here when Liam dropped the kids off too, so they met.'

'Was Liam on time?' Hannah asked.

'Early,' Stef admitted. 'An hour and a half.'

'Hmmm. But he didn't let himself in, right?'

'The front door was unlocked. But he's still hassling for a key,' Stef replied. 'I have to figure all that out. But, Han, you should have seen Liam when he saw Alex in the kitchen. Just standing there with your face and his old apron. It was priceless.'

Hannah chuckled. 'The Stunned Mullet?'

'Yep. His best impression,' Stef said.

'Oh I don't know,' Hannah deadpanned, 'I also like the "I'm Sober Drunk".'

Stefanie Fidler, you're needed in Lounge and Dining right away. Stefanie Fidler.

'Gotta go,' Stef said. 'I've left Dora from whitegoods in charge and she doesn't know shit about any of our upmarket lounges. But have fun with Alex tonight. And let me know how it goes, okay? Please tell me everything.'

'I'll make sure to take minutes and email them through,' Hannah said.

There was a pause.

'I wish we'd always known him, Han,' Stef said.

Hannah felt a sudden whoosh of emotion and found an image to use in her lecture. Simultaneously.

'Steffie,' she said softly. 'It's not too late.'

•

The lecture flowed well. Hannah tended not to watch the online repeats because it made her too critical of her faults, but she might even take a peek at this one later. The students had seemed engaged. There were no major interruptions other than a mobile phone that went off and took a while to silence.

Hannah spotted Ethan in the third row and – well, nobody else would know and it was a well-documented public speaking aid – she directed her knowledge, her deep understanding, to him. Facial features were hard to discern from the stage, so she had given Ethan the look of rapt attention she knew from tutorials.

On rare days like this, Hannah felt almost satisfied. She was connected to the broader world by her students. Her family was experiencing an awakening.

She looked back at the screen behind her, showing the final quote of her lecture. The terrifying notion that the very essence of existence was manufactured most often seemed to be at her core.

But tonight, with Alex coming over for dinner, Hannah felt, in a state that approximated faith, that she really might exist after all.

•

Hannah walked down the hallway with her brother. Side by side, strides matching. Alex paused under the skylight and looked up.

'I hope you don't mind that I chose to stay in a hotel, Hannah,' he said. 'It's just that this whole experience ... is overwhelming.'

He didn't look overwhelmed, but then again, people were always telling Hannah that her nerves didn't show. She wondered where Alex bought his grey suit. Perhaps it had been tailored? Underneath he wore an off-white T-shirt that tied in with his sneakers. Effortless flair.

'It's a lot,' Hannah agreed. 'But tonight will be low-key.'

'The burning question, new-brother Alex,' Rex called from the kitchen, 'martini – dirty or regular?'

'Well, as much as I can control it,' Hannah amended with a shrug.

•

As usual, Rex was charming and erudite. He sat in an armchair, leaving the couch for Alex and Hannah.

'How beautifully odd,' he said, 'to meet your long-lost sibling and find another version of you.'

'It is beautifully odd,' Alex agreed. 'I hope you don't mind if I borrow that phrase?'

'Not at all,' Rex said. 'It really is a marvel. Your bone structure in particular is strikingly similar, don't you think, Hannah?'

'Well, yes,' she said. 'That's what I've been telling you, Rex.'

'True, but there's no preparation for witnessing it in person.'

Rex gave the couch and its two tenants a wink. 'A cautionary tale, though,' he said, shaking his index finger. 'Did you know, there is a version of the myth of Narcissus in which he falls in love with his twin sister instead of himself?'

'Jesus, Rex,' Hannah said. That was a thing about Rex – it wasn't just that what he was saying was awkward, he also assumed knowledge that Alex may not share. Before she could rescue him though, Alex chimed in.

'I think it was Pausanias, a Greek travel writer, who recorded that version,' he said. 'Regardless of the small and subtle changes ...' He paused for a moment and faux-gazed at Hannah in a way that made both she and Rex laugh. 'The end result was consistent. A single Narcissus flower.' Alex motioned towards the gift he'd brought. 'But no need to worry, Rex. My small offering is chrysanthemums, not daffodils.'

Rex laughed heartily now, clearly delighted. He clinked glasses with Alex and then Hannah.

'Welcome to the family,' he said.

•

The conversation flowed so freely that Hannah forgot to stand outside herself in judgement of her own – or the others' – shortcomings.

Around ten, Rex stood up and excused himself.

'I have a Skype call coming in from Washington DC,' he explained. 'My son, Leo. After that, I might retire these old bones. It's great to meet you, Alex. I'm sure there will be many more evenings.'

Alex rose for a handshake. 'I'm sure there will, Rex. And thank you for the dinner. The company too.'

'Nightcap?' Hannah asked as Rex climbed the stairs.

Alex nodded. 'Scotch, neat, if you have it.'

Hannah poured two glasses of Scotch and resumed her position on the couch. Bursts of Rex's hearty laughter echoed from the study above.

'How old is Rex's son?' Alex asked.

'Leo is thirty-two,' Hannah answered. 'A lawyer. He mostly grew up in the States with his mother. He and Rex have only really reconnected these past few years.' She thought for a second about asking the question and decided against it. But Alex must have intuited.

'I'm sure Margaret would have told you I don't have children,' he said. 'It was never really a burning desire. And I didn't think I'd be very good at it.'

He paused. Hannah willed him to go on.

'My mother, Gillian, wasn't exactly maternal,' Alex shared. 'Not like Margaret.'

Hannah took a sip of Scotch. 'Interesting,' she said. 'I don't … I never really thought of Marg as particularly maternal. Don't get me wrong, she's always been supportive, but she's not exactly demonstrative. Dad's always been the softie. Kisses and hugs. Oodles of praise.'

'Really?' Alex replied. 'Well, I guess it's all relative. Margaret seems soft to me.'

'Did you … do you have an adoptive father?' Hannah asked bravely.

Alex put down his Scotch and Hannah's heart skipped a beat in case she'd pushed too far.

'Gillian never saw the need for such a beast,' he said with a wry smile. 'We had a patriarch though – Grandfather William. He didn't live with us, but he did drop in frequently to do inspections.'

Hannah could only assume from the inflection that Alex was being sardonic. She was wondering whether to pursue the comment when another burst of laughter came from the study.

'Sounds like Rex and Leo have a good relationship now. Even if it was a rocky start.'

'I guess parenting isn't all smooth sailing,' Hannah said, immediately feeling like an idiot for stating the obvious. But Alex took the mantle.

'I met Stef's kids last night,' he said as though it were a case in point. 'Seems like Rosie is going through a bit of a rough patch.'

Hannah shrugged. 'Our dear Rosie lives in a perennial rough patch.'

'The poor kid must be having trouble adjusting though,' Alex said. 'The divorce – and now her father in a new relationship.'

And of course, that was the right way to think. The empathetic way. Hannah chastised herself.

'What about you, Hannah?' Alex asked, and he didn't have to expand. She knew exactly what he meant.

'I've never had the desire for kids either.' As soon as she said it the image of the child she'd conjured up emerged, his eyes liquid with hurt and betrayal. 'Well, not enough,' she amended. 'Rex definitely didn't … doesn't want any more kids, and my career has been all-consuming. Plus, the planet is already overpopulated. Blah, blah, blah,' she added.

'Hmm,' Alex said, nodding. 'Mostly, I'm okay with my choice. But like any huge decision, it can come laced with regrets. Sometimes when you're least expecting them.'

He tilted his head towards the stairway and Hannah knew he was referring to Rex and Leo's shared laughter. There was a shorthand being developed between her and her brother. Embryonic perhaps, but there.

'For me, anyway,' he finished. 'Perhaps not for you?'

Weirdly, somehow Hannah wanted to share the desire for a child – her particular child – with her new brother. To hold it up for them to honour together before letting it go.

He would think her mad. Possibly.

Hannah changed the topic.

•

'What are you doing, Han?' Rex asked, rubbing his eyes as he stood at the door of their study. 'It's after four.'

Hannah tucked the sketch in a pocket at the back of her diary.

'I felt inspired to draw something,' she said, 'after Alex left.'

'That's nice, Han. It's been a while since you've drawn anything,' Rex said. 'Are you coming to bed now?'

Rex didn't ask to see the sketch. Hannah did not offer to show him.

CHAPTER TWELVE

'Is the pressure okay, Mr Carpenter?'

'Firmer thanks,' Alex replied, 'and more focus on my neck and shoulders.'

The strain had begun from their first night together. From the hallway photos, displayed with pride, that showed Hannah and Stef at various stages of their lives. Oh, to be celebrated like that. Ridiculous that he had tried to superimpose himself in that ordinary suburban house with ordinary suburban parents. That he had mentally interspersed the photos with ones from his own youth, replacing the smiles that never reached his eyes with the genuine article.

Alex had been abandoned. Forgotten.

Through the course of that evening, it was plain to see that the triumvirate – Margaret, Hannah and Stef – was solid. Seemingly impenetrable. The women's ease with each other pushed home what he was up against.

His performance had been worthy that first night. Alex knew he had done a good job at feigning spontaneous shock and surprise at his and Hannah's physical likeness. It had just been a matter of emulating his initial reaction to the photos the private investigator had sent him. But going through the motions had been taxing.

The tension his body carried had been exacerbated by the visit to Stef's home and then Hannah's. With their small problems and casual assumptions of the normality of being loved unconditionally by both their parents. Of the predictability of the childhoods that they took for granted. Of their stable connections with each other.

That his half-sisters welcomed him didn't matter. Family was shared history, not just blood. It was collective recall of pleasure and pain and all things in between.

Alex had felt like an adjunct. Worse still, an outsider.

So unfair it was sickening.

As the masseur worked his magic, the tension Alex had been carrying started to dissipate. A phrase ran through his mind.

You teach people how to treat you.

Obviously there were exceptions. It was laughable, for instance, to suggest that he or Ricky, especially as children, could have influenced the way Gillian or William had treated them. Alex had never, even as a young bull of a teen, issued a real challenge to his grandfather. The result would have been a fait accompli. He'd seen that first-hand when poor Ricky had been deluded enough to have a go at it.

And even at the end, Gillian had the upper hand. She made dying an extended performing arts piece with sporadic intervals and fake curtain calls. Even in her most reduced state, when she was confused and weak and emaciated, Alex never shared his intention to find his birth mother. He couldn't guarantee that the mere mention of such a betrayal wouldn't shock her back to full mental capacity. Rage had always empowered Gillian.

Yes, they had definitely taught him and Ricky how to regard them.

With caution.

With devotion.

With respect.

And with gratitude. Always with gratitude.

'Mr Carpenter, sir, we've gone over time.'

'Excuse me,' Alex said. 'I must have drifted off.'

The masseur rubbed Alex's temples. As a finale, he walked his fingers up to the centre of Alex's forehead, tracing two semi-ellipses that met in the middle. The third eye. Symbol of insight and higher consciousness.

Alex dismissed the masseur with a generous tip.

He wrapped himself in a cashmere robe and retrieved a bottle of Dom Pérignon from the bar fridge. As night lights blinked on, his choice to stay at Crown Towers overlooking the Yarra made sense.

Undoubtably there was work to do here. But unlike poor Ricky, Alex was capable. Tenacious. In all the criticisms that had been levied against him over the years, work ethic was never one of them.

Yes, it was too early to permit himself to celebrate a job well done.

But, in anticipation of what he knew he would achieve, Alex held a bubbling glass up to the window.

CHAPTER THIRTEEN

'I played with Anya at recess and at lunchtime I mostly played basketball,' Heath said into Stef's phone. She watched as he twisted his spaghetti legs around each other. 'I'm not exactly good at basketball though, Pop. I think I'm about … tenth best. Can you take me to the school on the weekend so we can practise shooting? Will you be back on the weekend?'

Heath nodded solemnly as his pop delivered the answer.

'That's okay,' he said. 'I can be tenth best for a bit longer. But do you think I should draw a face on the figurine you made for me? Or wait for you to come home?'

More of her dad's voice.

'Love you too, Poppy,' Heath said before handing the phone back.

'So,' her dad said, 'how are things going down there, Steffie? How's your mum?'

'I think she's fine,' Stef replied. 'She and Alex seem to be spending time during the day together. But it's all a bit overwhelming for her. There's not a lot of debriefing going on – not with me or Hannah anyway. Has she been … is she talking to you much?'

'No,' he said. 'Just the essentials.'

'And how are you holding up?' Stef asked. 'You know we all miss you.'

'I'm okay, honey. The fly-fishing is magnificent. Did you get the photos?'

'Of Uncle Bill and the trout? Yes, I'd like some of you though.'

'I'm looking a bit rough. I'm not sleeping well.'

'It will get better,' Stef said.

'Of course it will.' It sounded like he was trying to convince himself. 'But, Steffie,' he said eventually, 'it might take some time. So tell Heath to go ahead and draw a face on the figurine.'

•

'I hope you don't mind me dropping in,' Alex said a little later. 'I come bearing gifts.'

Stef motioned for Alex to come in. She did not mind. At all.

'How was your day at the Furniture Barn?' he asked.

Stef gulped down a sudden wave of annoyance. 'It was fine. Busy. But it's actually called the Furniture Gallery,' she said.

Alex paused, brow furrowed. 'Oh, that's odd. I tried to make a mental note about your place of business when Hannah mentioned it the other night. Guess I got it wrong.'

'You probably didn't,' Stef said, shaking her head. It wasn't Alex's fault he got the name wrong. Maybe she should start referring to Hannah and Rex's precious Melbourne University as school? Minimise her achievements in their brother's eyes.

But the way Alex called her workplace a 'place of business' eased some of the annoyance.

'We're having a bit of time in the garden,' Stef said, leading Alex down the hall and through the glass sliding door. 'It's such a beautiful evening.'

'It really is,' Alex agreed. 'And you've created' – he made a sweeping gesture taking in the lush garden jungle – 'the perfect place to be on such an evening. You have the artist's gaze.'

Stef briefly saw her garden through Alex's admiring eyes. Appreciated the subtle link between this comment and the Furniture Gallery misnomer. Perhaps she wasn't so stupid, so basic, after all.

She ignored the hole in the paling fence.

'See who can go higher, Rosie?' Heath suggested. Rosie sat beside him on the other swing. Sedentary. Alex handed a parcel to each of them.

'Sheesh!' Heath said as he unwrapped the gift. He held it aloft so that Stef could see. 'I totally cannot believe it. This is actually … awesome! And you remembered, Alex. You remembered exactly which of my PlayStation games freeze up. Thank you. Thank you. Thank you, times infinity!'

Rosie unwrapped her gift slowly, as though it was an effort. She held up a small box. And honestly, the kid probably should start playing poker, because her face hardly belied the joy Stef knew she must be feeling at getting a set of AirPods. Not to mention the leverage this would give her in pleading her case for a brand-new phone to match. Stef was relieved that she at least seemed to have muttered a thank you.

'I'm sorry Rosie is so ... ungracious,' Stef said when Alex came back to join her at the outdoor setting. 'It's incredibly generous of you.'

Alex put his elbows on the table and rested his head on his fists.

'I think Rosie is battling a few demons, poor kid,' he said. 'But I'll win her over,' he continued with a half-smile. 'Eventually.'

Stef blew out a breath. Eventually meant Alex was willing to persist. Still, Rosie was so rude these days. She definitely needed boundaries. So, when her daughter got up to go back inside, Stef tried to take the reins.

'I'd like you to hang out with Heath and Alex while I prepare a platter please, Rosie,' she said firmly.

Rosie glared at her mother. But she did head back towards the swing set.

'Let me show you complete control,' Stef whispered to Alex. And, despite the fact that her family was a complicated and imperfect unit, Alex's grin buoyed her spirits.

•

Stef had a couple of superb Australian cheeses she'd taken out of the fridge on Alex's arrival. Her buying habits were definitely being influenced by having a connoisseur brother who liked to drop in to her place (which was a home without being homely). Yes, she'd allowed herself some luxuries of late. Alex had openly admired the navy and tan designer dress and matching heels. She hadn't quite been able to take the price tag off the leopard-print chiffon shirt in case the sensible side of her decided to return it for a refund. She would have to start pulling in the belt very soon. It was less than ideal to have fallen behind in the mortgage and there were some hectic household bills she needed to catch up on. She couldn't expect her mum and dad to chip in after all the expenses associated with Rosie's shift to PLC. It would help if Liam was less erratic with child support payments. But if she was living week to week, Stef would choose to live these precious ones fully. You couldn't put a price on celebrating a new brother's entrance into their lives.

As she unwrapped the Berry's Creek Tarwin Blue and Woombye Blackall Gold Washed Rind and plated them up with fig paste and crackers, Stef could already feel Alex's approval.

And honestly, Rex and Hannah's dinner would have been fine but the ingredients wouldn't have been so carefully chosen. They wouldn't have had to forgo a thing to provide it either. Hannah and Rex had zero financial strain. No responsibilities beyond themselves.

Come to think of it, Stef couldn't recall Hannah saying anything about Alex bearing expensive gifts.

Perhaps, just perhaps, he felt a special affinity with her?

Stef was arranging rocket leaves when Rosie stormed into the kitchen.

'Alex is a dickhead!' she said, and honestly, Stef couldn't remember the last time Rosie had delivered a statement with so much passion.

'Why? What happened?' Stef asked. She crouched down so she was level with Rosie.

'He's just a dickhead, Mum,' Rosie reiterated. 'And you're a dickhead too, if you can't see it.'

Standing up straight, Stef was still a head taller than her daughter.

'Rosie,' she said, 'that's enough! You need to take a good look at yourself.' She lowered her voice to a harsh whisper. 'Your uncle just gave you a fabulous gift. And you want to know something else? He's trying to understand you. Though God knows, that's almost impossible these days.'

As Stef expected, Rosie stomped out of the kitchen. But instead of heading to her room, she went back outside. Stef watched through the sliding doors. Alex was sitting on the swing next to Heath, both of them chatting. Whatever minuscule thing had happened out there to piss Rosie off hadn't affected him.

Rosie grabbed Heath by the hand, pulling him up. She led him back past the kitchen. It was unlike her to take Heath's hand. Even more unusual for her to take him upstairs to her bedroom, slamming the door behind them. But then again, trying to piece together the puzzle that was Rosie was getting more and more difficult. It was probably just the best way she could think of to sabotage Alex's visit. Draw the attention back on herself.

So, Stef let it go.

•

'I'm terribly sorry, Stef,' Alex said. The platter was untouched between them. 'I didn't mean to upset Rosie. The last thing I want to do is cause distress in my new family.'

He put his head in his hands, massaging his temples briefly before looking up. 'I thought I was just suggesting a bit of healthy competition between siblings,' he said.

'It's okay, Alex,' Stef soothed. 'Chances are Rosie is in her room playing music through the AirPods you gave her. Honestly, she'll be fine.' She leaned forward and touched Alex's hand. 'They're really PC about competition these days. Play pass the parcel and everyone gets a prize.'

Alex shrugged. 'Musical chairs and everyone gets a seat?' he quipped.

'Practically,' Stef said. 'At Heath's last party we got pressured to divvy out the sweets from the Piñata, and there were still disputes.'

'Oh my,' Alex said. 'I'm officially a dinosaur.'

'Do dinosaurs eat delicious cheese?' Stef asked.

'This one does.' He added a small amount to a cracker and topped it with fig paste and rocket before tasting. 'Especially if it's Tarwin Blue,' he said with a wink.

•

Later that night when Stef went to check on Rosie, she found the AirPods on her dressing table.

Still in the box.

CHAPTER FOURTEEN

'You never told me you have a brother, Hannah.' There was more than a hint of recrimination in Katrina Head of Admin's voice. She'd been quite clear at work functions that should anyone have an eligible male in their lives, they were to volunteer him up. Katrina had been on RSVP and Plenty O' Fish and EliteSingles and even Tinder (don't get her started).

'Anyway, I thought I'd show him where your office is. It's a bit of a rabbit warren.' (It wasn't. Hannah's office was second floor, first door on the right.) 'It's so lovely to meet you, Alex,' Katrina said. 'You know, Hannah, I was telling Alex I've actually spent a bit of time in Adelaide and I don't mind it. I was staying with my brother and sister-in-law, she's from there originally, but don't get me started on them because my humble opinion is that they're in all sorts because of the—'

'Thanks, Katrina,' Hannah interrupted. A flash of confusion ran over Katrina's face before she recognised she was being dismissed.

'It was lovely to meet you too, Katrina,' Alex said, and if Katrina had been of an age where poking one's tongue out was an acceptable signifier, she may have let Hannah have it. But she could only employ her eyebrows to do the work.

'I saw online that you're giving a lecture on *Godot* this afternoon,' Alex said after Katrina flounced off. 'And I didn't want to just turn up unannounced in case it put you off your game. But I'd love to see you in action, if that's okay with you.'

Hannah had retrained herself years ago. Women were indoctrinated to play low status, to minimise the value of their skill sets and mitigate threats to the male ego. She refused to play. But this was her brother. And she had to wrestle anew before she put the tendency down for the count.

'If you would like to indulge in a little nihilism on this sunny Melbourne afternoon,' Hannah smiled, 'who am I to contest it?'

Alex threw up his arms. 'I'm passionate about nihilism,' he deadpanned.

'I'll be in the lecture theatre at two thirty.'

'What for?'

'Go away. Or I'll get Katrina to come sit with you.'

'I'm gone.'

•

Hannah couldn't see the back row from the stage, but she knew Alex was there. It struck her that even though her mum and dad were clearly proud of her, even though Stef sometimes talked about her work with awe in her voice, Alex was the only one who'd actually bothered to come and hear her speak.

Of course she'd given this exact lecture homing in on the role of society in *Waiting for Godot* before, but this time she felt it. In her nerve endings.

Oh, and wasn't it kind of cute that Ethan was there again, even though he'd already chosen the essay topic on symbolism in the play. Obviously he felt he could delve deeper by cross-pollinating. That was how densely propagated Hannah's lecture was. How rich.

And now, afterwards, with Alex still in the back row to witness, Ethan was practically tumbling down the aisle to the lectern to deliver accolades and admiration.

Except Ethan took a left turn four rows from the stage. There was an exit at the end and he must have been heading there. A little disappointing. Perhaps he had to rush to another class. But no – halfway down the row, Ethan stopped, his back to the stage. Hannah couldn't see who stood up in front of him, but she could definitely figure out what was happening.

In Hannah's day, it was called 'pashing'.

Whatever it was currently called, it killed any doubt.

•

'Extraordinary,' Alex said. 'I've spent a fair amount of time in lecture theatres, rarely have I seen a speaker so engaging. Is it too early for a drink?'

It was too early for a drink. And Stef had asked to meet Hannah halfway between their places for a debrief on all that had been going on. It was one of her nights without the kids.

Hannah – who had none, zero – was expected to be flexible. She could have asked Stef to meet them.

But.

Fuck it.

●

'They do a great espresso martini,' Hannah suggested as they bagged a booth in the Back Saloon at Cicciolina. Alex had enjoyed the tram ride. The St Kilda Esplanade had performed beautifully.

'Espresso martini it is.' Hannah watched how the bartender leaned forward to take the order – how she smiled and nodded at something Alex had said. The ongoing banter as she made the cocktails and slid them across the bar to him.

'I like this place,' Alex said, sitting opposite Hannah, 'it's got character.'

'It's a bit of a Melbourne institution,' Hannah replied, lifting her glass. 'To siblings, lost and found,' she said.

'To the sheer wonder of it,' Alex said, looking directly into her eyes as they clinked glasses. 'You know, Hannah, I didn't expect to feel so proud to watch you give that lecture.' He took a sip of his drink and shook his head. 'I'm not even sure proud is the right word. My reaction was surprisingly ... visceral. My God, I'm not explaining it very well. But I suppose it comes from understanding that my sister, my flesh and blood, is a woman of talent and purpose.'

There was a tingle at the back of Hannah's neck. She was a woman of talent and purpose, the judge of which couldn't be more qualified. She drained her glass and, almost without pause, the bartender placed another drink in front of her. 'That's a good trick,' she said with a smile. 'So, you've ordered ahead?'

'And, just like that, the compliment is deflected,' Alex said. 'Yes, I've ordered ahead. Nibbles and wine are up next.' The second espresso martini was even better than the first and something was expanding in Hannah's chest. She usually liked to choose from the menu but in this moment, she was satisfied.

'I feel the same way, Alex,' she tried. 'We are so alike, physically. But it's more than that, isn't it? It's our interests. The way we see things. What we want from life. The connection is ... fundamental.' She breathed in and out. The people at the adjacent booth were loud, but it was of no matter. 'Can you keep an eye on my bag while I nick to the bathroom?' Hannah asked. 'I don't want to be distracted by my bladder for this chat.'

'You are a woman of talent and purpose,' Hannah told her smiling reflection in the bathroom mirror. Walking back into the saloon, she could see the bartender lingering at their booth and a territorial feeling washed over her. She shook it off. There was a bottle of grenache on the table with two glasses already poured. A cheese platter, arancini and a plate of fried sardines. Hannah hated sardines. She slid into her seat.

'Enjoy. And please just raise your hand if you need anything else,' the bartender said, focusing solely on Alex. Hannah took a sip of wine. It was delicious.

'You're right, we do see things similarly,' Alex said, as though their conversation hadn't been put on pause. 'But Hannah, I have a confession. I haven't been entirely forthcoming with you about why I don't have children.' He stopped talking as the people from the next booth piled noisily out of the saloon, waiting until there was relative quiet. Hannah drank and willed him to continue. 'It's just that people tend to get on the quiz bandwagon, as I'm sure you'll know first-hand,' Alex said. 'Are you child-free or child-less? As if it's that simple. When sometimes it's neither. Or both. It can be very fucking annoying.'

Hannah poured herself another glass of grenache and topped Alex's up. 'Very fucking annoying,' she echoed.

'I would have had them with Cara,' Alex continued. 'Or one at least. I thought we were trying, actually, but nothing was happening. It was only by chance that … I found out she had a Mirena.'

'Jesus,' Hannah said. 'But why would she do that behind your back?'

'Cara was never clear about it, but I think it ultimately had to do with her not believing I was father material.'

'Did she … did Cara go on to have children with anyone else?' Hannah asked.

Alex shrugged. 'I don't know,' he said. 'I don't want to know either. We lost contact after our divorce. She moved interstate.' He gave a little snort. 'You don't stay in Adelaide when you've pissed off the Carpenter family.'

Another pause. A sip. It felt like no one else in the bar was talking. Although of course they must have been.

'I'm sorry I'm a bit emotional,' Alex said, not looking emotional. 'I've never shared that before.'

'Please don't be sorry,' Hannah said, holding Alex's hand across the table. 'Not for a single moment.' And perhaps the martini/grenache combination was playing with her inhibitions, but Hannah felt compelled to go further. 'I feel for you, Alex. And I understand, better than you might think.'

Alex squeezed Hannah's hand. 'Anyway,' he said finally. 'I've had some struggles with all that over the years. Wondering what could have been. I mean, you wouldn't be human if you didn't imagine what it would be like to have a kid.' His expression turned into a half-smile. 'Meeting Rosie helps ease the existential crisis.'

Hannah grinned. She felt perfectly comfortable here in this booth, sitting across from her brother. So, now there was to be honesty between them. No need for pretence.

'It's complicated for me too,' Hannah said eventually.

She reached into her bag, took out her diary and the sketch she'd stuck in the back pocket, and proceeded to tell her brother about her dream child.

CHAPTER FIFTEEN

Alex adjusted the incline on the treadmill in the hotel gym to maximum and reduced the speed. It wasn't a race he was after, but a solid climb. The burn in his quadriceps and calves was rewarding. Meant he was doing the work.

Similarly, he'd exacted great pleasure recently from the time spent with his sisters. Hannah and Stef weren't to blame for their trauma-free passage through life. Not really.

It seemed entirely possible that these women may become the inner sanctum that had always seemed to elude him, as long as he kept working to prepare the terrain. A reshuffle of the status quo would take time but that was of no matter.

Out of habit, Alex increased the speed. He kept jogging for thirty seconds before realising. He smiled wryly to himself and pressed the arrow back down. Down again.

Of course, there was an innate desire to move faster in terms of Hannah and Stef too. The women had their whole lives together as a head start. That was glaringly apparent. Their little in-jokes. The obvious affection despite their differences.

But evidence was emerging of private pockets, tucked away from each other. Everyone had them. It was why Gillian had bothered to become a confidante to both the powerful and the powerless. How she brought down some networks and restructured others. How she collected confidences which she could then strategically disseminate.

How she prevented Alex and Ricky from ever executing an alliance against her.

At Cicciolina on Thursday evening, Hannah had confided her struggles with what was supposed to be a mutual decision between her and Rex to remain child-free. Admittedly, having access to the diary that poked out of her handbag while Hannah went to the bathroom was a stroke of luck. The sketch that was tucked into the back pocket may as well have been captioned: *Woman in Crisis Over Reaching the End of Childbearing Years.* And here, Cara's betrayal had finally come in useful. Alex had managed to overlay his fury with a blanket of sorrow so heavy, so *palpable*, that the former was barely detectable. Alex had been empathetic rather than sympathetic, and Hannah was clever enough to discern the difference.

It was only he, Alex, Hannah had shared her secret with.

There was something going on behind the scenes with Stef too. Alex could sense difficult memories lingering in her house – most certainly in her pain-in-the-arse daughter. It was a little surprising Stef hadn't already off-loaded on him, since, unlike her sister, she had no shell. But it would come. Alex would make sure of it.

Tomorrow, he was meeting with both sisters. It would be a golden opportunity to see them interact again and further observe the chinks in their relationship.

Alex eased the incline back to zero and reduced the speed until it was time to press stop. As he wiped down the handles of the treadmill, a woman walked in. Despite there being a second step machine on the other side of the gym, she climbed onto the one right beside him. An objectively attractive woman of perhaps forty, with chestnut hair, brown eyes and leopard-print tights.

'Hi there. Are you here for the conference?' she asked. There was a familiar invitation in her smile. At another time, Alex would have pursued it. Now, he wanted to be well rested, focused, for tomorrow's endeavours.

He politely extracted himself.

Afterwards, in the sauna, Alex smiled at the recollection of the Furniture Barn sisterly glitch. He wondered if the effect could be amplified should he slip a casual mention of his and Hannah's visit to Cicciolina.

Alex was very much looking forward to tomorrow's excursion.

CHAPTER SIXTEEN

It was the first time the three of them had been out together. Stef had tried on several outfits. It wasn't like her, but she kept reviewing the options against Hannah's grey and black minimalist style and Alex's preference for muted tones. The red jumpsuit? It suited her, but she might look like a piece of ripe fruit. Floral wrap dress? They were going to an art gallery, not a community garden. Were her clothes gaudy? There was her black skirt and the tee with the lace inset. But this wasn't a funeral.

Self-talk was really annoying when it was so contradictory. Hannah had a style, Stef had her own. A curvy woman could never pull off Hannah's androgynous look anyway. Stef decided on the red jumpsuit and natural leather wedges. She had her look and she needed to own it.

Her phone pinged with a text from Hannah.

Exciting hey, sis? The three of us together! Xx

Hannah wasn't one to send texts with no purpose. Nor was she big on exclamation marks. Perhaps she was feeling bad about cancelling on Thursday night. But work was work, Stef understood that. Twice last week she'd stayed up until midnight finalising the new season orders from their Spanish and Italian suppliers.

They were meeting out front of the gallery in an hour so she had to get moving. She sent back a heart, grabbed her oversized sunnies and headed out into the afternoon sunshine.

Then she popped back in to change her shoes.

•

Hannah arrived at the gallery early and found a spot for coffee. She wished she'd arranged to meet Stef before Alex arrived so she'd have time to set the record straight. Even when they were teenagers and had so little in common they were practically speaking different languages, she'd hated lying to her sister. To be fair, her text cancelling their catch-up had been more of an omission than a lie. Still, Hannah didn't want anything just popping up in conversation that would give away the fact that she'd gone out with Alex instead.

It wasn't a big deal, of course. Hannah had decided to have a few drinks after work rather than driving to suburbia. That would be her rationale, should she need it.

She spotted Stef sashaying through the crowd on the Princes Bridge looking like a movie star in her red jumpsuit and giant sunglasses.

And now, to the right, her brother was approaching.

Hannah finished the rest of her latte and walked up the sheltered walkway to greet Stef. But before they could say anything, a commotion erupted.

A homeless guy had parked himself on the concrete ledge beside the footpath that ran between the Playhouse and the gallery. His dirty blond hair was matted, his feet bare and filthy. A grey blanket and hat were set up on the pavement in front of him.

'Fucking leech.' A young man approaching from the other side wore a Bintang singlet, trackpants and a snarl. 'Fucking parasite. Why should I give you money? Hey? What's wrong with you?'

The homeless guy murmured something Hannah couldn't hear. Whatever it was seemed to rile Bintang, because his volume and vitriol increased.

'Looks like you've got arms. And legs. So why don't you get a fucking job?' he spat.

The homeless guy bent over. He scooped up his blanket and the hat half-filled with coins and shuffled towards the gallery. Bintang followed, flailing arms behind the man's back.

Hannah and Stef watched.

'Could be ice,' Hannah whispered.

'Or just plain arsehole,' Stef said as Bintang leaped onto the ledge and disappeared into a grassed area.

Hannah felt just as on edge with Bintang out of sight.

The homeless guy took up position in front of the gallery moat. Alex joined Hannah and Stef just as Bintang re-emerged for Act Two.

'You're a fucking weasel,' Bintang taunted.

Hannah cringed as he reached into the hat and grabbed a fistful of coins. He looked around, seemingly pleased with the gathering audience.

Hannah glared at him, but she felt as paralysed as the rest of the crowd. People had their phones out and ready, but what had actually happened? Was verbal assault and the theft of a few coins enough to warrant calling 000?

Bintang clambered up the ledge in front of the moat, holding the coins aloft.

Just then, Hannah spotted Alex weaving his way through the crowd towards the two men.

'Yep. Let's make a fucking wish,' Bintang yelled, oblivious to Alex moving closer. He theatrically dropped a single coin. 'I wish you homeless fucks would do everyone a favour and kill yourselves.'

Then, Alex was right there, staring up at the maniac. Bintang looked thrilled to have a worthier opponent. He stared Alex down, dropping coins one by one.

Hannah couldn't see Alex's face. The homeless guy had dropped to his knees and appeared to be praying, hands together above his bowed head.

Bintang crouched down.

'Is that a knife?' Stef yelled suddenly. 'Hannah, does he have a knife?'

Hannah pulled Stef in tighter.

But then, in a deft movement Hannah could barely follow, came Alex's punch. A swift strike to the guy's solar plexus. The maniac was winded. He fell back into the moat.

'There's no knife, Steffie,' Hannah reassured her. 'It was just glare from the coins.'

Summoned by the splash, gallery security arrived. But Bintang's dip in the moat had rendered him tame. He was humiliated, hopeless. No threat to anybody. When the guards told him to move on, he obeyed, a water trail dripping from his singlet to the footpath.

Hannah took Stef's hand and they moved towards Alex. As they neared, the homeless man launched himself up on his haunches. He reached out a grateful hand for Alex to help him up.

But Alex shook his head. His eyes seemed suddenly hard as he straightened up to full height. 'I'm not your saviour,' he said. 'If you don't want to be hunted, refuse to be prey.'

In the ensuing pause, Hannah winced.

'Help yourself up,' Alex said.

CHAPTER SEVENTEEN

There were other men in the crowd – younger men. Bigger, stronger men – but it had been Alex alone who took action where it was needed. Their brother hadn't thought of his own safety. Of course, it had turned out that there wasn't a knife, but there could have been. If Liam had been there, he would have acted the same way. Sticking up for the underdog. For all the ugly moments between them, Stef knew this and it broke her heart a little.

'It's okay, Steffie,' Hannah said again, when she had actually been the one standing there like a fence post. At least Stef had yelled out. That was probably what alerted the security guards. Stef withdrew her hand.

'I'm fine, Hannah. Alex was so decisive. One blow and that arsehole was in the moat. I just ... well, I guess I'm proud.'

Hannah nodded but she looked preoccupied. 'Did you see Alex's reaction when the homeless guy wanted a hand to get up? Could you tell what he said?'

'No,' Stef replied, though it wasn't entirely true. She wasn't sure what to make of what she'd seen. Or thought she'd seen.

Regardless, she found herself wanting Hannah's take on it before she tried to frame it for herself. 'Why?'

Hannah shrugged. 'I'm pretty sure he said something about not being a saviour, and that the homeless guy should help himself up. But the bit that kind of freaked me out was when Alex said, "If you don't want to be hunted, refuse to be prey." Don't you find that a bit weird? After all that happened? I mean, Steffie …' Hannah's voice was a whisper, though the crowd had dispersed and nobody was listening. 'I just got a creepy feeling about it. It seemed like, I don't know … a command.'

A shiver ran up and down Stef's spine. She would have preferred to just feel proud. But there was something in Hannah's assertion that resonated.

'I think I did hear some of that,' Stef conceded. 'And it was a bit odd. I guess we don't know him very well yet. I mean, there's a huge emotional connection for sure – you, me and Alex together. It's … amazing. He's half our blood, our DNA. That will never stop astonishing me. But that last bit was weird.'

People were stopping Alex as he made his way back to them. Stef saw a pat on the back, a thumbs up. 'We can talk about it later, Han,' she said, setting her face to open approval as Alex approached.

'Talk about what, later?' Alex asked and Stef cursed herself for being too loud. 'Your bravery,' she managed.

'Well, that will take about ten seconds.' Alex smiled wryly. 'Let's get the requisite shot of ourselves reflected in the waterwall, then we can finally go inside and see the exhibition.'

They did need some sibling photos. Stef had a sudden desire to take all the regular tourist shot opportunities.

'After the exhibition, how about we jump on a tram and head to the St Kilda foreshore?' she suggested. 'We could get a shot in front of the Luna Park mouth for Mum.'

Alex nodded. Then he turned to Hannah. 'We didn't get to walk along the beach on Thursday, did we? We were too keen for a cocktail.'

Stef's jumpsuit was definitely gaudy. Her sunglasses were too big. She was too big. She didn't fit in here, at the National Gallery Waterwall, with her chiselled-cheekbone siblings.

•

As they wandered through the exhibition separately, Stef stared at each piece blankly. She wished she hadn't worn red. It was so easy to spot her.

The sculpture Stef stood in front of now was a giant ball of twine made from wire. Art reflecting life. How could anyone unravel it when you couldn't find the beginning?

So Hannah had ditched her. On one of Stef's child-free nights when she could easily have joined and the three of them could be together, Hannah chose to exclude her. The protectiveness she'd just tried to demonstrate was skin deep. Hannah probably wanted Alex to herself. Maybe she thought Stef brought down the tone of the conversation. Jesus.

Stef blinked away a tear and bit her lip to stop more. God she was lonely. In her heart, her soul, her body. And fuck it, but she missed Liam most at times like this.

And here was Hannah, walking towards her. Eyeballing the twine as though she was the only one smart enough to figure out where it began and ended.

'Steffie, I'm sorry about Thursday night. It was a bit of a misunderstanding.'

'Not really. I think I understand pretty well.'

'It actually was work-related. I had a bit of a rollercoaster day ...'

As she expanded on her bullshit excuse, Stef breathed in. On the exhale, she cut Hannah off. 'You know, Hannah, I work too. And not at a furniture barn. It's called Furniture Gallery.'

Hannah stepped back. 'Okay. I should have known that.'

'You should have known a lot of things. Maybe you're not as smart as you think. Maybe you're just ... smug.'

'Steffie, where's all this coming from?' Hannah asked.

'I'm sick to death of the way you treat me, Hannah. You have no respect. How about you try to bring up two kids and still have a career?'

As Alex walked towards them, Stef tried to compose herself. He looked from sister to sister, clearly registering the tension. And God, she didn't want it to happen, but her voice cracked. 'I think I'm going to call it a day.'

'Please don't, Stef,' Alex said. He took one hand and then the other. 'I hope I haven't caused any distress.'

Stef shook her head. '*You* haven't Alex,' she replied.

'Jesus, Stef,' said Hannah. 'A bit of an overreaction, don't you think? You know what, you guys stay. I have work to catch up on.'

And if Stef still nursed a wisp of uncertainty about Alex's parting words to the homeless man, the desire to talk about it with her sister had evaporated.

•

After Hannah left, Stef and Alex made their way to the gallery cafe. 'I'm sorry you saw that, Alex,' Stef said.

Alex shrugged. 'It's what happens with siblings,' he said. 'I'm sure it will pass.'

Stef had a sip of her cappuccino and looked around.

'You said you had a brother?'

'Yes. Ricky. He passed away when he was nineteen. I miss him like hell, but that doesn't mean there was no sibling rivalry.' Alex paused and it looked to Stef as though he was remembering his brother fondly. 'There was plenty.'

Stef looked up at an abstract painting. Her instinct told her it was of the sky, so it was probably the ocean. She tried for a smile. 'I love Hannah to bits,' she said.

'Of course you do, Stef,' Alex said. 'And she loves you back. But perhaps she also feels a little overshadowed by you.'

'Really?' she replied, willing him to continue.

'Well, yes. I mean, you're earthy and creative and beautiful. You have two delightful children. You're clearly valued at work and you connect with people easily. You're warm, Stef. I feel like I could tell you anything.'

The way Alex framed Hannah's mixed feelings about her made sense. It calmed Stef down and gave her perspective and confidence. Thank God he'd walked into her life.

The painting was of the sky. Stef confirmed it when she read the title.

'Thank you, Alex,' she said. She reached across the table and held her brother's hand. 'Thank you.'

CHAPTER EIGHTEEN

On the way home, Hannah tried to wrangle her thoughts. Maybe Stef had a point? Maybe she had been dismissive. But it cut Hannah to the quick to think she'd hurt her sister.

A flush rose through her body as Hannah thought about Stef's work. She actually had thought it was called Furniture Barn. And she got how Stef might be offended.

Perhaps she did come across as smug? But she'd never felt superior. She'd never even felt good enough until Rex.

Hannah was definitely proud of what she'd achieved. What Stef probably didn't understand was that this self-pride had been a long time coming. Hard fought. When Stef was a child, a teenager, her popularity had taken zero effort, but Hannah had to work for every morsel of friendship. In her scarce romantic experience, it had always seemed the guys were looking over her shoulders for something better.

Her dad could tell when it got her down. 'Just be yourself, Hanny,' he'd say. 'A bright spark of a girl. You're enough.' But her father had to love her. And she *was* being herself. At least, she didn't know how to be any other way. And it was a self that people could take or leave.

As teens, Stef thought Hannah chose to live that way. That books and academics were her lifeblood. And Hannah supposed she nurtured the perspective. What was the alternative? Sympathy from her baby sister?

There had been more private ways of getting relief.

God, what an unsettling day it had been. Hannah needed to debrief with Rex. From the incident with the homeless guy and the weird things Alex said to him, through to her argument with Stef. Hannah understood she wasn't the most magnanimous of people, but Rex provided that quality for both of them. He could calm Hannah's negative energy and turn it around with his generous interpretation of people's motivations. Even hers.

Especially hers.

Perhaps Hannah had lost sight of that temporarily, but as soon as she decided she would tell Rex everything about her day, she felt lighter.

•

When Hannah arrived home, Rex was in the kitchen on a call with Albie.

'Oh buddy,' he was saying, 'I really am sorry. But what did Sonia say she couldn't handle about you?'

There was a pause then Rex roared with laughter. 'Well, obviously she had to go anyway. I can tell you in all honesty' – he looked over at Hannah and winked hello – 'your storytelling skills are unrivalled. And your moccasins are ochre, not tangerine. A person who can't distinguish the vast difference simply deserves no more of your time.'

If Hannah needed reminding that she had a partner who was able to process life's little catastrophes with humour and grace, it was right in front of her.

There was another pause and Rex gave Albie a few words of consolation before hanging up.

'Sonia has broken up with Albie,' he confirmed. 'He's feigning broken-heartedness while swiping right.'

'Poor Albie. But I wasn't a big fan,' Hannah admitted.

Rex grinned. 'My darling, I'm aware of that,' he said. He poured her a glass of pinot gris. 'How was your day?'

Hannah took a sip of wine and then another.

'It was weird, Rex,' she said.

Rex took his wine into the lounge and sank back into the couch, ready to listen. Hannah took her time, providing a detailed narration of the incident with the homeless man. It was a relief to lay it out like this. She still baulked at repeating what Alex said after the culprit moved on – it felt almost disloyal to her brother. But the whole point of telling Rex was to have her doubts assuaged.

Hannah took a deep breath and urged herself on. 'He also said something I found a bit odd – "If you don't want to be hunted, refuse to be prey."'

Rex said nothing. He got up and brought the wine bottle to the coffee table, topping up each of their glasses.

'I'm probably overreacting,' Hannah prompted, but Rex's silence was making her feel more and more discomfited.

'Obviously, Alex thinks people should be proactive about fending for themselves. My initial reaction was that he was making a kind of ... command, I guess, and it seemed a bit creepy. But of course, when I rationalise it I can see it's inevitable that there will be times where Alex's thinking doesn't coincide with my own. It's not like his mental processes are going to be as similar as our physical features. He's had a different upbringing, different life experiences. I guess the most important thing is that his first impulse was to help.'

Hannah waited for Rex to chime in. And finally, he did.

'Actually, Han, I think that was an extremely odd thing for Alex to say,' he said. 'It reeks of control. And I know that discovering a long-lost brother feels amazing for you, but I think you should slow things down a bit. We don't really know this person.'

Rex lay a hand on Hannah's leg.

We don't really know this person? Maybe he didn't, but Hannah did. This *person* was her flesh and blood.

Rex grimaced, as though he was about to say something he'd prefer not to.

'Han, I also have a suspicion that Alex has been following me.'

Hannah's heart thumped. That was the opposite of what she needed from Rex. Where was the reassurance that Alex was a great guy? Smart and sophisticated and a fabulous addition to Hannah's life? And it was deeply disappointing that Rex would bring the conversation back to himself when she needed him. She hadn't even got to the falling out with Stef yet.

'What do you mean?' Hannah asked, her voice remarkably even. 'When? Where? Why?'

'I don't know why,' Rex said. 'But I was in the uni cafe at lunchtime on Thursday and there was Alex – in the quad, looking through the window. He pretended not to see me. It was ... disconcerting.'

Hannah shook her head. 'Well, I know this might come as a surprise, Rex,' she said, 'but Alex was at uni to sit in on one of my lectures. "The Role of Society in *Waiting for Godot*", actually. One you've threatened to come to several times without ever making it.'

Rex removed his hand.

'Okay, okay, Han. I'll accept that. And I'm sorry I haven't made it to that lecture because nothing makes me prouder than to watch you excel. But, honey, on Friday afternoon I was in the pub with a few students and there he was again, looking through the window. I waved but he just took off.'

Frustration and anger rose so high in Hannah that she had to stand up to unleash it. A version of her imagined child, around Heath's age now, cheered from the sidelines.

'Jesus, Rex,' she said, 'that's very fucking self-centred. You really think you're so important that a wealthy and accomplished man would bother stalking you? How about this for an idea – you're jealous because I've become close to Alex. There's another man who is truly interested in what I think, what I say, who I am. I wish I'd never even tried to confide in you about what happened today. I was after a bit of reassurance, but that only goes one way in our relationship, right?'

Rex stood up. He walked to the kitchen counter and picked up his keys. So fucking obvious.

Hannah had time for one parting shot.

'And you might want to rethink hanging out with students at the pub, Rex. It's pathetic.'

•

Hannah heard Rex come home at 5 am. She heard the tap running for teeth-cleaning.

Then the door to the spare room closed behind him.

CHAPTER NINETEEN

Alex hadn't been behind the wheel for months. In Adelaide, with Ray as his driver, he preferred to use his time as a passenger to catch up on work. But here he was, in a generic rent-a-car. A white Suzuki Swift, the likes of which were dotted all around him in the lanes of the Nepean Highway. The car he was following, on the other hand, was its own version of look-at-me. A maroon Chevrolet with chipped paintwork and a noisy clutch that Alex imagined was supposed to project casual quirkiness.

Everyone, Alex knew, had their own repertoire of signalling. The trick was whether they were able to align their signals with others' perceptions. Rex's charming dishevelled intellectual pose was, in Alex's opinion, rather exaggerated. But it obviously piqued interest in younger generations. Alex supposed his success often relied on a hapless sidekick for contrast. Looking through the window of the pub the other day, he had identified such an example. One didn't need to hear what he was saying to know that the tall youth with the sparse beard and terrible teeth was pontificating to the point that his fellow drinkers were suppressing yawns. It was in the eager slant of his eyes, the emphatic hand gestures.

And there was Rex, sinking into the bench seat with his beer, issuing a laconic one-liner that woke the other students from their torpor and brought life back into their eyes, while the unfortunate bearded youth cast around, unsuccessfully, for an opportunity to hold the floor again.

Alex tapped the wheel, changing lanes to pre-empt a right-hand turn. The person in Rex's passenger seat had long hair and a habit of reaching up to ruffle the top layer. When she bobbed her head, Alex had to assume she was laughing.

Rex did, Alex had to admit, emanate a relaxed goodwill. This was not a man who lured. But should an attractive woman climb into his web voluntarily, Alex guessed Rex would accommodate. Perhaps there was an understanding between him and Hannah?

Alex's tapping against the steering wheel increased in both speed and pressure as he turned into Cummins Road. He probably shouldn't have voiced his advice to the homeless man after the incident at the art gallery. Not loud enough for Hannah and Stef to hear, anyway. Perhaps, given they had been raised with soft, unconditional parental love, they would have perceived it as harsh? As one might if they had never really had to struggle with the basics. But there were no free rides in this life. Not for some, anyway.

Alex breathed in. Stef had been okay afterwards. She hadn't even mentioned the incident other than to say he'd done well. Then again, Alex suspected that Stef may have had experience of surviving in murky waters. The first time he'd seen Stef and her ex interact, witnessed the proprietary way Liam waltzed in and out of her life, Alex had suspected their history included trauma that kept them both repelled and attached to each other.

But murky waters seemed only part of the reason Stef hadn't been as fazed as Hannah. Her headspace had been in a different zone. She had clearly been upset with Hannah for failing to ask her to join them for drinks at Cicciolina. She'd tried to put on a brave face, but Alex could practically see Stef attempting to shed her own body as she walked around the gallery. As one who had experienced the real thing, Alex understood this was a very mild case of sibling rivalry.

Clearly, Stef had embraced his Psychology 101 interpretation of Hannah's jealousy. She would keep basking in her reflection through his eyes. It had been their first bonding experience of critiquing another family member together. An exclusive. And Alex knew that with a little massaging, the intimacy between them would bloom. It was only a matter of time before Stef spilled the details of what had gone on between her and Liam before they separated.

No. Stef was okay with Alex. Heath too. The thorny girl-child, Rosie, was the one in that family he still needed to win over. Obviously, she was not buying the signals he'd put out. But Alex had an idea on how to override her doubts. Everyone had their currency, and he was pretty sure he'd be able to peg Rosie's.

But Alex had definitely seen misgivings in Hannah's eyes and it probably resulted in a shift of her perception of him. Still, perhaps that wasn't entirely a bad thing? If Hannah understood that her new brother was no toothless tiger, she might also understand there was strength in her revised corner, should she need it.

Alex hadn't attempted to hide when Rex saw him at the pub window. Nor at the uni cafe. He wanted Rex to suspect he was under scrutiny. If he was being duplicitous, if he wasn't treating Hannah with respect, Alex would find out.

Even today, as Rex's Chevrolet pulled out of the car park, Alex had been tempted to let his presence be known. But he'd changed his mind in case that knowledge influenced Rex's movements. This time, there was no gaggle of students. There was one person in his car and they were far from the campus and the university's local pub.

It would have been more pleasant if they'd taken the scenic route along Beach Road to Black Rock. It gave Alex the impression that they weren't out for a casual drive. That there was a destination.

Up ahead, the Chevrolet's indicator blinked left and turned into a car park on a suburban shopping strip.

Alex pulled in behind, with one car between them. The ocean loomed large at the end of the street.

The passenger-side door opened first and Alex leaned across for a better view. The woman bounced out with the spring step of youth. She was dressed in the kind of grey drill overalls a tradie might wear. Underneath, a bright purple shirt that looked to be made of a delicate fabric, perhaps chiffon or silk. On her feet, white Doc Marten boots. A carefully curated outfit to signify an eclectic personality.

As Alex zoomed in on his camera phone, he saw that her hair wasn't long as he'd supposed from the back view. Or rather, it wasn't all long. The left side of her head was shaved. On the same side, her neck was fully tattooed. Even with the camera at full zoom, Alex couldn't make out the form. A dragon, perhaps?

And now, from the driver side, with the creaks and groans of being middle-aged and overweight, Rex emerged. In his navy chinos, white shirt and Timberland loafers, he could have been her father. Perhaps about to take his rebellious offspring for a reconciliatory lunch at the little Vietnamese cafe they were now walking towards.

Except, no. Arms linked they walked straight past the cafe.

It was only then that Alex turned his camera to the signage of the shopfront next to the cafe. He took a series of photos as Rex held the door open for the young woman. As they disappeared inside.

Extraordinary.

Alex patted the dash of the Suzuki Swift. Wound down the window and breathed in the sea air. It had been a productive couple of hours.

He would definitely reward himself by taking the scenic route back to the hotel.

CHAPTER TWENTY

Stef checked the time on her phone again. She walked up the hall to the front door. The white stretch Hummer was parked in the street.

'I am beyond sorry,' she told Alex. 'I asked Liam to drop the kids off at two o'clock sharp. I didn't say why because I'm trying to keep things to myself. Liam thinks he has the right to all the details. But maybe I should have told him specifically.'

'Please don't stress, Stef,' Alex said. 'For what it's worth, I think that's the right decision. Liam seems to have an entitled attitude about keeping in the loop. Especially when he can't respect a simple timetable.'

Stef looked down the street and tried not to cry. Alex had gone to so much trouble. The kids were supposed to come home and drop their stuff off way before the Hummer arrived. They were supposed to walk into the street and be wowed. Alex and Stef were going to reveal the destination once they were en route.

And there was Liam's car, ambling up the street.

Stef marched towards him, arms folded, while Alex stayed in the house so the kids could drop their gear off before he locked up.

Liam wound down the window.

'Hooley dooley,' he said casually. 'Is that your Hummer, lady?'

Stef waited until the kids had jumped out.

'That's it, Liam,' she hissed. 'You're late and you've ruined our afternoon. This will not happen again.'

Liam looked chastened. Then again, a look was pretty easy to manufacture.

'Prue had the car. She was late back from Zumba.'

'Jesus Christ, of course she was,' Stef said. 'I'm sure she's a natural.'

Stef hadn't meant that to be funny, but Alex gave her a half-smile.

'Stef, if you'd told me your rich brother was hiring a Hummer to take the kids to … where?'

'None of your fucking business,' she replied.

'To none-of-my-fucking-business, I would have made sure they were here on time. I'm sorry, Stef. Truly.'

'You always are,' she said. In front of her, Alex and the kids were getting into the Hummer. Alex held up Stef's purse and indicated he'd locked the front door. The guy really had his shit together. Thank God someone did.

'A basketball match,' Stef told Liam. 'It was supposed to be a surprise.'

Then she got into the Hummer with the others.

•

'I love this car so much,' Heath said, taking a Coke from the bar fridge. 'I could probably live in here and be, like, the King of the Hummer.'

Stef waited for her daughter to say something snide, but even Rosie was too lost in the moment to comment. As they drove through the backstreets of Burwood, a group of four kids appeared on the sidewalk. It took Stef a moment to realise one of them was Lara, Rosie's supposed bestie.

The kids looked to see who was inside.

'Oh my God,' a boy said, 'that's Rosie Simmons!'

'Rosie!' Lara waved.

Rosie pushed the window button. The chauffeur slowed down even further, letting his passenger have her moment. Stef could have hugged him.

'Oh, hi,' Rosie said. The kids jogged beside the car.

'That is the coolest.'

'I wish I could get in.'

'Where are you going?'

'My uncle got us tickets for the basketball game today.' Rosie's reply was delightfully understated.

'Box seats!' Heath added, leaning over Rosie. 'Melbourne United versus Sydney Kings!'

Rosie pulled Heath back to his own seat but Stef could tell she was glad for his addition.

It was perfect. Stef could practically see Rosie's status soaring. If anyone needed that, it was her daughter. Perhaps Liam's lousy timing was a blessing in disguise.

Stef looked over at Alex and he nodded.

'Are you ready to get going, Rosie?' he asked.

She gave a last wave to the admiring group.

'Yes,' she said. Then, without a single prompt, 'Please.'

•

'I think Heath might be a little hoarse tomorrow,' Alex said as he and Stef settled on the back verandah that evening.

'I just hope my ears stop ringing by then.' Stef laughed. 'They loved it, Alex. I'm sorry that we missed the pre-match entertainment though. Liam has never had a sense of urgency about anything. We've even missed a couple of planes over the years – before the kids, when we backpacked around Australia.'

Alex tilted his head. 'You two were childhood sweethearts, right?'

Stef nodded. 'We were seventeen when we started going out. Sometimes it feels like we were always in each other's lives. I think that's what's made the separation so tricky.'

'It's like an almost-separation, hey?' Alex replied. 'Liam still takes liberties?'

Stef considered for a moment. 'That's exactly what it's like,' she said. 'I legally reverted to my maiden name, but even that felt symbolic rather than practical. It just seems that whatever I do, our boundaries are blurred.'

'I had to get Cara out of my life in one fell swoop or I would have gone nuts,' Alex offered. 'For me, there could be no half-measures.'

'Hmm,' Stef said, 'maybe that's the right way to do it. If you can.'

'Perhaps.' Alex shrugged. 'But of course it was only possible to make a clean break from Cara because we didn't have kids,' he said.

'You would have made a wonderful father,' Stef replied softly. 'Perhaps you still can.'

Alex made a scissor-snipping motion. 'I'm afraid that's off the cards,' he said. 'I had a vasectomy after we split.'

'That's heavy shit,' Stef said. 'But it can be reversed, right?'

'I was very much in love with my wife, Stef. Our divorce was devastating. I've never had the desire to have a family with anyone but Cara.'

'How did it end?' Stef asked.

Alex leaned forward. 'Is this just between us, Stef? Can it be?'

There was a buzz of satisfaction in being the one he chose to confide in.

'I believed that Cara and I were trying for a baby. I was full of anticipation, so ready to experience the joy of a child who would be part of each of us. Being adopted, I'd never experienced that biological connection. Even though we were a year down the track, we weren't panicking.'

Stef nodded. She didn't want to speak – just for Alex to continue.

'One night we were at a party. Cara's best friend was drunk. And while the three of us were talking, Bronwyn just burst out with this thing. This thing I'll never forget. "I'm still bleeding every month since I got that fricking Mirena. What about you, Cara?"'

Stef felt the blow in her own gut. 'Oh Alex,' she said. 'Why would Cara do that? Why would she lie to you?'

Alex's shrug still couldn't dislodge the hurt, even all these years later. Stef could see it.

'She couldn't explain. Ultimately, explanations wouldn't have mattered anyway. Cara did not want to have a child with me. The marriage was over for me as soon as I learned that.'

Stef sighed. She looked out at the willow bottlebrush where the stringybark tree had been. Then at the hole in the back fence.

She could hear Rosie talking with Lara on the phone in the kitchen. Connected, for the time being at least, because of Alex's thoughtfulness.

'Our marriage ended with a bang not a whimper too,' she said.

Yes, she'd made a vow with Liam that neither would breathe a word about what happened. At the time, it had felt like the right thing to do. To forget. But forgetting was hard. Forgetting burned inside her. And, ultimately, Liam was more to blame than she was. He'd brought the whole possibility into their house, their home.

And now, finally, Stef had found a true and trusted confidant.

CHAPTER TWENTY-ONE

Alex pulled into Liam's street, parked the Suzuki Swift and walked up the driveway where a battered canary-yellow ute was parked just short of the garage. He briefly looked inside. Boxes were stacked from floor to ceiling. Alex suspected a great proportion might be fragments of the past, random and unclassified. Things Liam could not let go of but didn't want to bring into his new life.

Stef's garage was practically empty. Clean, spick and span. No relics.

He had timed the visit with Prue's Wednesday evening Zumba class. It was a shame not to meet her in the flesh after hearing various characterisations. To ascertain for himself what kind of woman Liam had chosen after the disintegration of his marriage. There had been no next for Alex after Cara. Dalliances, yes, but he had not allowed any of them to stay overnight at Hughesdale, let alone cohabitate. He would never open himself up to be crushed like that again.

Alex walked across the lawn, past the mower that had been abandoned halfway through the job and up a few stairs to the brick veneer house. There were holes in the flywire he opened to knock.

After a minute or so, the door opened inwards. Liam's eyelids drooped as though he had either been asleep or was stoned. Alex suspected the latter.

'Alex?'

To which Alex nodded.

'Is everything okay with Stef and the kids?'

It was best to reassure at first. The impact was greater that way. 'Everything is fine,' Alex said and Liam's shoulders dropped noticeably.

'Well then,' he said. 'Phew. Do you wanna come in? I was just watching a rerun of the game. I'll get you a beer.'

As Liam headed for the kitchen, Alex looked around the lounge. Taking pride of place was a giant TV on mute atop a cabinet, AFL players frozen in time. There was a pink, three-seater velvet couch and matching armchairs, an IKEA coffee table and an open beer. Underneath, a glass bong that had been pushed to the far corner, stashed but not quite hidden. It was a handy find that Alex immediately added to his arsenal.

Below the bay window at the back of the room was a makeshift nail salon with two chairs either side. If Alex needed further proof that the house was predominantly Prue's domain, it was on the wall opposite the TV. The lovebirds sported matching white shirts with collars turned up, denim jeans and cheesy smiles. Alex had to repress a snort of laughter as he recalled Rosie bemoaning the 'lame' pictures scattered around her dad's place while she mimed putting fingers down her throat. The kid might be brittle, but since the Hummer and basketball match she was beginning to trust him with her perspectives.

Everyone had their currency.

Alex was compelled to follow Liam into the kitchen to see how honest and accurate Rosie's take was. Completely on point. The magnets his niece had spoken of were right there on the fridge. Four of the same prints as the one in the lounge, shrunk to fit. Pinned underneath was a notice for a seminar entitled, 'How to Help your Child Transition to High School' and a seven out of ten spelling test with Heath's name on it. Clearly, they were invested in the kids. Which should make this transaction fairly simple.

Back in the lounge, Liam downed the last of his old beer and opened the next.

'So, to what do I owe this pleasure?' he asked, pressing play on the remote so that the game continued in silence.

Alex remained standing as he pointed under the coffee table.

'Do you smoke when the children are here?'

Liam put down his beer and leaned forward.

'Beg your pardon?' he asked.

'Do you smoke dope when the children are here?'

Liam did some manspreading on the pink velvet couch.

'I don't see why that's any of your business, Alex,' he said through his teeth.

'You don't see why the welfare of my niece and nephew is my business?' Alex replied, keeping his tone measured. 'I have friends who I suspect might advise differently. Family law barristers, for example, who deal with custody arrangements and the like.'

Given a more sophisticated target, he would have danced around the subject. Made it an art form. Alex sat on an armchair, legs crossed. He opened the beer and held it up in cheers. On the couch, the true colours Stef had spoken of were emerging. Liam's fists were clenched. Nostrils flared. A blue vein appeared over one temple. And perhaps he shouldn't have smiled, but this was ... amusing.

'There's also the question of inconsistent child support payments,' Alex said. 'Of course, I can and will step into that financial void. None of us wants Heath and Rosie to do without. But it does, I think, escalate the premise that your business and mine are interwoven.'

Liam rose to better unleash his gesticulations.

'Who the fuck do you think you are?' he demanded, jabbing a finger in the air. So crude and unanswerable that Alex could only ignore it. The cat and mouse with Rex was proving way more interesting.

'If I was to involve lawyers on behalf of Stef to sue for sole custody, I'm fairly certain that the possession and use of an illegal substance would be a black mark on your parental slate.' Alex paused. Waited a few beats. Liam's mouth hung open. The timing was right. 'As would possession of an unregistered firearm should you ever have had one, say, in the garage. Especially one that was accessible to children.'

Liam's mouth snapped closed. He collapsed into the couch.

Alex finished his beer and stood.

'All I currently ask, Liam, is that you recognise and respect the boundaries between you and my sister. Drop-offs and pick-ups should be timely and there is no need for you to hang around Stef's house. Can we agree on that?'

Liam stared at the TV and nodded.

'Excellent,' Alex said. 'Thanks for the beer. I'll see myself out.'

He began walking down the hallway. Stopped and turned around.

'Oh, and Liam,' he said, 'Stef and I have had the locks changed.'

•

This was the first group email Alex had written to his biological mother and sisters and it felt like a landmark. He'd ticked the boxes to make sure it was doable. Margaret was free of commitments, especially so since her husband had gone AWOL. Hannah would be on university holidays. Stef's bosses had been very accommodating when he called them. And, although it was officially Stef's week with the kids, Alex was sure Liam would be amenable to switching.

He attached digital copies of the airline tickets and pressed send.

Truly, he didn't much care about Margaret. Every time he looked at her, Alex felt revulsion. Rejection. But the Fidler women came as a package deal. There was intimacy building between Alex and his sisters. But with the late-in-life start, these relationships couldn't just mosey along. They required acceleration.

And that work could only be done at Hughesdale.

PART TWO

RUPTURE

CHAPTER TWENTY-TWO

Hannah took the window seat with Stef in the middle and Marg in the aisle seat opposite. The take-off was smooth. The last few days with Rex had not been. She stared out until Melbourne became a doll city then disappeared completely.

When Rex returned to their bed two nights ago he'd asked Hannah to reaffirm their agreement – that they were two autonomous people coming together by choice. That neither should attempt to dictate the way the other chose to live. That notions of control and one-upmanship were the province of the weak-minded.

He hadn't retracted the accusation about Alex but neither had he mentioned it again. Hannah was weak-minded enough to take that small victory.

So, they'd fallen back into a semblance of their relationship where the gloss was dulled. Rex had been sincere when asking Hannah to take care on the trip to Adelaide. He'd assured her that he was on the other end of the phone for her any time, but Hannah couldn't shake the feeling that he was relieved in anticipation of a break from her.

Other men had told her she was too intense. Never Rex. He'd insisted that her intensity was inseparable from her intelligence and therefore welcome. But his parting kiss had been passive, and it made Hannah wonder how he'd said the final goodbye to Leo's mother all those years ago. The woman who had supposedly forfeited her intelligence for a child. His child.

'How do you like business class, Mum?' Stef's question brought Hannah back to the present.

Marg accepted a glass of sparkling wine from the flight attendant. 'Jim would call it fancy,' she said. 'Have either of you spoken to your dad lately?'

'Yes,' Hannah and Stef said in unison.

'As we know, he's a man of few words when it comes to his own emotions, but it sounds like he's doing okay,' Hannah added.

'I rang Uncle Bill too,' Stef said. 'He swore Dad was taking it easy and that he'd let me know if there was anything to report.'

'Good. Bill would be the perfect companion for Jim right now,' Marg said. 'He and your dad are peas in a pod.' She smiled wistfully. 'I know exactly what Jim would say about business class.' She sat tall as though trying to channel their giant dad. 'He'd say it was a waste of hard-earned money.'

'Well, I don't think money is an issue for Alex,' Hannah said.

Marg put her drink on the tray and her hand seemed to rise to her heart involuntarily.

'I don't really know what is or isn't an issue for Alex,' she said. 'It's different for you girls, I can see that, but for me, his boundaries seem impenetrable.' She cleared her throat before continuing. 'He's shut down all my attempts to explain what happened, why I gave him up for adoption. And he's told me very little about his life. It's his prerogative, of course. I'm trying to take the cues from him, not force things, but it's difficult. I guess all I can do is keep trying.'

It was the first time their mother had offered a hint of her relationship with Alex that wasn't bordering on the generic.

'I think Alex is just a private person,' Stef said. 'He keeps things close to his chest.'

Hannah choked back a response. Before their tiff at the gallery, perhaps she would have contested that statement. She would never have betrayed Alex's trust by revealing the specifics of the disintegration of his marriage, but she could at least have hinted that he'd been willing to share confidences. Now Hannah worried it might seem she was implying a greater intimacy with Alex than her mother or sister.

There was no way she could tell them about Rex's accusation either. Maybe they'd reject the idea that Alex had purposefully shadowed Rex, as she did. But it might also appear that Hannah believed she and Rex were worthy of such targeted attention. In other words, it could appear … smug.

Yet, surely this was the time to share their thoughts about Alex – positive or negative. They should be open and honest and give each other licence to toss their perspectives in the air, knowing they could retract them later if it turned out they were wrong. But it felt like they were all harbouring their own points of view.

They knew so little about Alex's past and even less about how his pieces fit together. When he arrived in their lives, Hannah had expected change, but she hadn't really anticipated the possible shifts in the dynamic between them. Something, or maybe many things, seemed to be holding them back from speaking as freely as they were used to.

'Why so serious, Han?' Stef asked, nudging her and clinking her half-full glass of sparkling. A speck spilled over onto the lapel of Stef's navy and tan dress and she immediately dabbed a serviette in water to sponge it.

Hannah hadn't seen the dress before. It looked expensive. So did her tan leather boots, now she thought of it. She might have to dig a little at some point in their time away to make sure Stef wasn't overspending. It would be very irresponsible if she were to lean on their mum and dad any more than she already did. Hannah probably didn't know the half of it.

'We're on bloody holidays,' Stef reminded her.

Hannah smiled. Stef was right. She needed to relax and enjoy the time ahead. Even if there were hiccups and adjustments along the way, the expansion of their family was going to be a good thing. After all, Stef didn't seem to be carrying an iota of resentment from their argument. Stef could – had always been able to – shake it off.

Hannah needed to be patient and let things unfold. The point of going to Hughesdale for a whole week was for the Fidlers to truly get to know Alex and help him fit into their family.

They were all present. All hopeful.

And now they were landing in Adelaide.

•

As Alex had advised, a driver was waiting for them at the airport. With his grey hair closely clipped and black shoes polished to maximum shine, he had the aura of an ex-military man. But as Hannah offered her bag to put on the trolley, he couldn't camouflage his surprise.

'Terribly sorry, miss,' he said, recovering the slack jaw. 'It's just that your resemblance to Mr Carpenter is a little startling.'

'I was a little startled myself,' Hannah replied, glancing at his name tag. 'Nice to meet you, Ray. Do you know Alex well?'

'I've known Mr Carpenter since he was small,' he said. 'Hughesdale has been my second home for many years.'

'So, you'll be able to give us the lowdown,' Stef joked. 'All the family goss?'

Suddenly Ray's military demeanour was restored.

'Despite their public standing, the Carpenters have always been a private family,' he said stiffly. 'Please follow me.'

Hannah was relieved that their mum was in the front passenger seat of the black Maserati sedan. Judging from the frequent glances in the rear-view mirror, Ray still seemed taken aback by her likeness to Alex. As Stef chatted away, Hannah looked out the window. The Adelaide Hills were magnificent undulating slopes of green. Houses became sparser, largely hidden from view behind ample foliage.

Then they arrived at a wrought-iron fence with the signage, Hughesdale.

Ray pressed a remote and the gates opened slowly. The Maserati glided under an arched canopy of purple wisteria. Across the beautifully manicured lawns, Hannah glimpsed the clay surface of a tennis court. To her right, glistening in the twilight, was an infinity pool. At the end was a sweeping circular drive. The mansion behind it looked like something from a British period drama.

And there he was. Alex looked very much the master of his domain in a crisp white shirt, beige linen suit and white loafers.

Stef was barely out of the passenger seat when she began raving. 'Oh my God. You don't know this, Alex, but I used to be a pretty hot tennis player,' she said. 'We'll have to have a hit. It's a bit of a shame that it's too cold to use the pool. Unless it's heated? And Mum, aren't the gardens above and beyond?'

'It's lovely, Alex.' Hannah hoped the interruption would give Stef the cue to tone it down a notch, but Stef hadn't finished.

'Wow. It's pretty much a castle. I knew Hughesdale was impressive. I mean, I googled it of course. But I had no idea of the scale.'

'There's a lot you don't know about my life, Stef,' he said. 'I trust that's what this week will be about. The four of us getting to know each other properly.'

Stef nodded but Hannah could see that, in her awe, she was skimming over Alex's words when she should have been taking them in.

'Will that be all for the moment, Mr Carpenter?' Ray asked.

'Yes thanks, Ray,' Alex said.

As Ray transferred to the ute parked in the driveway and took off, Stef rebooted.

'Mum, you dark horse,' she said. 'Why didn't you tell us how ridiculously grand this place is?'

Marg looked to Alex, and Hannah thought she saw him nod permission before she spoke.

'Alex wasn't quite ready to introduce me to Hughesdale on my last trip,' she said. 'This is new to me too.'

Her mum had mentioned to Hannah that she hadn't stayed at Hughesdale, but she hadn't intimated that she'd never even visited.

As the group reached the front verandah, Marg touched Alex's elbow. 'It's beautiful,' she said softly.

'It is,' Alex agreed. He retracted his elbow, but that could have been in readiness to open the door. 'And it's been home for all of my fifty-six years, with the exception of my short-lived marriage.'

Hannah took her mother's arm instead. 'If the walls could talk,' she quipped.

Alex pushed open the teak double doors to the cavernous entry foyer where three chandeliers hung low and wide.

'Oh but they will, Hannah,' he said. 'The walls ...' He gestured with his right hand. 'The halls,' he continued with a gesture from his left. 'Even the chandeliers,' he finished, lifting both hands palms up. 'They've been silent for too long.'

Nobody spoke.

'Be careful though,' Alex said into the vacuum. 'At the slightest touch, the fittings and fixtures may bleed.'

•

Truly, the house wasn't to Hannah's taste. Old mansions were too dark, too staid and airless. Hughesdale could have used a skylight or two. And Alex was obviously trying to be funny when he made that strange quip about the fixtures and fittings, but everywhere Hannah looked, she could visualise a scarlet trickle.

After a brief tour though, there was no doubting the grandeur, even if it did feel more like a museum than a home. Rex would have been in seventh heaven over the scale of the library. If it didn't belong to Alex.

'This is your wing, Hannah,' Alex said a little later. The bedroom was enormous. It was relatively light because of the floor-to-ceiling windows overlooking the eastern side of the grounds with its lush jungle of plants and white gazebo. Two giant, fresh bouquets rose out of bronze vases in opposite corners. A third, miniature version sat in the centre of an antique dressing table.

The bed was a four-poster, the canopy in pink and lemon. Fluffy white towels were laid out among a sprinkle of rose petals matching the canopy. Hannah doubted these touches were Alex's or Ray's handiwork.

'Cecilia dressed the room,' Alex said, as though reading her mind. 'You'll meet her soon. Ray maintains the grounds here and provides the flowers, while Cecilia takes care of the house. She's also our cook. We're very lucky to have both of them.'

Alex cleared his throat. '*I'm* very lucky,' he corrected, and Hannah was struck with the understanding that Alex's family losses remained fresh.

'Here,' he said, opening a door, 'is your ensuite, Hannah.'

The bathroom was almost the size of the bedroom. There was a giant oval bath in the centre. A gilt-framed mirror sat above two gleaming white basins with gold taps set in a marble bench. The towels were pink and lemon doubling down on the bedroom theme.

'Oh my God,' Stef said, taking Hannah's arm. 'I love this too much. But it's wicked you get it all to yourself. I'll be visiting to use that bath.'

Alex straightened. 'Your own wing has all the amenities you see here, Stef,' he said. 'As does yours, Margaret. There will be no need for you to visit each other for baths and the like.'

Hannah had no idea how to respond. Even Stef was silenced.

'Enjoy some down time, Hannah,' Alex said eventually. 'I'll get Margaret and Stef settled. Dinner will be served in the dining room at seven.'

●

Hannah checked her phone – 6 pm. There were no new messages. She considered taking a bath. There were quality salts in the vanity, but she felt too antsy – or was it vulnerability – to give over to the pleasures of a soak. She decided on a shower instead.

As she changed into fresh clothes and brushed her hair, Hannah felt the urge to go and find Stef's room. But hadn't she been discouraged from doing that?

She tapped tinted moisturiser under her eyes, onto her cheekbones. She was being uptight. Alex's statement had been a bit odd, but she'd probably misunderstood his intention. The prospect of being host to a long-lost biological mother and two half-sisters for a week had to be daunting. Hannah was probably overreacting because of Rex's suspicion. She just needed to recalibrate her thoughts.

Still, it was a relief when her phone buzzed with a text from Stef.

> FYI: To get to my room, turn left at the end of the hallway. There's a painting of children dancing around a maypole. Don't look too closely or their eyes will follow you. I'm first door on the left. X

Hannah grinned. Sometimes Steffie just nailed an atmosphere.

She looked at herself in the gilt-framed mirror. Alex looked back.

Then, at 7 pm sharp, Hannah went downstairs for dinner.

CHAPTER TWENTY-THREE

Stef's suite was just as fabulous as Hannah's with its extravagant, Versace vibe. She'd taken a Moët piccolo from the bar fridge and was luxuriating with bubbles on bubbles in a giant round bathtub. To have a whole hour to herself was a thing to cherish, so it was a tad annoying that she'd left her phone on the charger and out of reach. She had to get out of the bath to read the text from Liam.

> Rosie left her basketball uniform at your place. Ok for me to drop her there to collect?

Neither Alex nor Liam had told her what had gone down between them, and Stef hadn't asked. But it was clear something had. It was in Liam's sudden shift to punctual pick-ups and drop-offs where he no longer came inside the house or began personal conversations. It was in his polite but distant texts. It was a relief to be able to rely on Liam and make firm plans. Finally, thanks to Alex, her ex-husband had become manageable.

Stef texted her permission and got back into the bath, but it was harder to relax now. In telling Alex, she'd set something in motion that seemed irreversible. After the incident at the NGV, Stef suspected Alex might act instead of just listen. She'd gone ahead regardless. She could hardly feign surprise. But why did she feel she'd lost something now that Liam was following the rules? Why did she feel forlorn about the shrinking of an intimacy she no longer wanted?

Whatever Alex had said or done to change the dynamic between her and Liam, it was a good thing. Timely. Stef just needed to wrap her head around a new normal.

As she changed into her emerald-green wrap dress, Stef checked the time. That it was already 7.10 pm made her heart skip a beat. But that was ridiculous. She'd be there by seven twenty. Alex was persuasive, not tyrannical.

Still, Stef sped through her hair and make-up routine.

•

The others were already seated in the dining room. Marg was opposite Alex, Hannah next to her. Alex motioned to the seat beside him.

'You're late,' he told her. Stef had to assume he was being flippant.

'It takes a long time to look this good,' she tried, but Alex didn't smile.

An array of beautifully presented roast meats and salads seemed to have appeared magically on the table.

'Cecilia,' Alex said as though reading Stef's thoughts. 'I've sent her home now, but you'll be experiencing more of her wonders.'

Alex poured a shiraz for Marg and waited until she'd had a sip before filling the other glasses. 'A toast,' he said, clinking glasses with Marg, then Hannah and finally, Stef. 'Here's to getting to know each other.'

'Hear, hear,' the Fidlers agreed toasting each other. As they talked about how beautiful the room was, Alex looked impatient.

'Remember what I said about the fixtures and fittings,' he said. 'Please, let's eat.'

Stef forced a smile, but this time, the joke had fallen flat. She turned her attention to the feast. The beef tenderloins were melt-in-the-mouth, mushroom wine sauce complementing them perfectly. The salads were fresh and flavoursome. But Hannah seemed to be more focused on something behind Stef than the amazing food. Stef put down her cutlery and turned around.

On the wall was a large framed photo. A distinguished older man with clear, cold blue eyes and a neatly trimmed grey beard sat with a sandy-haired, hazel-eyed toddler perched on his knee. Standing next to him was an elegant blonde woman who looked to be in her mid-thirties, top to toe in Chanel. She wore only one statement ring on the middle finger of her right hand. The emerald and diamond cluster was as large as it was stunning. On her hip was a second toddler with similar colouring to the other, but a much rounder face. Stef recalled a comment Alex had made that first evening they met – that in the sixties, adoption was virtually a smorgasbord from which you could choose babies who had physical similarities.

'There's definitely a resemblance between you and your brother,' Stef said. 'Which of those gorgeous kids is you, Alex?'

'The man is my grandfather, William Carpenter,' Alex replied. 'He was a self-made mining magnate and rather a large icon in Adelaide. On his knee is yours truly.'

Stef smiled. She couldn't ease the sadness Alex must have felt at losing his entire adoptive family, but she could at least pay tribute. 'Look at your darling little shirt with the Peter Pan collar, Alex,' she said. 'Oh and the braces. So sweet. You have the same outfit as your brother too. Mum used to make Hannah and me matching outfits back in the day, didn't you, Mum?'

Alex put a finger up to his lips. 'This is a time for listening,' he said.

Stef gulped. Why did she always feel the need to gush? Across the table, Marg delivered an almost imperceptible wink.

Hannah didn't gush. Hannah would not be shushed.

Stef banished the threat of ensuing tears with a mouthful of pear, walnut and gorgonzola salad.

'As you have gathered, the other little boy is my brother, Ricky,' Alex confirmed. 'And the young woman is my mother, Gillian.'

'Gillian looks very beautiful,' Marg said tentatively. 'She seems to have a lot of character. It's her eyes, I think. And you, Alex, look very sweet.'

'Gillian definitely had character,' Alex said. 'And Ricky and I were both sweet at times. When it was possible.'

He paused and Stef wondered whether he might expand on the comment, but it didn't happen. There was an awkward silence in which Stef thought of her own kids. One sweet, one not so much. She missed them equally.

'And where is Gillian's husband?' Margaret asked. 'I was led to believe you were going to a couple. Well, there was no mention of it being otherwise. I just assumed ...'

'That you had to be married to adopt in the sixties?' Alex interrupted. 'Well, I gather the rules were bent a little for Gillian. I mean, it was clear she had the resources. And Grandfather William was involved with raising us, but it suited our mother to be a single parent.'

Stef steeled herself. If she didn't dive into this conversation now, she may not find her way back. 'Gillian must have been strong-minded to want to raise two boys,' she ventured.

'You mean two boys who weren't her own?' Alex asked and Stef wondered if everything she said at Hughesdale was going to come out clunky. Underneath the table, Stef reached out a foot and rested it against her mum's.

'You're right, Stef,' Alex said. 'Gillian was very strong-minded.' Though he was replying to Stef, his eyes were on Marg.

'Will you tell us more?' Marg asked. 'About all your adoptive family?'

Alex nodded. 'I'd like to, Margaret,' he said. 'But it's difficult to describe family dynamics. I think especially so in regards to the Carpenters but perhaps it's the same for the Fidlers. And I'd also like us to do more than just go through the motions.' He lifted his hands, palms upturned. His smile was charming. 'I'm suggesting a bit of quid pro quo, Margaret. In fact, I've designed a game to help us make this process more interesting. I do hope you'll indulge me.'

Stef sensed her mum's reluctance in the tensing of her foot. But perhaps a game would lighten the atmosphere, smooth down the rough edges of small misunderstandings. All three women nodded their agreement.

'Excellent,' Alex said. 'We'll begin after the dinner dishes are cleared. Perhaps, Hannah and Stef, you could take care of that?'

Of course, it was fair and reasonable that Alex asked for their help. But it was also quite clearly an order more than a request. That Hannah silently accepted was jarring. She was usually champing at the bit to call out anything that reeked of patriarchy. And wasn't there an implicit instruction for Marg to stay put?

Stef stacked some plates and followed her sister towards the kitchen. They paused just outside the door of the dining room, curious as to what might be said in their absence. It was Alex who spoke first.

'You will come to know much about my life, Margaret,' he said.

His tone was cool enough to prompt a wince, but not quite cold enough to raise her concern with Hannah. Truly, Stef wouldn't know how without divulging her and Alex's recent shared history and opening a can of worms.

So, she and Hannah exchanged small frowns and went to do the dishes.

•

'It's pretty simple,' Alex advised when Stef and Hannah returned to the dining room. 'In the jar, as you see, there are several pieces of folded paper. A year is written on each. The idea is that you choose a song from that year along with a personal anecdote.'

Stef finished her wine and Alex immediately poured her another. He seemed fine. Maybe she should interpret the shushing as an indication that he was becoming more comfortable around her? That they were beyond the stage of politeness. It was a reassuring thought.

'I wonder if you wouldn't mind doing the honours, Stef?' Alex asked. 'Youngest to oldest.'

Stef fished around in the jar Alex offered. She leaned back in her chair to open the paper. The wine was kicking in beautifully. 'Can we use our phones to check song release dates?'

'If you must,' Alex said.

'Ah, but I must not,' Stef said. 'Nineteen eighty-seven. I would have been six.' She clapped her hands together. '"Walk Like an Egyptian"! It had been on the charts since the year before, so everyone knew it off by heart. We played it over and over at my birthday party.'

'You invited the whole class,' her mum confirmed. 'I tried to whittle down the numbers but you insisted they were all your best friends.'

'Haha,' Stef said. 'My twenty-five besties were in seventh heaven, doing all the actions.'

Stef couldn't resist jumping out of her seat when she brought the song up on her phone. There was plenty of room to walk like an Egyptian around the table and there she was, doing something she was good at – making her mum and sister laugh. She would keep trying until she had the same effect on Alex.

'What about your anecdote?' Hannah asked. 'Or is the performance a replacement for that?'

'Not on your life,' Stef said. 'I've got the floor and I'm gonna use it.' She focused on Alex.

'It was a birthday tradition that Dad's mum would come for dinner. Gran Dorothy always bought the best presents. So, when the party ended, I was probably extra hyper and excited because on my wish list to her was a Sylvanian Caravan.'

'Sylvanians are little animal-like toys,' Hannah explained to Alex. 'Stef was obsessed with them.'

Alex was still not looking particularly engaged. Stef needed to ramp it up a bit.

'I was dying to get my hot little hands on that van,' she agreed. 'But Gran Dorothy just passed me a card. Inside, it said, "IOU a Sylvanian Caravan". She explained that all the toy shops were out of stock, and she'd put in an order but it would take six weeks. Despite the trauma, I thanked her – Hannah and I were taught good manners. But six weeks was an eternity.'

'You kept it together, Stef,' Hannah said. 'I remember. I was so proud of you.'

'It took a toll,' Stef said with a smirk, turning her attention to Hannah. 'But do you remember what happened after dinner?' Hannah shook her head. 'You took me up to your bedroom,' Stef continued. 'Dad had made you a doll's house and, typically, you'd used it as a home for a million of those tiny books you used to create. He was making one for me too, but it was still in the early stages. You took all your little bookshelves out and told me I could borrow it until the Sylvanian Caravan arrived.'

'Really?' Hannah replied. 'I don't remember that at all, Stef.'

Stef blew a kiss to her big sister. 'But I do,' she said. 'It's one of the reasons I forgive you when you're being a cow.'

Hannah hung her head, pretend-humbled.

'What a delightful sibling story to start the game,' Alex said. 'I do hope when it's my turn I'll be able to find something even nearly as charming from my memory bank.' He looked at the family photo and Stef fancied he was giving a nod to his own deceased sibling before continuing.

'Next up – Hannah.'

CHAPTER TWENTY-FOUR

Hannah reached into the jar and pulled out a year – 1996. She had been eighteen and the most outstanding memory was of throwing away her virginity in the backseat of a car at a drive-in movie theatre in Coburg. Her partner was an engineering student with a tendency to mansplain proceedings – narrating the penetration with more precision than performing it. Hannah had returned a few nights later to catch up on what she'd missed of *Trainspotting*. It wasn't a memory she would share here though. Stef already knew about it and maybe Alex would find the details fairly entertaining, but some things were better left unspoken between parents and their offspring. Talking about sex had never been part of their relationship and that seemed the best way to go now when the product of their mother's teen union was their host.

Besides, after Stef's anecdote, it seemed right to choose a story that repaid her sister with kudos. She could couple what she had in mind with a moderate display of vulnerability. Was that what Alex wanted from this game?

'"Killing Me Softly" by the hip-hop group, Fugees,' Hannah began. '"Macarena" kept it from going to number one on the charts, but that was for lightweights anyway. I was deep. This was my song.' She looked around the table getting satisfying recognition of her self-deprecation before continuing. 'I was standing in line at the Prospect Hill Hotel with my first legal ID and my friend, Ronnie, who was equally deep in her allegiance to the Fugees and her desire to be seen as indie.'

'Ah, I remember Veronica,' Marg said. 'Big Catholic family. Her mother, Lilith, used to do canteen duty with me. Poor Lilith. She'd have to lug along three little ones and honestly, it would have been easier to manage without her. One of them had—'

'Some women keep their little ones close,' Alex interjected, 'even if it's not convenient. May I suggest we stick to exposition of ourselves and our immediate family?'

There had been so little emotion in Alex's voice that Hannah, especially after so many wines, was not absolutely sure she'd heard correctly. But if she needed confirmation, Marg's twisted expression gave it. Hannah raised her eyebrows and Marg replied with a shake of her head. Although part of her itched to take it up with Alex, let him know she thought his comment was unnecessarily brutal, her mother clearly wanted to avoid sinking into such a major and fraught topic on their first night at Hughesdale. So, Hannah continued with her anecdote.

'A few spots ahead of us in the queue, there were two guys we recognised from around the traps. We'd never had the courage to actually talk to them, but they were fascinating from afar. One wore denim overalls and a choker, the other rocked the grunge look in all black. They had swag, but not the kind we were used to. Theirs was more stylish and less blokey. And the way they smoked cigarettes was an art form in itself.'

Hannah paused, and although her mum was stone-faced, Stef and Alex nodded their encouragement to continue.

'Ronnie and I vowed we'd pluck up the courage to talk to them that night. And we did. We were a couple of beers in and the music was loud, but we managed to introduce ourselves. Julian and Dominic were so open, so interesting. We talked about the Fugees and favourite books and gap years. Then, well into the evening, we landed on the topic of love.'

'So did you have a bit of a crush on one of them, Hannah?' Alex asked.

'Dominic,' Hannah admitted, 'and Ronnie was keen on Julian. But it turned out they were both in love already. With the same person.'

'That's unfortunate,' Stef said. 'And did you find out who?'

'It was a girl who'd sold them CDs at the Brashs store in Elizabeth Street. They'd go in some Saturday mornings to buy stuff just so they could talk to her.'

'I used to work at that Brashs on Saturday mornings,' Stef said.

'Tick, tock,' Hannah joked as she waited for the penny to drop.

'Oh no!' Stef squealed. 'That sucks. I'm sorry, Han.'

'It's okay, Steffie. I've worked through the damage in my own time,' Hannah said wryly, and it was a relief that her mum also managed a smile.

'An interesting choice of anecdote, Hannah,' Alex said. 'I appreciate your display of vulnerability and the nod to Stef's appeal.' He looked from Hannah to Stef, finally settling on Marg. 'Your daughters have very distinctive personalities,' he said. 'I wonder if that has been the case since they were small? What was the famous quote? "Give me the child until he is seven and I will show you the man."' Alex paused. 'Would you agree with Aristotle, Margaret?' he asked.

'Yes,' she said, and it seemed her pause was to gather confidence to continue. 'At least I think the most salient features of the seven-year-old are still present in the adult.'

Alex stroked his chin as he nodded. 'So, the bigger question for an adopted child,' he said, 'is how much of us is nature and how much nurture?'

He didn't wait for thoughts on that question. Instead, he reached into the jar.

•

'Nineteen seventy,' Alex read. '"Bridge Over Troubled Water", Simon and Garfunkel. I don't have to look it up because Gillian played that record over and over. Interestingly, I was seven years old, as was Ricky. Perhaps, as Aristotle suggested, the writing was on the wall as to the men we would become. In those days we shared a bedroom – that is, whenever Mother allowed it.'

'That's very sweet,' Hannah offered. 'Stef and I could never share a bedroom. She was always shouting out in her sleep, weren't you, Stef? She was obsessed with Humphrey B. Bear and used to play noisily with him in her dreams. Midnight picnics and the like.'

'I was bananas for Humphrey.' Stef laughed.

'How cute,' Alex said, but his tone suggested the aside wasn't particularly welcome. His eyes scanned the three women and rested on Marg again. 'Nineteen seventy,' he repeated. 'Mother had always told us we were adopted. The phrase she repeated most often was, "I adopted you and you adopted me."'

'That's beautiful, Alex,' Stef said. 'Did it make you feel special to be chosen? It sounds like that's what it was meant to do.'

'Yes,' Alex agreed. 'There was a strong sense of belonging in that phrase. But until nineteen seventy, it stood alone, without much context. That year, Gillian started to fill in the blanks.'

Next to Hannah, Marg's leg jiggled. Marg, who disapproved of any form of fidgeting.

'I know we were seven because it was Ricky's birthday. We'd had a party, just the three of us, though William had already given him a drive-on electric car. A Mercedes-Benz, shiny and red. The housekeeper at the time had made a train cake with carriages that went on forever. I was jealous. For my last birthday I'd received a book from Grandfather and a supermarket sponge cake. So, I'd stolen a whole carriage and hidden it in our bookshelf. Ricky hadn't noticed. He wasn't one to dwell on inequities or small betrayals even when they weren't in his favour. But when Mother came into our room, I was on high alert. I thought I was about to get my comeuppance. Instead, she sat down on my bed with her clinking clear drink and talked about the first time she'd met each of us.'

Alex looked back at the photo. 'She started with me. She told me that when the deaconess showed her the first baby, she was instantly besotted. She said the nurses had clearly taken a shine to me, that I was clad in a hand-knitted lemon jumpsuit and smelled like lavender. That my hair, which was quite long for a baby, was freshly washed and combed. She said she took me in her arms and I was her very own, darling boy.'

Alex paused and took a sip of wine. Marg's leg-jiggling halved in tempo. Her shoulders dropped.

'Of course, Ricky pleaded for his own story. It was, after all, his birthday. So Mother got up from my bed and sat at the end of his. She told him their meeting was five months later. That she'd wanted a proper family – two boys, because girls were too much trouble. That she was excited to meet him, but this time, the deaconess pulled her aside. She was told there was a baby ready for her, but there was no obligation to accept him. A prospective mother had apparently already baulked upon meeting him, and she was perfectly within her rights to wait for another baby.'

Hannah felt a prickling at the back of her neck. Across the table, Stef barely suppressed a gasp.

'Mother told Ricky that when she saw him, she understood why the deaconess had warned her. Poor baby Ricky had eczema all over his infant body and smelled of vomit. I remember Mother saying the vomit was even in his ear canals, and that he was dressed in a second-hand gown, grey with overuse. Clearly, Ricky hadn't been a nurse's favourite.'

Alex looked around the table and it occurred to Hannah that, during his anecdote, he'd almost forgotten the Fidlers were there.

'Then Mother assured Ricky that she never had a thought to leave him behind. That Ricky belonged to her, just as I did. That we all belonged together.' Alex cleared his throat. 'She promised she would never abandon us as our birth mothers had,' he finished.

Hannah gulped and stared into Stef's widened eyes.

Marg froze, mid jiggle, one foot suspended.

Nobody spoke.

Alex shrugged. 'Straight after that, we chanted together. *I adopted you and you adopted me.* Over and over. And all through it, our Ricky sobbed. Do you think that's beautiful? Margaret? Hannah? Stef?'

Still, nobody spoke.

'I do fear,' Alex said eventually, 'that your energy is waning after a big day and it must be time to retire. It's unfortunate that we didn't get around to you, Margaret. Let me do the honours of picking a year for you and we can finish the game tomorrow evening.'

Without waiting for her agreement, Alex reached into the jar. As he handed it to Marg, her hand trembled. She opened it slowly.

'Nineteen sixty-three,' she said flatly. 'The year you were born.'

CHAPTER TWENTY-FIVE

Despite the comfort of the bed and the absence of disturbances from children, Stef tossed and turned. Alex's anecdote had rattled her. Why would Gillian choose to tell that backstory to her children, even if it was the truth? How could she allow such disparate birthday gifts to her two sons? Surely it smacked of a mother who wanted to divide her children?

It was too hot. Stef kicked off the covers.

If she was prepared to judge Gillian's mothering, she would have to be open to judgement of her own. Oh God. What she'd put her kids through. Rosie particularly. She'd placed most of the blame on Liam, but it was her fault too. Their family unit was fragmented and Rosie was showing the battle scars. Maybe Heath had them too, but they were not so apparent yet. She was supposed to teach her children how to live by example. That was a mother's job.

Now it was too cold without the covers. Stef reached down to the floor and pulled the blanket back up so that it covered her lower half. Her phone told her it was 3.30 am. She was dehydrated. Thankfully there was a jug of water and a glass on the bedside table. She chugged some down and tried to resettle.

Hannah's decision to remain childless meant she didn't have to worry about the wounds she caused or the scars they left behind. How light that must feel. How unburdened.

But tonight, sturdy, reliable Marg, who had been there for Stef and her kids through thick and thin, was in line for judgement. Alex seemed so casual when he threw the barb about some mothers choosing to keep their children close. But the choice of 1963 as Marg's year to build an anecdote from seemed deliberate. Alex was finally inviting her to tell the story of his conception, birth and adoption for the first time. But it was obvious that he would remain in charge of the parameters.

The biggest imprint Marg made on Alex must have been her total absence from his life. How deep were his scars? In Melbourne, apart from the incident with the homeless man, Stef hadn't seen them. But at Hughesdale, they were becoming apparent.

Mothers.

Gillian.

Margaret.

Stef.

She turned onto her side and pulled the covers over her head so she was cocooned.

Marg had a big night ahead. They all did.

•

'Steffie, wake up. Breakfast is ready and you'll be punished with fifty lashes if you're late.'

Reluctantly, Stef opened her eyes. Hannah was lying next to her, on top of the covers. She was wearing black leggings, a singlet and a thick layer of sweat that would be seeping into Stef's bedclothes.

'Gross,' Stef said. 'Jesus, Han, you're a machine. Have you already been for a run?'

Hannah nodded. 'Yes, I have brushed out the cobwebs. The day is magnificent.' She leaped up and opened the curtains to prove her point. Stef sat up drowsily amid the sunshine. 'Mum and Alex are sitting on the verandah. Cecilia, the woman Alex mentioned yesterday, is serving up produce from a local farmers' market. You're going to be in seventh heaven when you see the offering, Stef. And Mum and Alex both seem fine.'

'Really?' Stef asked. 'Because last night Alex seemed a little tetchy, especially with Mum. And his anecdote was ... well, it was a worry.'

'It was definitely an odd evening,' Hannah said. 'I do think Alex is a more complicated equation on his home turf, but maybe he needed to get a couple of things off his chest. I guess we just try to ride the waves. He wants us to join them on the verandah for breakfast. I think I'll suggest we explore some local wineries and have lunch out. Perhaps Ashton Hills or Mount Lofty Ranges? I'm sure Alex will know the good ones.'

Stef got up and rifled around in her suitcase to pick an outfit for the day. If she showered before breakfast, she should probably choose something that would be nice enough to go for lunch in. Perhaps the tangerine culottes with the cream

V-neck tee? They were a little creased, but that would fall out once she was wearing them.

'What do you think?' she asked her sister.

Hannah jumped up from the bed, the corners of her mouth twitching.

'Nice. Oh but, Stef, Alex has casually suggested we be at breakfast by eight thirty.' She tapped an imaginary wristwatch.

'Oh my God.' Stef laughed, checking the time on her phone. 'We have thirteen minutes.'

'Twelve minutes and fifty seconds,' Hannah replied.

'Twelve minutes and thirty ...' Stef tried, but she couldn't get the rest out.

The paroxysms of laughter lasted a full seventy seconds. Time well spent. Stef and Hannah made it down to the kitchen on time, dressed but not showered, arms linked.

●

Cecilia looked to be in her early to mid-sixties, with a grey bob and an aura of no-nonsense efficiency. Stef lingered in the kitchen making breakfast choices while Hannah went straight out to the verandah with a haphazardly chosen bowl of fruit.

'Would you like me to add a little camembert from our local farmers' market to your omelette?' Cecilia asked.

'Is the Pope a Catholic?' Stef replied.

Cecilia's reaction was a minuscule nod, but the obvious care she'd taken in choosing the array of food on the kitchen counter more than made up for a lack of humour. Stef could already taste the flavours.

'Ray said he's known Alex since he was little. How about you, Cecilia?' Stef asked.

Cecilia added red onion, peppers and chilli to the steaming skillet. She did not turn around.

'No, he would have been nineteen when I was employed,' she said. 'It was shortly after the tragedy ...'

Stef supposed it had something to do with Ricky since he'd died young, but Alex had never told her what happened to him. She walked to the other side of the kitchen bench to stand next to Cecilia. 'What was the tragedy?' she asked gently.

'I'll bring this out to you. Mr Carpenter is waiting,' Cecilia re-routed.

The subject was clearly off limits, so Stef helped herself to some beautifully ripe strawberries and an already prepared half-mango and walked out to the verandah to join the others. The day was crisp but sunny. Full of promise.

'How did you sleep, Stef?' Alex asked with no mention of her being late to breakfast. He was clearly more relaxed than the previous evening. Hannah was right, except that in the light of day, what had gone down seemed more of a ripple than a wave.

'Really well,' Stef lied. The first strawberry was ridiculously good, ripened to perfection. Alex poured a coffee, adding milk and one sugar without having to be reminded.

'Excellent,' he said. He leaned over to hand her the coffee. 'I think people sleep well when they're relatively free from responsibilities.'

'You mean kid responsibilities?' Stef asked. 'Because even though I miss Rosie and Heath so much, I must say I'm not missing the cooking and cleaning and all that.'

'Yes, of course,' Alex agreed. 'But also, I think you're going to have fewer burdens over the coming days. Just call it a hunch.'

'That's a tad cryptic,' Hannah joined in, cutting a Granny Smith in segments, though the fine specimen really called for being held as a whole and crunched into. 'What burdens?'

'We all have them, Hannah,' Alex said with a smile. 'But I guess we should be more focused on gratitude. I'm so delighted you're all here with me.'

The omelette Cecilia put in front of Stef was extraordinary.

'We are so very glad to be here too, Alex,' Marg said. 'Thanks for your generosity.'

'We are,' Hannah agreed. 'And given it's going to be such a lovely day, maybe we could do a tour? I mean, we can't be this close to the Barossa Valley and not visit some wineries. Do you have any particular favourites, Alex?'

He put down his cup and leaned back in his chair. 'Is there something lacking here at Hughesdale, Hannah?' he asked evenly. 'Is the wine inferior? The food not up to scratch? Or perhaps it's the accommodation?'

Stef could see that her sister was taken aback by Alex's sudden change of mood.

'Oh, I'm sure that's not what Hannah was implying,' Marg said. 'Everything here is exquis—'

'Of course that's not what I was implying, Alex,' Hannah interrupted. 'Actually, I don't understand how you could take offence at the proposal of a little sightseeing. It's a very ordinary thing to suggest.'

Stef wasn't sure what to make of Alex's twitching mouth. His delayed nod was accompanied by a small smile.

'Of course it is, Hannah,' he said eventually. 'I'm sorry to be abrupt. Honestly. But please let me explain myself.'

The oozing camembert in among the fluffy texture of the omelette was nothing short of brilliant. And comforting. Stef took another bite.

'Cecilia will be delighted that you're enjoying one of her specialties, Stef,' Alex said.

Stef felt she was somehow being blessed by Alex this morning. It seemed she could do no wrong today. She had to admit she was glad it was Hannah rather than her who'd brought up the prospect of a winery tour.

'My vision of having you all here at Hughesdale,' Alex continued, 'does not involve sightseeing. Not this trip, anyway, though I'm sure there will be others and, with some forward planning, I'd love to do just that. But, to begin with, Hannah, my presence at any of our local wineries would be noted at any time, more so should I arrive with my doppelganger. The press would be alerted, and it wouldn't be long before the story was splashed everywhere. I don't think that's the kind of time we're after together, right?'

Hannah nodded. 'I hadn't thought of that,' she conceded.

'Of course you hadn't,' Alex replied. 'Why would you? But this time together is special.'

Stef finished her omelette and popped a mango chaser in her mouth. 'I understand,' she said.

'Thank you, Stef,' Alex said, looking around the table. 'Now, I have a couple of hours of urgent paperwork. Finish up here and when you're ready, Ray will give you a tour of the grounds.'

•

Stef took off her shoes and dangled her feet in the infinity pool. If Heath was here, he'd stay in the water forever, even if it meant his teeth chattered with the cold. Behind her poker face, Rosie would be impressed too. Stef could imagine her daughter awkwardly donning bathers before forgetting to be self-conscious and embarking on a game of Marco Polo.

Being away from them, Stef couldn't feel the burden of parenting. Sure, the financial side was stressful, especially lately, but there was nothing in the world she loved more than her children. As she looked at Marg, up ahead with Ray and Hannah on the footbridge, she tried to imagine, again, the impact on her mother of giving up her child. But Stef could only feel resistance. Even though she'd never say it aloud, she felt a kernel of disgust that Marg could have allowed anyone to take her baby. That if it was her, Stef would have found a way to fight for her child. The thought was immediately trailed by guilt. As much as Marg was a part of her, Stef could never know the myriad feelings she'd suffered over the years.

Stef rose. Now was the time for celebration, not lingering criticism of a situation she would probably never really understand. She walked over to the others.

'The plants,' Ray was saying as he pointed at the giant goldfish in the pond below the footbridge, 'help keep the environment oxygenated. As you can see, the fish are flourishing.'

'Flourishing is an understatement,' Hannah whispered to Stef. 'Goldfish aren't supposed to be that big. Like everything about this place, they're too much.'

Stef frowned. Sometimes Hannah could be so … snarky. Ray walked over the footbridge and past a lush apple tree. Stef had an urge to outpace her sister and walk with her mother and Ray instead, but it would have been awkward.

'I wonder what Alex meant when he suggested our burdens might be eased in the coming days,' Hannah said when the others were out of earshot. 'I mean, are we supposed to guess? Sometimes he talks in riddles, right? I'm probably going to have to call him out on it. Especially since we're trapped here with no escape.'

Stef upped the pace. Alex had said that *she* would feel a burden being eased over the coming days, not Hannah. A small thing, perhaps, but it was annoying that her sister didn't acknowledge the distinction. The one time he'd singled Stef out for positive attention had clearly rattled Hannah. And she understood that Hannah was trying to be funny when she said they were trapped here, but that pissed her off too. It was so … ungrateful.

'We're hardly prisoners, Hannah,' Stef said sharply. 'I mean, you've been for a long run this morning. And Alex has a good point about avoiding publicity, for the moment at least.'

Up ahead, their mother and Ray were inspecting a bed of blue, pink and white delphiniums. The gardens here could truly lift the spirit, if you were able to open up enough to appreciate them.

Hannah put a hand on Stef's shoulder. 'Are you okay, Steffie? I mean, are you okay with me?' she asked. She paused and Stef saw her concern. 'Us Fidlers were all fine before Alex came along, weren't we?'

The icy feeling Stef had towards her sister moments ago melted instantly. 'Of course we were, Han,' she replied. 'And after things settle, after we truly get to know Alex, we'll be even better.'

In the pocket of her culottes, Stef's phone beeped with a message.

'It's work,' she told Hannah.

'Well, that burden hasn't vanished,' Hannah quipped.

Stef shook her head and waved her sister on. She answered the text about a delayed shipment of armchairs from Milan. Then she browsed her emails.

There was a new statement alert from the bank. With the familiar stomach lurch, Stef brought up her home loan account. She scrolled down.

She leaned against the trunk of a giant oak tree to double-check.

There was a new figure in the credit column: $286,761.

The balance was zero.

CHAPTER TWENTY-SIX

Alex sat at his desk, reviewing the two emails he'd drafted. The Donovan Foundation, which dealt with mental health issues for teenage boys, had been a pet project. Alex liked to think that Ricky could have benefited from something similar all those years ago. Unfortunately, a rookie director had recently made an oblique but public criticism about the lack of environmental sustainability of one of the most lucrative mines William had established. A clear case of biting the hand that feeds you.

The replacement beneficiary was a local youth centre. And who knows? Perhaps that would have been more effective in helping Ricky find the belonging he craved.

Alex pressed send on both emails. Then he stood up and looked out the window.

Ray was showing Margaret and Hannah some of Hughesdale's flourishing flower beds, but it was Stef who Alex focused on. She was alone, leaning against the apple tree right of the footbridge, staring at her phone. Stef placed the screen against her heart for a few beats before returning it to arm's length and giving a restrained but visible fist pump. Really,

Stef would have been a perfect actor for silent films because it required no effort for Alex to interpret what was going on. She must have detected movement because she looked up. When she saw Alex, she raised her hands in prayer position.

Alex nodded acknowledgement. Put his index finger to his lips. It was unlikely that Stef would want to tell Margaret or Hannah he had paid her mortgage. For starters, judging from the pile of bills Alex had taken photos of and studied in private, Stef clearly lived beyond her means. Now she'd be free to indulge her whims without fear of falling short. But more than that, even Stef would see the potential disharmony between sisters that could arise from the revelation.

Favouritism, whether perceived or factual, was a powerful force.

Alex walked away from the window and back to his desk. From now on, he was not only Stef's brother, but her benefactor. The time for Alex to challenge the foundation of his sisters' connection was approaching. He could barely withstand another assault of the untrammelled, in-joke laughter that had spewed down the stairway that morning. Their cutesy anecdotes from shared vanilla childhoods.

For such a small sum, Alex expected his investment would yield excellent returns.

•

The rest of the afternoon had been smooth sailing. There had even been a quiet and peaceful hour where all parties relaxed and read books in the cabana, though it was hard to concentrate for Stef's frequent, grateful glances.

That evening, Alex chose a maroon paisley shirt and black pants from his extensive wardrobe. Although the very thought of setting Margaret loose to spout the tale of his birth and adoption made him queasy, it was time. He doubted there was anything to separate it from the generic – in which the birth mother was the real victim, forced to abandon their darling offspring. But it was important that Hannah and Stef were present. The sisters would, at the very least, truly register the significance of their changed birth order. That he had been the first resident in Margaret's womb.

That, in the natural order, they were destined to be followers.

Alex went into the bathroom to shave. As the razor hugged the contours of his cheek, Gillian's spirit echoed. His adoptive mother didn't need a body, a mouth, to express disgust.

I'm the only woman who has ever loved you.

Not your slut of a mother.

Not your fake bitch of a wife.

Not your novelty half-sisters.

You want to know your story? Look where that got Ricky.

Alex opened the bathroom cabinet and took out the Dolce & Gabbana scent Gillian had been allergic to. He dabbed his cheeks and sprayed the bathroom thoroughly.

Gillian couldn't control him now. Nobody could.

This was his time.

•

In a floral linen and silk dress, Stef was the first to arrive for dinner. A small but satisfying change that signalled a welcome shift in her priorities.

Hannah wore black pants and a maroon shirt. Not paisley, but sometimes their synchronicity came as a shock. All three siblings noted it, but Margaret remained silent. She looked pale too. The impending divulgence was obviously weighing heavily on her, but Alex was determined not to provide a verbal prompt back to the game.

It was not until Stef had helped herself to seconds from the seafood platter and Alex and Hannah were close to finishing their first that Margaret finally interrupted their small talk.

'Nineteen sixty-three,' she said suddenly, and conversation immediately stopped. 'The song – "Our Day Will Come", Ruby & the Romantics.' There were tears in her eyes, but they hovered without overflowing.

Margaret tapped the table, index finger to little finger and back again. Alex made fists to thwart an urge to copy the action.

'I was seventeen and madly in love. You know his name. Antonio. He was eighteen and the most beautiful boy. I can see his influence in the way you carry yourself, Alex, in the cut of your shoulders and the raw power of your presence.'

Alex said nothing. Waited.

'I was naïve about some things,' Margaret continued. 'But I knew what sex was. I knew how a girl got pregnant.' She paused. Gulped. 'We both did.'

A tear slid down her cheek.

Hannah should not have put a hand on Margaret's knee, but Alex refused to let it rile him.

'My parents didn't approve of Antonio,' Margaret continued. 'He was Italian. Poor to our middle class. In my parents' opinion, altogether unacceptable. But they weren't as vigilant as some. We seized every opportunity to be together. We vowed that we would be each other's always. And we made what we thought was a plan to help achieve it.'

Beside him, Stef let out a small groan. 'Dad,' she said under her breath. 'He would be—'

'This is not about your father,' Alex said and Stef had the gall to wince. He gestured for Margaret to continue.

'There was no way our parents would allow us to marry. Unless I was ...' Margaret paused. She closed her eyes and cleared her throat. 'We thought we were the first teenagers ever to fall in love. We believed that, together, we could conquer society's prejudices. It was crazy, of course. But Antonio and I planned the pregnancy. We wanted you, Alex. We thought it would force my parents into letting us marry. We thought we could set up house together. Play happy families.'

Alex felt the words circulate in his chest. A rancid mess of long expired possibility.

He could have been the one born into love. The sisters would have been erased.

'We were deluded,' Margaret said. 'The night I gave birth to you, Antonio was already on a boat back to Italy. I never saw nor heard from him again. The midwife told me to thank my lucky stars that no one need know I was a fallen woman.

She insisted you were going to a respectable family who could give you everything I couldn't.'

The tears were flowing freely now. Little rivers that trickled through the grooves of Margaret's wrinkles.

'There was no way I could raise you on my own, Alex. My parents would have disowned me. I thought I was making the best decision by you.'

And there it was. The self-sacrifice spin.

'That's what the adults told me,' Margaret said.

Alex despised the lovestruck teenagers who had created him. The self-centredness was staggering. He was their flesh and blood, not a pawn to be surrendered when obstacles arose.

'I still don't know whether I did the right thing,' Margaret said.

If she was fishing for affirmation, there would be no satisfaction coming from him.

Alex stood and retrieved the jar from the mantelpiece.

'Bonus round,' he said.

•

Alex checked the paper – 1968. He shut his eyes and let a memory rise to the surface.

This one would do.

'Ricky and I were five. The song was "Hey Jude", The Beatles. It must have been late January. We were about to start school at Prince Alfred College. Grandfather William was their most celebrated alumni. In anticipation of the special occasion,

Gillian had let us share a bedroom. Our uniforms were hanging on the closet door. Caps, blazers, grey pants, ties. I'd been buzzing with excitement for weeks, but Ricky was anxious about it.'

Alex paused. He took a sip of wine.

'Ricky was anxious about quite a lot,' he continued. 'When Mother came in to wake us, I leaped out of bed, but Ricky pulled the covers over his head. Mother had to prise them off him.'

'It's hard to start school,' Stef interjected. 'I remember Rosie telling us she was going to try it for a week and if she didn't like it—'

Alex raised a hand. He shouldn't have needed to. This was his turn.

'Ricky had wet himself,' he said. 'Mother was furious. She called him a disgrace to the Carpenter name. I can't remember her exact words, of course, but I remember the gist. She told us that our blood was bad. She said we needed to be taught right from wrong. Then she told Ricky he had to wear those piss-soaked pyjama shorts under his school pants.'

There was gasping around the table. Good. If Hannah and Stef wanted a tale of sibling advocacy to obliterate their own, here it was.

'I begged Ricky to stop crying. By that age, I knew it would only make things worse. But when I pleaded with Mother on his behalf, I made my own mistake. Because Gillian peeled off Ricky's soaked pyjama shorts and threw them at me. She told me to get dressed. And so began my very first day of school.'

Alex stared directly, methodically, into three sets of widened eyes, one after another. How little it took to invoke a reaction.

'Cecilia will clear the dishes in the morning,' he said. 'It's been a big day. Time to retire.'

CHAPTER TWENTY-SEVEN

Hannah sat on the bed, head in hands. The music coming from Alex's quarters was faint, but she could make out the song. Amy Winehouse's voice was too distinctive for there to be any doubt. It was her version of 'Our Day Will Come', on repeat.

Hannah could only speculate as to why he was playing it. Upon hearing his birth story, Alex had been impassive. It had seemed that Stef was the one to feel the greatest impact, that she was the one carried away by the tale of a passionate and romantic love, sadly thwarted by fate and leaving baby Alex in its wake.

Her parents had been, at least until Alex turned up, a grounded and caring couple. There was love there, for sure, but their relationship had never struck Hannah as impassioned. She wished she'd never heard Marg's tale of romantic doom. She would have to work hard to erase the image of Antonio that her mother had brought to the table tonight.

Her poor dad.

And again, the dulcet tones of Amy Winehouse surrounded her.

What would Alex be mulling over as he listened to those lyrics in the privacy of his room? Of the cruelty that their day never arrived? Perhaps he would be thinking that his conception, though misguided, was both joyous and purposeful? Or would he be angry that they had been reckless with his life?

Hannah knew she was hard to read. But Alex was on another level altogether. He seemed to have ultimate control over what emotions, what reactions he imparted. In theory, Hannah admired it.

But the bonus anecdote he'd shared certainly came across as punitive. That it supposedly emerged from a random year suggested there would be a plethora of examples of Gillian's brutality. Because it wasn't just fucked up to send Alex to his first day of school wearing piss-soaked pyjama shorts under school trousers as a punishment for sticking up for his brother, it was a deeply divisive parenting strategy. If there was a lesson at all in there, it had little to do with bedwetting.

But God, what happens to someone who's been mothered like that? And why the fuck would Alex share such a deeply unsettling story with them?

In Melbourne, Hannah had been impressed by Alex's insight, intelligence and self-control. But she still recalled, verbatim, what he'd said to the homeless man at the art gallery and now it ran in loops alongside the Amy Winehouse track. *If you don't want to be hunted, refuse to be prey.*

What imprint had Gillian's mothering left on Alex? What damage? Yes, Alex was blood, but he was still a stranger.

As the song started again, Hannah lay down, but she tossed and turned. If the child of her mind's eye had become a reality, what sort of mother would she have been? What imprint would she have made?

Hannah looked at her phone – 1.22 am. Rex often had wakeful periods during the night. He would go into the kitchen, pour a Scotch and listen to talkback radio. He said he loved the callers. The drunks. The shiftworkers. The lonely. According to Rex, talkback radio in those hours was humanity in its purest form.

She could call. Even if she did wake him, wasn't that what partners were for? To lean on when there was need? Perhaps her mixed feelings about the visit to Hughesdale so far would become clearer with the telling.

Hannah cradled the phone.

No.

That Rex could be entirely uncritical of the drunks, the shiftworkers and lonely while being so quick to call Alex out as some kind of stalker was a testament to his jealousy. Hannah had always been able to confide in Rex. She'd always valued his feedback. But confidences about Alex's upbringing and the context in which he let them seep out would only confirm Rex's bias and give him opportunity to camouflage his feelings as concern.

No.

Stef had been uncharacteristically evasive all afternoon. Hannah had always been able to tell when she was withholding something. The Fidler women needed to come together and try to process the day's events. They were the only ones who had skin in the game. Or, more accurately, blood.

And it had to happen right away.

•

Stef had been wide awake when Hannah came to her room. She hadn't been able to shake the creeped-out feeling Alex had triggered with his pyjama story. Every time she closed her eyes, she'd visualise the fucked-up situation. Still, when Hannah suggested they go to see their mum in her room, she'd been reluctant.

Today, Alex had changed her life. It was only possible to fully understand the weight she'd been carrying on her shoulders after it was lifted. The last thing Stef wanted was to betray – no, that was ridiculous – *disappoint* her brother. So she had pleaded the late hour. She'd thought of bringing up Alex's comment about there being no need to visit each other's quarters, but on second thought that seemed disloyal. Of course Alex hadn't forbidden them. Stef had clearly misunderstood his intention.

Regardless, Hannah was strident. Hannah won.

Stef didn't knock on Marg's door though. That the sound might reverberate seemed unnecessarily risky.

Stef's and Hannah's rooms were grand, but Marg's was next level. The bed was a four-poster with a billowing canopy of shimmering rose gold. Behind it, the curtains were open to a view of the footbridge, with fairy lights casting a spell over the surrounding gardens. In a baby-blue nighty and matching slippers that Stef had given her for Christmas, Marg crossed the great expanse between the bed and the door. Her eyes were red rimmed.

'Mum,' Stef said, thankful now that Hannah had made her come, 'are you okay?'

As the three women sat down on a white leather couch, Marg sighed heavily. 'I'm so sorry if I implied Antonio was the only love of my life,' she said. 'Hannah, Stef, I adore Jim. I love your father.'

'We know,' Stef said gently. 'He loves you too. And he will come back. I just know it.'

Marg seemed not to hear. 'I'm sorry for a lot, but how can I be sorry for everything? Should I be sorry for everything?' she asked, her voice cracking.

Stef gulped down the lump in her throat. This wasn't the mother she knew. Marg wasn't one to ask advice on how she should feel. Marg was pragmatic and solid.

But here she was. The same mother. Lost.

'If it had turned out differently, if our absurd plan had somehow worked, I wouldn't have you girls,' Marg said then. 'So I can't be entirely sorry. But what did I leave Alex to? Who did I leave him with?'

'I guess we're finding that out together,' Stef said. 'But, Mum, you couldn't have known what kind of family you were giving Alex to. You were told so little.'

'I was told little and I chose to believe it,' Marg said.

'You didn't have an option,' Stef replied, and maybe it was amplified by guilt about her earlier thought that she would never have allowed her baby to be taken, because both Hannah and Marg shushed her. 'Anyway,' she continued in a whisper, 'there are obviously good things about the way Alex has been brought up too. I mean …' She paused and gestured around the room and beyond. 'Look at all this. He would have wanted for nothing.'

'Perhaps, Stef,' Hannah said, 'but material wealth doesn't compensate for emotional trauma.'

Last year, Hannah and Rex spent three months in France and Italy. Stef took her kids to Rosebud for a week. She resisted a sudden urge to mimic her sister, show her what a twat she could be.

'It's not just the bedwetting story that rattles me,' Hannah continued, 'it's that Alex chose to tell us. I wonder what he wants us to take away from it? And I wonder who he has become given those shocking experiences with his adoptive mother. It seems that Gillian was a bit of a monster.'

Stef bit her lip. Oh, Hannah would have been the perfect mother, as long as the exercise was theoretical. Academic. It was a relief when Marg chimed in.

'I don't feel in a position to criticise the woman who adopted Alex after I gave him up,' she said.

Stef nodded. 'Who can tell what challenges Gillian faced in motherhood?' she added, trying to keep her voice down. 'You don't know unless you've been—'

Suddenly the door swung open. Alex was wearing a grey cashmere robe. His feet were bare. As he leaned on the doorframe, Stef's heart skipped a beat.

'Well then, what have we here?' he asked, tilting his head. 'A clandestine meeting in my own home?'

'It's hardly clandestine,' Hannah objected, standing. 'We're just catching up.'

Stef couldn't look at him. She wished she'd never let Hannah talk her into coming to Marg's room. Wished, for once, she could disappear.

'That's interesting,' Alex said as he walked over to the couch. 'It begs the question why' – he made air quotes with his fingers – '"catching up" should be a priority in the middle of the night when you've had the opportunity to do so all your lives.'

Alex stood over Stef and Marg, but Hannah's palpable annoyance seemed to make her grow taller as he spoke.

'It's disappointing to be excluded, especially when I've missed out for fifty-six years,' he said. Stef shifted on the couch. There was no comfortable position. 'But I like to think I'm a fair man, so I ask myself why you're wanting to gather right now. And the answer, of course, is that you feel the need to discuss me behind my back. I understand that you can hardly do that in my presence.'

Hannah didn't miss a beat. 'It's not about going behind your back, Alex,' she said. 'You're right. Hughesdale is showing you in a different light. And that's natural since it's been your home pretty much forever.' She paused and threw up her hands. 'We're trying to figure out what's gone on for you in the past. And what you're feeling now,' she finished.

'My backstory is probably not best understood through the limited prism of the Fidler experience,' Alex said.

'Really?' Hannah challenged.

'I apologise,' Alex said. 'I didn't mean that. It's just … it's bordering on impossible to give you a sense of how I grew up. But that's what I want. That's what I need.'

Finally, Stef willed herself to meet Alex's eyes. 'No, we're sorry,' she said. 'Nobody is judging you. We're just trying to understand you, that's all.'

'It never is all,' Alex said. 'We're all hawking a narrative about our past, checking to see who will buy it. Wondering how much it will cost us in the end.'

For a horrible moment, Stef thought Alex might bring up the payment of her mortgage. But he only pinned her with his eyes. Until Marg rose from the couch.

'We want to know you, Alex,' she said quietly. 'To know your adoptive family. To understand the experiences that have formed you.' She paused to clear her throat. 'Personally, I ache for it.'

Alex walked over to the bed and sat.

'Okay,' he said. 'Well, this is … was, Gillian's wing.' Alex's gaze narrowed as he focused entirely on Marg. 'Perhaps it's time my two mothers got to know each other?' He shrugged, this new attitude bordering on playful. 'Granted, one of them is dead, but I don't think that entirely precludes the idea. Do you?'

Marg shook her head.

'I've replaced the bed,' Alex continued. 'As you might imagine, in her younger days, Gillian often had company in here. She was a beautiful woman. A wealthy socialite. Many tried to catch her, but Gillian would not be caught.'

Alex rose from the bed, hands in the pockets of his robe as he continued.

'Committed relationships were … are, not really a thing for us Carpenters,' he said. 'Gillian's mother died when she was very young and William raised her alone. He always had a date for functions, but there were never any long-term prospects. Ultimately, I don't think either of them were able to sustain such intimacy.'

Alex walked to the window and looked out.

'I thought I might break the mould with Cara,' he said, and perhaps her mother and sister couldn't see his pain, but Stef could. 'It wasn't to be, though. So it seems that Gillian's primary relationship was with her father. And I guess, despite not being blood-related, mine was with her.'

Alex walked back to the couch and stopped in front of Marg again. 'Mother did love me,' he said. He continued towards the enormous walk-in wardrobe and emerged holding a blue-grey gown on a hanger. 'Hubert de Givenchy,' he said. 'Haute couture one shoulder silk dress.'

Stef gasped and was glad she did when Alex shot her a smile. Thank God. He carried the gown back to the window.

'Ricky and I were ten when Grandfather and Mother hosted a mega charity gala at Hughesdale.' He pointed out the window. 'A giant marquee was erected out there with the footbridge and pond as the central feature. We were forbidden to go inside, but we managed to scoot under the tables, playing cat and mouse, and the staff pretended not to notice. The week had been plain sailing. Better than plain sailing. We'd never seen Mother so consistently happy and excited.'

Alex turned around.

'She would have been forty-one, Hannah,' he said. 'Like you are now. Mature, but still beautiful and lithe.'

Stef was not lithe. She tried to hide the sting with an encouraging smile.

'Gillian had a trial run of hair and make-up the day before the event,' Alex continued. 'And maybe there was someone special set to attend the gala or perhaps she was just excited to show off Hughesdale, but Gillian was bursting with *joie de vivre* when she modelled this dress for me and Ricky. She even fashioned a red carpet in the hallway and let us stride up and down with her, laughing at our faux model moves.'

As Alex hung the dress on the window frame, Stef held her mum's hand and squeezed. He returned to the front of the couch, but Stef kept her eyes on the magnificent dress, suspended in time and place. She imagined trying it on, but of course it would be too small.

It would fit Hannah.

But her sister was clearly imagining no such thing. Hannah looked agitated. 'That's all very nice, Alex,' she said. 'But it's late. I'm going to bed.'

Alex frowned. 'I haven't finished telling you about the evening,' he said. 'Please, Hannah. It won't take long.'

Stef saw Hannah look at their mum, her begrudging change of mind.

'Five minutes,' she said, and now Alex looked a little amused at being given a time limit. Stef could never have done that.

'On the day of the gala,' Alex began, 'Grandfather William and Mother had an argument.'

CHAPTER TWENTY-EIGHT

The manipulation stuck in Hannah's craw. Although Stef was obviously seduced by the gown and the impending party story, Hannah had had a gutful. She was dead serious about the five-minute allocation.

'Ricky and I were in the playroom having a table tennis tournament,' Alex continued, 'but we heard them.' He shook his head. 'No,' he corrected, '*they* weren't arguing. William was berating Gillian for arranging a percentage of profits from the gala to go to a domestic violence charity. He wasn't yelling, but his voice carried down the stairs when he called her an idiot and asked why she dared to link his good name to a bunch of man-haters.'

Alex wasn't yelling either, but Hannah still felt buffeted by the forceful undercurrent of his words. The story seemed to be headed south. Marg didn't need that. Not tonight. Hannah narrowed her eyes to indicate these feelings, but Alex forged ahead.

'That night, as the sole heirs to Hughesdale, Ricky and I were to make an appearance. We were dressed in suits and bow ties and instructed to front up to the stage at eight so the MC could introduce us. As planned, Ray escorted us to the marquee.'

Alex stared out the window again.

'It was a sight to behold,' he continued. 'Hughesdale had never looked so opulent. The guests were glamorous. Many were famous. Many were rich. Very rich. You might think Ricky and I would have been complacent about wealth by the age of ten, that gowns and jewels and attitudes would hardly register. But we had often been reminded of what poor was. How it stank. How it could well have been our fate.'

Butterflies began a disturbing performance in Hannah's chest. She willed Alex to stop but couldn't find the words. Beside her, almost imperceptibly, Marg shuddered.

'When the band had a break, the MC beckoned us onto the stage. As he introduced us, I searched the crowd for Mother.' Alex ran his fingers along the hem of the gown before continuing. 'Gillian was wearing the same uniform as the waitresses – a short black dress with puff sleeves and a flared skirt. A frilly white apron and flat practical shoes.'

Alex shook his head as though the very idea of his adoptive mother wearing flat practical shoes was an anathema.

'Mother's hair was limp, unstyled, and she wore not a skerrick of make-up. She wove her way through the crowd with a tray of drinks,' Alex continued eventually, and only then did Hannah realise she'd been holding her breath. 'Ricky laughed. He thought it was some kind of joke. But I could see that Grandfather William was watching her every move and I knew better. This was Mother's punishment.'

His hand dropped from the gown to his side. His eyes were vacant; the same eyes Marg had when she went elsewhere emotionally.

Hannah would have liked to scream *cut* on this whole situation, but, Marg's eyes were urging her not to. It was as though her mother needed to listen to the whole fucked-up story as penance.

'I'm so sorry, Alex,' Stef said, dripping pure sympathy as she stood up. 'You shouldn't have had to see that.' She held out her arms and Alex stepped forward for a hug. 'It must have been humiliating.'

God, Stef was useless. She had a backbone of jelly. It was as though she was beholden to Alex regardless of how upsetting the things he said.

'Humiliating is an understatement,' Hannah said, and now she was furious with herself for staying to hear this as much as at Alex for the telling. 'It was absolutely dysfunctional. Completely fucked. Bordering on—'

'I'm sorry, Alex,' Marg interrupted, tears rolling down her cheeks.

'That's enough for tonight,' Hannah said, sharply now. Fuck the penance. She put an arm around her mother's shoulders. 'It's hardly the ideal bedtime story for Marg. For any of us. Can't you see that, Alex?'

He blew out a breath and shook his head. 'Please, Hannah. According to your own stipulation I still have just over a minute.'

Marg sank back into the couch.

'The party ended late,' Alex continued, mirroring Hannah's crossed arms. She could practically see him sliding back behind his eyes, as though he was able to control even that. 'I hadn't slept a wink. Every time I thought about Mother carrying the tray of drinks and the bemused looks on the guests' faces, I felt sick to my stomach. And I'll admit, I was worried it would send Mother on a downward spiral too. Her downward spirals worked out badly for me and Ricky. But ...' Alex held up his index finger, 'instead of crying into my pillow, I worked up the courage to go to her.'

Alex walked over to the dressing table and sat in the olive velvet chair. 'She was right here,' he said. 'I told her I was sorry about what Grandfather had made her do. I told her I loved her and I wished I could make things right.'

Alex spun the chair to face them, and Hannah could almost see Gillian sitting there. The tracks of her tears. 'Mother drew me in and held me tight,' he said. 'She told me that what happened that night didn't matter. She said what really mattered was me, and I was the best thing that had ever happened to her. She vowed that she loved me endlessly and kissed my cheek.'

As she looked at her own mother's teary smile, Hannah felt the tension in her shoulders ease. It was probably for the best that she hadn't walked out before the ending.

'I'm sure Gillian loved you very much,' Stef said. 'That was beautiful.'

'It was,' Alex agreed. 'So Hannah, Stef, time for bed?'

•

Nobody talked as they walked up the hallway, but it was a companionable silence. Alex and Hannah said goodnight to Stef outside her room before continuing on.

At her door, Hannah turned to Alex. 'I'm glad I stayed,' she said. 'I'm sure you can see that Mum is fragile. She really doesn't need any more traumatic recounts, so I was concerned about how that story was going to end.'

'It must have been a relief for you then,' Alex said.

Hannah blew out a breath. 'Well, yes. But a relief on your behalf too. I'm genuinely glad Gillian told you she loved you and kissed your cheek.'

'Did I say that, Hannah?' Alex asked, and was that a smirk on his face? 'Or it could have been that Gillian said I was a random mistake that she would forever be responsible for cleaning up. Perhaps she told me I was nothing but a burden to her and slapped my cheek.'

In a gentlemanly gesture, Alex opened the door for Hannah.

Then, he was gone.

CHAPTER TWENTY-NINE

*D*ysfunctional.

Alex cradled the word in his mind. Rocked it like a baby. It had been Hannah who dared to use it to describe the punishment William had meted out to Gillian at the gala, but he could tell that it had been swirling around the consciousness of all three Fidler women. It was hardly the first time the label had hovered unspoken.

Oh, but it burned. It was so reductive. So generic.

The arrogance was stunning.

While he'd allowed himself the indulgence of Amy Winehouse and a sliding-door fantasy that saw Margaret and Antonio as his loving parents – a paltry half-hour of delusion to Hannah and Stef's cushioned lifetime – the coven was in Margaret's room, talking behind his back.

Oh and he was still angry. But Alex couldn't help but smile as he recalled Hannah's expression after his alternate story ending last night. He'd seen how the confusion and outrage intermingled. It was one thing for her to speculate and theorise about his upbringing, entirely another to sample a little emotional whiplash first-hand.

In some respects, it had been flippant. A spur-of-the-moment decision for instant gratification. But now Alex saw that it could be part of the bigger picture. Hannah needed to experience being thrown off balance. And she was almost due for a much bigger trigger.

The year, song, anecdote game had begun with Stef. The new game would be way more sophisticated. It would require self-restraint. Pacing. Strategy.

The Fidler women were not exempt from dysfunction. Alex would take great satisfaction in holding up a mirror. Beginning with Hannah.

He had been misguided in attempting to physically prohibit the women gathering without him. It would be much more effective to diminish their desire to do so.

Opening the curtains, Alex let the light of a new day infiltrate his room. Then he went downstairs for breakfast.

●

'Mum is staying in her room for a while,' Stef told Alex as she watched Cecilia prepare her eggs bearnaise. 'She's expecting a call from Dad.'

Alex's shoulders tensed. Jim's retreat had been timely. Should he walk back into their lives, the dynamic Alex was working towards would be sullied. He could not allow that.

'I'm glad Margaret and Jim are communicating,' he lied.

'Are you?' Hannah's first words for the day were little bullets.

Alex chose not to reply straightaway. Instead, he handed her a plate of fruit and led the way to the gazebo. Ray had set the table with a white cloth and the silverware glinted in the streaming sun. Stef sat next to him. Opposite, Hannah's jaw was clenched.

'What's up, Han?' Stef asked and Alex knew it was his cue. He needed Hannah back in his fold for her to experience the full impact of being flung out.

'Hannah is cross with me,' he said, making sure his tone was conciliatory. 'Justifiably so, I'm afraid.' Hannah's jaw remained locked as he continued. 'I gave her an alternate ending to last night's gala story.'

'Yes, you did,' Hannah said sharply, staring him down. 'An alternate ending that was the antithesis of the first.' She broke the stare to look at Stef. 'This one culminated in Gillian telling Alex he was nothing but a mistake and a burden, then slapping his cheek. Very close to the original, right? No wonder the confusion.'

Sarcasm was cheap. Alex chose to rise above it.

'Let me explain,' he countered. He paused for a moment, choosing his words. 'I guess I was trying to convey something of the extremes of my relationship with Mother. The dual ending was supposed to give you insight. I see now that it was clumsy. But it's so difficult to convey the nuances, to do justice to the intensity of what Gillian and I were to each other.' Alex shrugged. 'And I suppose I was aiming for a touch of catharsis.'

Hannah's eyes narrowed. Her chilli scrambled eggs remained untouched. A token of her lack of gratitude. 'Fuck your catharsis, Alex,' she said.

It was, on all levels, a disappointing response.

'I'm sure Alex didn't mean to upset you, Han,' Stef said, giving him a glance of collusion before she continued. 'Sometimes people just need to unburden.'

Alex poured Stef a coffee, putting the last chocolate dipped strawberry on her saucer. A small but clear reward for loyalty.

'What can I do to make amends, Hannah?' he asked.

'The truth would be a start,' she said.

'Then I'll start with a truth,' Alex said. 'Before I came to Margaret's room last night, I had been indulging in a sliding-doors fantasy. Yes, I'm a mature man, yet there I was, immersing myself in a fiction that Margaret and Antonio kept me. It's not an excuse as to why I may have gone off-track last night, but it may be at least part of the reason.'

It was a painful admission, but Alex could already see a softening in Hannah's demeanour he could build on.

'Another truth,' he continued, 'is that I'm not sure which memory was correct. Gillian was capable of either. In reconstructing the event, each seems equally likely. Mother's behaviour was … erratic. Maybe you can both relate to that on some level since, from your own account, Margaret checked out at times.'

'Mum wasn't erratic.' Stef's reaction was knee jerk. She even saw fit to put down her knife and fork. 'Marg just needed a little rest sometimes,' she said, more gently. 'And now we know that it was mostly on your birthday, Alex.'

One day per year was all the thought Margaret had spared him. One puny day. Worse still, Hannah rode right over the revelation.

'We don't have versions of historical events,' she said – and oh, weren't she and Stef making a cohesive team now there was a smidge of criticism around their own backyard – 'we just have events.'

Alex felt the fury first in his gut. A black pit of swirling, clanging, sharp objects.

On his face, a smile. It was crucial that he draw both women back into his orbit.

'Other mothers seemed so different from ours,' he said. 'They were predictable and safe. Ricky and I used to fantasise that our birth mothers were coming to rescue us. I told him stories of how my real mother was crossing oceans in search of me. I would rhapsodise about how she was nearly here and when she arrived, there would be only love. There would be no more talk of being a mistake or a burden or lucky to be rescued, because she was my real mother. I belonged with her. She would think me perfect.'

Beside him, Stef was melting. Hannah was still holding on to righteous indignation but Alex could tell that her grip was faltering.

'Ricky would echo that his real mother was also on her way. But he was never particularly grounded, our Ricky. The birth mother he imagined was ephemeral. She would have wings like an angel and fly away with him into the soft clouds and all would be peaceful.'

'Oh Alex. That's so sad, but understandable,' Stef said, and she was back with him.

'Or could it be another unreliable memory?' Hannah challenged.

The fury had abated a little. In a way, Hannah's scepticism was admirable.

'Come with me,' Alex urged. He led Hannah and Stef over the footbridge and past the infinity pool. Finally, he opened the gate to the clay tennis court. They walked to the far corner, where the grooming brush never quite reached. Then, he knelt and brushed aside the loose clay.

'This was my end,' he said, uncovering the small drawing. Faded but still intact, Alex's mama totem was a stick figure in a skirt. Her eyes were arched windows and streaks of curls billowed from her head.

'I used to touch her before every match,' he said. As they crouched to look, Alex could see that even Hannah was softening. That she could sense a minuscule portion of the yearning Alex had lived with, always.

Not one day per year.

He led them to the other end and uncovered Ricky's picture. It was a simple outline of a woman, with wings.

'Please don't show Mum,' Stef begged.

'I don't think she could handle it,' Hannah added.

Hannah's jaw was slack as they all stood. She leaned in, head resting lightly, forgivingly, against his shoulder. On the other side, Stef. Alex stood tall in the middle.

How it should be.

Not for a fleeting moment like this, but for the rest of their lives.

CHAPTER THIRTY

Before the discovery of parties and boys, Stef had been an excellent tennis player. Her coach had speculated that she was capable of making it to the top should she commit, and it had been music to her dad's ears. Stef could easily recall his beaming smile and praise, shared with everyone around regardless of whether they were interested, after she'd won a match. Embarrassing, yes, but she'd never had the heart to ask him to tone it down. A grand final win would mean pizza out. She could ask her tennis mates and it was his shout.

Stef had never had to draw pictures of her dad to keep her company, because he was always there.

As her mum and sister watched courtside now, Stef tossed the ball in the air and served to her brother.

Of course her dad had been disappointed when Stef told him she wanted to quit. She was sick of missing the first half-hour of *Heartbreak High* on Wednesday evenings and having to rely on friends to fill in the gaps. She wanted her Saturdays free for hanging out at Forest Hill Chase, or joining groups at Gardiners Creek Reserve where bottles of Blackberry Nip in brown paper bags were furtively passed around.

Stef told her parents together, but it was her dad's face she watched. His eyes turned liquid and he'd taken a deep breath before telling her it was her life. He insisted he would always be proud of her and support her no matter what her choices. Marg had agreed, albeit reluctantly. There were digs, but no withdrawal of support.

Their love was unconditional. Solid. For Stef and for Hannah.

'For the sake of momentum, I think you need to have mercy on me, Graf,' Alex called out as Stef aced yet another serve.

She smiled. She really had been good. Perhaps, had her parents responded differently, she could have taken that talent somewhere. Perhaps she could have been someone special. The Grafs and Dokics didn't have fathers who allowed them to back down from the relentless hard work of making it happen.

At least Stef was a flexible person, able to go with the flow. She would adjust her play so they could get some decent rallies in. Spending this special time at Hughesdale with Hannah had forced Stef to acknowledge her sister's rigidity. It had been difficult to watch how hard she'd made Alex work to recover from a small transgression. There had probably been a playful element to his alternate story ending that Hannah, despite all her bookish smarts, hadn't picked up on.

And of course, now she looked at it, Stef understood that Hannah's negativity had always been there. It was always other people's fault they hadn't liked her as a teen. Always other people's shortcomings.

As the hours ticked by, Stef became more and more convinced that telling her mother and sister about Alex paying her mortgage would be wrong. Stef could almost hear Hannah switch the blessing into a curse, making her feel unnecessarily conflicted.

No. Stef wasn't one to look a gift horse in the mouth. She would lean into the freedom of owning her house outright. Alex had empathised with her plight and acted upon it. Hannah hadn't been the one fretting when a new power bill came in. Hannah hadn't felt ashamed as she asked her parents for loans she would most likely never pay back.

Hannah and Alex looked alike, but that was just the surface.

There was little doubt that Alex had been forced to overcome obstacles within his adoptive family, but the result was that he was impressive. Powerful. Decisive. Perhaps a little adversity could go a long way.

Who got it right in parenting?

Stef went easy this time and Alex's return was pretty good. The constant spin he employed didn't faze her. With her next hit, Stef planned to make him run to the net. She could see the play several shots ahead.

In tennis, at least.

For the final game, Alex was back at his home end. Before he served, he walked to the far corner and crouched down.

Marg would have assumed he was doing up his shoelaces.

•

197

'You were actually quite nimble out there, Stef,' Marg said as Hannah took her turn at singles with Alex. The not so hidden meaning was that she could be very nimble should she drop a few kilos, but Stef refused to dignify that with a response. She felt more comfortable with herself today. Almost worthy.

'I was fabulous!' she said instead. Despite her general fitness, Hannah was awkward on the court. Flummoxed by Alex's spin, she returned another ball into the net.

'Jim used to get so excited about your potential,' Marg said. 'Nights before the finals, he had to take a tablet to get to sleep.'

There was a tug on Stef's heartstrings. Was it good that she'd been able to provide her dad with such hope for a time? Or was that ruined by the choice to stop training? There never really was another father/daughter activity that replaced tennis.

'What's the latest with Dad?' she asked.

On the court, Hannah and Alex were chatting and laughing at the net as though this morning's argument had been struck from the record. Long lean twins. Hannah wore black leggings and a singlet and Alex was in white shorts and a polo. Stef's tennis dress was pink with a stripe of maroon at the hem and sleeves. The feeling of self-worth was dissipating a fraction at a time. Her stomach rumbled.

'Jim seems a bit more settled,' Marg said, 'though that's just my interpretation. He did talk a lot about trout.'

She looked at Stef and both grinned with the mutual understanding that, other than his grandchildren, fishing was the only subject that inspired him to wax lyrical.

'But did Dad give you a hint as to whether he was getting closer to sorting out his emotions?' Stef asked. 'Fishing metaphors welcomed.'

'Jim did tell me I was angling for decisions he couldn't make yet,' Marg said.

It was lovely to laugh with her mum, even if it was short-lived. Stef waited for her to continue.

'I think he's reconciled that I had a relationship and a child before we met, and he understands why I didn't tell him before we married. Jim was a man of his time. He may well have seen me as damaged goods. But he's still struggling with why I didn't confide in him in the years after. He hopes he would have been big enough to accept it.'

'He is a big man,' Stef said softly. On court, Hannah and Alex were squabbling about a line call, like siblings. Stef resisted the urge to interrupt.

'I think the thing Jim's grappling with the most is that our first child wasn't my first child,' she said.

There was a long pause. Stef imagined her mother cradling a newborn Hannah. She could visualise her dad's Cheshire Cat grin.

Marg's first and second born rallied on the court. They were much more evenly matched than Stef and Alex. Hannah was beginning to read Alex's spin.

'Did Dad say anything about when he would go home?' Stef asked. 'He is going back, right?'

'I think so, but he hasn't confirmed when. He wants to wait until he feels genuinely ready to welcome Alex into our family.'

They were grooming the court now. At the net, Alex passed Hannah the broom. The surface behind him was pristine. Except for the two corners.

'Jim mentioned he spoke to Liam,' Marg said, and it seemed to Stef that she was speeding up so she could get in whatever she wanted to say before the others joined them. 'He said that Liam was evasive when he asked about Alex, but that he got the impression something was wrong between them. Do you know anything about that, Stef?'

There was a hollow passage from Stef's chest to her stomach. Something snake-like slid down it.

'No,' she said. 'At least, I don't think so.' Because how could she speculate about what might have happened between Alex and Liam without the rest tumbling out in its wake? 'Maybe Liam just feels more accountable since Alex has been around,' she offered. 'He's taking more responsibility.'

Marg shrugged. 'I'm not quite sure how Alex's arrival would have prompted that, but I guess it's a good thing. Liam has always been wonderful with the kids. You both have. Rosie and Heath are lucky in that way. So, the responsibility he's taking more seriously is financial? That would be a great relief for Jim and me.'

Stef gulped. There were so many false assumptions that she couldn't correct. When did omission become lie? Why was there so much room between the lines?

'Yes, Mum,' Stef said. 'Liam is finally growing up. You don't need to worry about him honouring his responsibilities.'

Hannah and Alex started to walk over to join them. A shaft of sunlight beamed behind Alex's head, momentarily presenting him as some kind of demigod, before disappearing.

'It's all taken care of,' Stef said.

CHAPTER THIRTY-ONE

Hannah got out of the shower and languidly combed her damp hair. She hadn't felt this relaxed since arriving at Hughesdale. The physical exertion of tennis in the sunshine had put roses in her cheeks, but it was more than that. In calling Alex out over his dual ending, she seemed to have navigated a corner in their relationship.

The off-white silk shirt floated down onto her body. Hannah drew her hair out from the collar and let it fall.

There were times in all relationships where you needed to delineate boundaries. It hadn't been easy. Hughesdale was Alex's domain and Hannah was a guest. But clearly, calling her brother out had been the right thing. Before that point, the stories about Alex's past seemed curated to evoke certain responses. Having Marg stew in guilt was a staple. After all, it was a conditioned emotion that was always just below her surface. But if Alex wanted empathy from Hannah and Stef, he couldn't just bombard them with random tragic but unauthenticated tales.

In challenging their brother, Hannah had finally managed to trigger a genuine, substantiative relic from his past. You'd have to have a black heart not to empathise with his childish attempts to summon a mother who never appeared. Alex was appreciative, and Hannah could sense his heightened respect, the channel of communication she'd opened between them. She just had to make sure she maintained the integrity of her approach. Make her boundaries clear. If Alex tried to revive the game again tonight, she would object. It was no longer, if it had ever been, a useful framework.

Hannah thought about going to Stef's room to borrow her hairdryer but decided to let her hair dry naturally. It tended to fall better that way, retaining its natural shine. On hair-washing days, Rex would pretend to be overcome with animal instinct, sniffing the fragrance of her shampoo like a bloodhound. God, she missed him. She would call him tomorrow. Smooth things over.

Hannah switched off the bathroom light and went down to the drawing room for the promised pre-dinner cocktails.

•

'I guess we drew the pictures so there was something tangible to our fantasies,' Alex was telling Marg as Hannah arrived. 'If you look carefully, you'll see the totems dotted all around Hughesdale, not just on the tennis court.'

While she accepted a martini, Hannah looked at Alex askance. The fury rose in her chest but there was no opportunity to release it. Not in front of their mother.

Alex put his martini on the bar and Hannah on hold. He peeled back a wood veneer panel on the bar skirting and pointed. Marg had been drawn in close, but even from a few steps away, Hannah could see the icon Alex was showing was essentially the same as the one on the tennis court.

'Oh,' Marg said, as though it was the only word in her current vocabulary. 'Oh.'

Alex picked up his martini. 'Hannah, I know you and Stef asked me not to say anything about this to Mum,' he said.

For a moment, Hannah was struck silent. Perhaps Alex hadn't verbally agreed to their plea to keep the totems a secret from Marg, but he hadn't objected either. And calling Marg Mum? She was sure she'd never heard him use it before, but there it was. Dropped without ceremony.

'I think it's best not to harbour secrets,' Alex continued. 'I want the three of us to know each other fully. And that means opening up. Sharing.'

'Do you and Stef think I need you to decide what I should and shouldn't be exposed to, Hannah?' Marg asked, and now that she'd found her words, they were blunt. 'Do you think I'm weak?'

'Who would ever think you're weak?' Stef asked, landing in the drawing room like a small tornado. She had definitely put the hairdryer to good use. Coiffured waves fell around the shoulders of her gold, diamond-embossed dress.

'Perhaps both you and your sister,' Marg replied. 'Though Alex seems to think I can withstand some truths. Which I can. I can.' She downed the rest of her martini. She seemed to be trying to convince herself she had the strength to cope.

'We're sorry, Mum. We won't do it again.' That Stef spoke

on Hannah's behalf was presumptuous, but there was nowhere else to go with this. Alex had made sure of that.

Marg turned to him. 'I wish I had been there for you,' she said. 'I wish I had been this magical mother who'd swooped down to rescue you in your hour of need.'

It was too much. They'd had a deal. Perhaps not signed and delivered but the terms had been set by both sisters. Hannah poured a refill from the pitcher. Marg's reaction seemed to be abating as her own discomfit rose in degrees.

Hannah sat in a mustard velvet armchair.

'What can I do to help now, Alex?' Marg asked. 'How can we move forward?'

Alex was hovering behind Hannah's chair.

'I want to be part of this family,' he said. 'But not as an adjunct or afterthought – as a fully functioning son and sibling. I think how we get there is to shake up the status quo.'

'How would that work?' Stef asked.

'One thing I've noticed about us three siblings is that we all seem to struggle with maintaining honest and lasting partnerships,' Alex replied. 'Perhaps we can examine that together.'

When Hannah looked over her shoulder and saw the set of Alex's jaw, she knew, at a gut level, that her earlier complacency had been premature.

'What would you say, Hannah, are the main tenets of your partnership with Rex?'

Hannah wanted to take a sip of her martini, but her hands were deadweights. 'They're not unusual,' she said quietly. 'Mutual respect. Trust. Honesty.'

Alex pretended to stifle a yawn. 'They are stock-standard principles,' he said. 'But what I find interesting is what hasn't been included in your Holy Trinity. Fidelity, for instance. Can you speak on that for us, Hannah?'

She was silent. She hadn't told her family about that aspect of her relationship with Rex and she didn't choose to now. She was big enough to understand that physical attraction was a different entity to a primary, committed relationship. That the two could exist in parallel.

But there they were. Her dad's words, swirling inside her.

Just be yourself, Hanny. A bright spark of a girl. You're enough.

'It's important to own our choices,' Alex said. 'And one of yours is to be in an open relationship with Rex. Isn't that right, Hannah?'

'That's not ...' she began and faltered. 'It's an over-simplification,' she tried.

'Okay,' Alex said. 'Of course, it's important not to be glib. So can you please tell us about the nuances of your partnership with Rex?'

'We respect each other's individuality,' Hannah said. 'We don't pretend to own each other and we try to resist getting bogged down by convention,' she continued, but now it felt that with each word, she was digging herself into a deeper hole.

'That's admirable,' Alex said, 'but let's not be coy. This lack of ownership manifests in a certain way. My understanding is that it means that both you and Rex are free to pursue sex outside the relationship. Would that be a fair statement?'

Hannah nodded but kept her mouth closed, not trusting the words swirling around her mind.

'What I find most interesting,' Alex said, walking around to the front of Hannah's chair, 'is that Rex actively exploits this clause, while Hannah's right to sexual freedom is purely theoretical.' He shrugged. 'In less *evolved* circles,' he said, addressing Stef in particular as though they had a shared interest in what was coming next, 'Rex's deal could be referred to as "having your cake and eating it too".'

Hannah's hand shook, martini lurching from side to side in the glass. Alex was being so cruel. He had lured her into this trap. And yet, had she, on some level, been feeding herself a false narrative? Yes, she believed that people shouldn't try to own each other. But had she agreed to the structure of their relationship so that she could bask in Rex's appreciation? His admiration that she was determined to be more than a ticking biological clock? To demonstrate that she was *a bright spark of a girl.*

Was she enough? Had she ever been?

Stef got up. Crumbs from the cheese platter dropped to the carpet.

'Stop, Alex,' she said. 'It's Hannah's place whether she wants to talk about this. You don't have the right.'

Alex shook his head. 'I'm not assuming the right, Stef,' he said, 'but the obligation. I'm trying to find my place in this family too. All I'm asking for is truth and transparency. For Hannah to take an honest, intelligent look inside herself. Especially because she and Rex regard themselves as ... what term did you and Liam coin for them?' He paused and clicked his fingers. 'That's right,' he said. '"The Intellectual Giants."'

Now Stef looked stricken. She opened her mouth to protest, but closed it again. Liam and Stef had judged Hannah's relationship so derisively, so frequently, they had coined a phrase for it.

Hannah looked down. The carpet had become ocean, swelling, grey and wild. Unpredictable.

Stef shakily poured herself another drink.

Alex raised his index finger. 'It was a good-humoured sibling jibe, as I'm sure you'll understand, Hannah,' he said. He was really using the space now. Walking around. Posturing. He shifted focus back to Marg and Stef.

'Let's take a deeper dive,' he continued. 'We've established that Hannah has negotiated rights to sexual freedom that she will, most likely, never use. An extension of that anomaly is a badge that our Hannah wears so proudly. The one that shouts CHILDLESS BY CHOICE.'

Alex reminded Hannah of herself presenting a lecture. He was circling, about to home in on the prize point.

'When the choice,' Alex said, drawing out the finale, 'belongs entirely to Rex.'

Hannah dropped into the carpet ocean. She drifted. Was pulled under. It was all the same, really.

No one spoke.

It was Marg who stood up, finally.

'You've got that wrong, Alex,' she said. 'Ever since she was a little girl, Hannah has always maintained that she didn't want children. I've checked in several times over the years and her position on that has never changed.'

'That's right,' Stef agreed. 'That part is not dependent on what Rex wants or what has been negotiated. It's one of the fundamentals about Hannah. It's at her very core. We've known it forever.'

Alex paused, as though considering Marg and Stef's input.

'Well, this is where things become interesting,' he said. 'The underlying assumption is that because you've known Hannah longer, you know all of her. But this is the exact assumption I would like to challenge.'

It was sport. Hannah could see that clearly now. Alex was dredging her up from the ocean floor, but this was not a rescue, just a reprieve. He wasn't finished toying with her. And Hannah wasn't one to lay down and be stomped over. She hadn't been passive in her life for many years. But this? How could she refuse to expose values she had willingly accepted? Wasn't that a betrayal of self? Of Rex?

'Please,' Alex said, 'we have plenty of time to catch up with Hannah's updated philosophy on children. Let's wash up for dinner now. Then we will meet in the dining room and enjoy the wonderful meal Cecilia has prepared.'

Hannah took a deep breath. She would use the break to collect herself. If Alex was about to throw another home truth her way, she would make sure she was ready to own it.

CHAPTER THIRTY-TWO

In the short break between drinks and dinner, Stef went upstairs to her room to refresh her hair and make-up. That the lipstick she chose to apply was labelled 'Sexual Healing' made her wince.

Hannah had clearly found it hard to hear Alex's take on her relationship with Rex. But if her sister assumed she hadn't already pegged Rex as a philanderer, Hannah must have thought her stupid. The man was a hot mess of roguish charm. A great people-lurer. By Hannah's admission, he was always 'working late' with his students. It was a no-brainer that Rex would go through the haul every now and then and take his pick.

The only thing Stef hadn't understood was that the arrangement was formal. God, her sister had never been more than lukewarm about any guy before Rex came along. It was hardly likely that Hannah would embrace sexual liberation elsewhere. With this new understanding, Hannah's unfettered adoration of Rex broke Stef's heart a little.

But it was brave, really, for Alex to call it out. It was best for Hannah to own where she was. In the past, Stef had thought to broach the topic of Rex's infidelity, but she hadn't been able to bear the idea of popping Hannah's bubble.

She wished, though, that Alex hadn't mentioned the 'Intellectual Giants' thing. She still wasn't sure why he did. It had been a confidence between them. Surely that was implied?

Stef put some more gold glitter on her eyelids and smoothed it out with her finger. There were confidences between her and Alex that should never be mentioned. Ever.

But she was getting ahead of herself. Alex had brought Hannah's situation to light for her own benefit. Nobody would benefit should he share what had happened in her own family. Not a soul.

She was safe in Alex's hands. He was trying to build, not destroy.

Stef would do some mollifying at dinner to make it up to Hannah. But Alex had certainly got the bull by the horns regarding Hannah's position on having children. Honestly, there was not a maternal bone in her sister's body. There never had been. And Stef would have known, instinctively, if that were to magically change.

Stef took a last look in the mirror. She made sure there was no lipstick on her teeth and went downstairs for dinner.

•

The pan-seared gnocchi with burnt sage butter was delectable. Stef would have to ask Cecilia for tips since her own attempts tended to be gluggy. These morsels were crisp on the outside and fluffy within. Each one a little symphony in the mouth. As the others made small talk, acting as though what had just gone down in the drawing room was no big deal, Stef rose to get a second helping.

'Stef, do you really need that?' Marg asked.

She'd managed to refrain from remarking on Rex and Hannah's arrangement, but this attracted comment. Stef understood. This was an area Marg could manage. Black and white.

'After the trouncing Stef gave me and Hannah today, I'd say a second helping is well deserved,' Alex said.

Perhaps it was a small thing, but it felt good to have her brother onside. Stef added an extra spoonful. When she sat down, she gave Hannah an extended blink that she hoped would stand in for an apology. Hannah acknowledged it with a slight upturn of her mouth.

Alex must have intercepted their non-verbal rally. 'That was a nice touch of sibling shorthand,' he said. 'Simple facial expressions that are only readable to one. I had that with Ricky many moons ago. But I do want you to understand that I have, in a disproportionate amount of time, been able to take some deep dives in getting to know my sisters. And I hope the experience has been, and continues to be … enriching.'

Stef put down her fork. It seemed a respectful thing to do, though there were still two pieces of gnocchi on her plate. Alex had certainly enriched her life. Firstly, with his interest and understanding. Secondly, thanks to him, Stef was no longer a mortgage slave. No longer would she feel guilty about buying new boots. New lipsticks. Things for the children. And it was good that this was just between her and Alex. She owed nobody an explanation.

When Alex took a deep dive into Stef's life though, he had surfaced with more than a problematic bank statement. Even more than the mortgage payment, that needed to remain under wraps.

'The reason I'm aware of Hannah's desire to have a child is that we discovered a commonality and chose to explore it,' Alex said. He turned to Marg. 'Stef and Hannah know a little about this, but I think it's important you do too, since it's an integral part of who I am today. Twenty years ago, my wife and I were trying to start a family. At least, that's what I believed. As far as I was concerned, there were no qualms. We were in love and obviously financially stable. We were as ready as anyone could be. And, as you can imagine, I longed for that biological connection. I longed for my own flesh-and-blood baby.'

Marg placed her hand on top of Alex's. He didn't acknowledge the gesture.

'I found out, by accident, that Cara had a Mirena implanted. A contraceptive device that is ninety-nine per cent effective.'

'Oh Alex, I'm sorry. That seems like such a betrayal,' Marg began, but Alex freed his hand and held it up in a stop sign.

'Yes. Another betrayal,' he said.

Silenced, Marg put her hands in her lap.

'The biggest commonality,' Alex continued, 'is that both Hannah and I chose partners who did not want to have children. Or, more specifically, partners who didn't want to have children with us.'

His voice trailed off. With a nod, he handed the mantle to Hannah.

'It's a little different since Rex already has an adult son. But essentially, Alex is right. Rex has no desire to have a child, but I've had a change of mind. A change of heart, actually. A few months ago, I dreamed of a baby boy. And he's been haunting me. I've been longing for him. I know this will be a shock for you, Mum and Stef. It's a shock for me too. And perhaps I could move past it, but Rex refuses to even talk about it. I've felt so alone. It was a relief to unburden to Alex.'

Stef could hardly believe what she was hearing. Not wanting children was at Hannah's core. It was practically her anthem. But to confide the change of heart in Alex above her? Jesus, Stef was a mother herself. She was Hannah's sister.

Perhaps Hannah didn't think her capable of navigating the complexity. Hannah, who had been present at the births of both Stef's children. A privilege Stef had reserved, just for her.

'You're not ...' Marg didn't need to finish the question.

'No,' Hannah replied. 'Not on Rex's watch.'

Stef tried to push through the hurt. 'So, what will you do?'

Hannah shrugged. 'This *Intellectual Giant* has no fucking clue.'

'Language,' Marg admonished, and the absurdity morphed Stef's hurt into laughter. It was a millisecond before Hannah joined her.

It took Stef a moment to see that Alex was unmoved by the hilarity. Even though his expression was neutral, Stef sensed anger. Perhaps it was frustration that he could not gatecrash this sibling shorthand? He picked up his phone, firstly scrolling, then holding it up.

'Knowledge is power,' Alex said, and there was something in his tone that trumped any remnants of frivolity. 'I do hope, Hannah, that you will receive this information as a gift.'

He put the phone face down on the table in front of Hannah and nodded for her to take a look.

It seemed to be in slow motion. Hannah turned the phone over. As she studied the screen, her face paled. She gasped. There was the sound of the phone hitting the table leg before falling onto the carpet.

Without a word, Hannah ran from the dining room.

'What?' Stef squeaked in her sister's wake. 'What did you just do?'

CHAPTER THIRTY-THREE

Hannah locked the door of the closest bathroom. She splashed water on her face and tried to slow her breathing. Sat on the toilet. Got up. On the vanity was a marble figurine of a woman standing in a pond with an umbrella, fragrant soaps at her feet. Hannah picked frangipani and threw it hard against the wall. She considered opening the window, pitching the statue and watching it shatter into a million pieces in one of the multitude of courtyards of this godforsaken property.

The image was burned into her brain. Fuck this. Was it really so easy for Rex to have his cake and eat it? While she was stuck here, catapulted back to her teenage years when she had never been anyone's first choice. She might as well try to get relief the way she'd found it then. Hannah rummaged through the drawers.

Would Rex really do this to her? Could he?

Alex was right. She'd never once taken advantage of their agreement. The one time she'd ever thought to, with Ethan, had nothing to do with lust or freedom. It was to prompt Rex into realising what he had in her. To make him jealous. How very fucking sophisticated. The Intellectual Giant who fed herself bullshit and swallowed it whole. Even as she declared independence and autonomy, adoration had made her compliant. And on some level, she knew it. She had always known it.

But this?

Hannah lifted her shirt and felt her hipbone. Despite the gastronomic decadence of their time at Hughesdale, her stomach was flat.

Rex liked to compare it with his own paunch, pointing out the similarities and ignoring the differences. It always made her laugh.

Scarlet blood appeared in a jagged line across Hannah's hipbone.

She was forty-one. Babies were for women without crow's feet. Given a much younger partner, were they also for aging men with wit and charm and a half share of a very sexy Carlton townhouse, complete with skylight?

Hannah was Rex's first choice. She believed that. She had to. But even if the photo could be explained away, the fact that she'd entertained the possibility of such a betrayal would taint their relationship forever.

Oh, but Alex was enjoying this. He had certainly succeeded in lulling Hannah into a false sense of security before giving her the old one-two. Hannah was reminded of the incident at the art gallery. His callous words: *If you don't want to be hunted, refuse to be prey. Help yourself up.*

He was still out there, in the dining room, trying to peddle the fruits of his stalking as evidence of brotherly love. There was something broken inside Alex and the sharp edges were more dangerous than any razor blade. Hannah saw that now.

There was a knock at the door. She tossed the bloodied blade back in the drawer.

'Han,' Stef said. 'Are you okay?'

'Go away.'

'I won't do that. I'm going to sit right here, outside the door. I'll only come in if you want me to. But please, talk to me.'

In the mirror, Hannah's face was ragged. Tears she hadn't felt coursed down her cheeks. The white and gold hand towel she used to wipe them was luxurious. She had an absurd urge to check the label and order some for the luxury townhouse she shared with Rex.

She dabbed at her hip and watched the tears and blood combine.

She could hear Stef slide down the other side of the doorframe. The bump as she leaned against the door. Hannah couldn't face her sister yet, but she slid down to the cool, tiled floor, head resting where she thought Stef's would be.

'It might not be what it looks like.' Stef's words were muffled but Hannah knew her cadence. She could fill in the gaps.

'What else could it be?'

'Do you know the girl?'

'I'm not sure.' The image burned into Hannah's brain included a belly but not a face.

Stef slid her phone under the door. Alex must have shared the photo. Perhaps the whole family could get copies for their wallets? It had been taken at street level in what looked to be an ordinary shopping strip. There was a Vietnamese cafe. Next door, the signage read *WUMe. Women's Ultrasound Melbourne.*

The logo looked like a cross between a boomerang and a wave. Rex was holding the door open. Hannah zoomed in on the woman beside him. Half her head was shaved, the other half, shoulder-length hair, dark and shiny. Hannah could just make out the tip of a tattoo emerging from the collar of her purple shirt.

Bethany. Fucking Bethany. Who had never scored higher than a credit for essays in Hannah's class because her analysis, unlike her quirky self-presentation, was bog standard.

So, this was honesty. This was respect. This was mutual trust.

'What, Hannah? What is it?'

It took seconds before Hannah realised she'd been laughing.

'She's one of my students,' Hannah said. 'Not one of Rex's. That would be … unethical.'

'Han, please let me in. Mum and Alex are worried. They wanted to come to you, but I asked them to give us some time.'

Hannah stood up. She opened the bathroom door and Stef fell in. She locked it behind them. How much time did they have?

'There's something very wrong with our brother, Stef,' she said quickly. 'Rex told me Alex was following him. I didn't believe it, but obviously it's true. And it's seriously fucked up.'

Stef lifted Hannah's shirt. She looked at her hip with concern, but the wound was shallow. Not much more than a scratch.

'Oh Han, not this,' Stef said. 'Please, not this.' She shook her head and let the shirt fall. 'Why didn't you tell me you'd changed your mind about having a baby? Why confide in Alex and not me? I'm a mother myself, Hannah. Rosie and Heath are my world. I could have helped.'

'I thought we just ended up talking organically, Stef. Now I'm not so sure. Alex seems to have some deep agendas. Please listen to me,' Hannah urged. 'Alex *stalked* Rex to get those pictures.'

'Come on, Han. *Stalked* is a very loaded word. Maybe Alex was just trying to be a protective older brother. Maybe he just wanted to confirm a suspicion. You're in shock. I get that. But this is about Rex. Alex is just the messenger. And it's best that you know the truth.'

'Perhaps,' Hannah said. 'But one of the main tools of an abuser is to isolate and alienate people from the ones they care about. And even Liam has backed away since Alex came on the scene, right?'

'Alex is no abuser,' Stef protested. 'And Liam needed to back away. You said so yourself.'

'I did,' Hannah agreed. 'But Liam has never been one to make himself scarce. So, the question is, what method did Alex use to make it happen?'

Stef sighed. 'Alex is not exactly a heavyweight,' she said. 'He's not a standover kind of guy.'

'No, he's not,' Hannah said. 'He's more strategic than that.'

'Whatever strategy Alex used, I'm okay with it,' Stef said.

'You mean, as long as you don't know what it is,' Hannah countered. Stef's shrug was truly frustrating. She was like a brick sometimes. Impenetrable.

'Stef, listen,' Hannah urged then. 'I understand I have a lot to think about where Rex is concerned. If he could actually do this …' She stopped. She decided to re-route to what was most urgent. 'But Alex has been toying with me. With all of us. His adoptive mother and grandfather were psychos. Charming perhaps, but Machiavellian. It's how Alex has learned to operate.'

Hannah paused. She hadn't meant to shoot off such a glib statement.

'It's not all DNA, Stef,' she tried again. 'It's nurture as much as nature that informs who we are.'

'We all have our foibles,' Stef argued.

Hannah sucked in her annoyance. 'I'm not talking about foibles, Stef,' she said. 'I'm talking about real and affecting damage. I'm talking about methods of dealing with life matters that are way short of okay.'

Stef wasn't getting it. Or refusing to. Hannah tried again. 'Can't you see how Alex reeled me in to pack this punch? His motivation in showing that picture was far from pure. He even said he wants to reset the way our family operates. He wants to be the pillar, and for that to be possible, it's important that I self-detonate. He's practically already achieved it with Mum. She's a shadow. But you'll be next, Stef. I can feel it. I can feel it. I can feel it.'

'Hannah, stop. Please,' Stef begged, rinsing a washer and dabbing at Hannah's hip. 'It's your choice whether you self-detonate. You're reading too much into it. Alex just wants you to know the truth. Now you can get to the bottom of this with Rex and make your own decisions.'

'Knowledge is power, right,' Hannah scoffed. 'But what do we really know about Alex, other than the poor little rich boy tales he sees fit to tell us.'

'We know that he's generous!' Stef's reply was too quick, too emphatic, to be related to a few bottles of wine and an airline ticket. Hannah looked Stef in the eyes and her sister looked away.

Hannah breathed in through her nose. Out through her mouth. She visualised cutting deeper and deeper into her hipbone until she found a degree of calm. Stef was withholding something and only a show of empathy would extract it.

'It's okay, Stef,' she soothed. 'Did Alex give you something? Something special?'

'No.' Stef was lying. The tell was as it always had been. In the upward inflection at the end of such a small word. In the twitching of her bottom lip.

Hannah waited. Stef couldn't bear silence. Hannah could practically see the swelling of a confession rising up her sister's throat.

'Alex paid my mortgage,' Stef said quietly. 'Be happy for me.'

Hannah opened the palm of her right hand and clenched it again. She had a sudden flashback of an argument over a Polly Pocket doll when they were about five and three, during which she pulled her little sister's hair and made her howl. She remembered the odd combination of horror and deep satisfaction at what she'd done.

Footsteps sounded up the floorboards of the hall passage. The clip-clop of Marg's court shoes. The dull reverberation of Alex's loafers.

'You can't let him pay your way,' Hannah said.

'Alex paid my mortgage, not my way. And I didn't let him, he just did it,' Stef replied.

'So, you're going to leave it as is? You'll just accept all that money from Alex?'

'He wanted to give it. I never even mentioned my mortgage. But Alex must have seen the statements on the spike in my kitchen. And Hannah, it's amazing. It's great for me. It's great for the kids. You don't know how hard it's been.'

'How hard, Stef?' Hannah demanded. 'So hard that you could only buy two designer dresses at a time? Only a couple of pairs of boots. So hard that you've used Mum and Dad as your own personal ATM?'

'That's not fair,' Stef said. 'Maybe you're jealous, Hannah. Alex thinks so.'

'Jealous?' Hannah exclaimed, and she could imagine Alex planting that idea and watching with satisfaction as Stef gobbled it up. 'What, exactly, could I be jealous about? You're a pretty basic model.'

'Fuck you, Hannah,' Stef said and Hannah had to refrain from grabbing her shoulders and shaking her. 'Maybe you're pissed that Alex hasn't done something like that for you.'

Hannah tried one more time to make Stef see logic.

'I don't *want* Alex to do anything that huge for me. I wouldn't take it if it were offered. You don't think there'll be strings attached?' Hannah heard herself hiss. 'You don't think Alex paying your debt will colour your already dubious judgement?'

Stef shook her head so vehemently that her ridiculous teased hair started to drop unevenly.

Hannah glared at her sister and Stef froze, mid shake. Good. Since Stef thought truth was the way forward, she could have it.

'You're a fool, Stef,' she said. 'Worse. You're a greedy fool.'

Then, Hannah opened the bathroom door.

CHAPTER THIRTY-FOUR

Hannah and Stef had been spinning their sisterly webs around each other in the bathroom for close to forty minutes. It was beyond disrespectful. Alex knew instinctively that the door would be locked too. Another deliberate exclusion from their inner sanctum.

Well, Alex had the master key and he would use it if necessary. There wasn't a room in this house he could not enter at will. Not a crawl space he didn't know intimately.

As he shepherded Margaret down the hallway, Alex had to remind himself to still his boiling blood. It took time for hard truths to sink in. He hadn't been ready to confront Cara for three days after the Mirena revelation. In that time, silence ruled their house. When Cara attempted to speak, inauthenticity choked her. Each time, Alex had visualised snakes falling from her mouth.

When he finally broke the silence, it was with resolve. The prenup William had insisted upon made the split simple and effective. There were no children to muddy the waters. It was best that Cara left Adelaide and, after a brief conversation with William, she did. The Carpenters had been lenient. She could have lost more. Alex had put out the word that he did not care for updates. Cara Romano no longer existed for him.

Hannah would likely object to his methodology in following Rex, but Alex had no such qualms. The end justifies the means. It had been as easy a choice as his visit with Liam. Both men were albatrosses around his sisters' necks, just as Cara had turned out to be.

Gillian had stepped up in the wake of Alex's failed marriage. In his worst circumstance, she had uncharacteristically but devotedly given him the gift of unswerving support. She had rebuilt his courage and, finally, the resolve that he would never allow anyone to sap his strength again.

Allegiances must be defined and protected. Alex had stepped in as a true brother. Eventually Hannah would appreciate the gift he'd given her and when that happened, she would be grateful.

Their time in Hughesdale, Alex hoped, would eventually be seen as a gift for all the Fidler women. A time in which they woke from their slumbering states to a new awareness. They did not know themselves, let alone each other. Their assertions of unconditional love would remain vacuous while flaws and weaknesses were papered over. Because what was unconditional love without the testing?

For now though, Alex would have to endure the banality of Hannah's pain.

And here it was, spilling out into the hallway. On parade.

●

Alex saw it all at once.

The cut on Hannah's hip. The misdirected, futile fury with which she took in his presence. The way she teetered on her high horse, hanging onto the reins for dear life.

It seemed that Hannah had said something that couldn't be unsaid. Stef had gone into the bathroom with doe-eyed empathy and emerged with cold glassy resistance. Oh, he was curious, all right. But there was no rushing the moment. Alex would let Hannah believe she was in control of how the scene unfolded.

'Hannah,' Margaret said. 'Your shirt. What happened?'

The church pew had run the length of that hallway for as long as Alex could remember. The kneeler was tucked underneath. He imagined bringing it out, giving them all a taste of the hours of penance he and Ricky had endured, their bony knees throbbing.

Margaret sat down, unknowingly atop one of Alex's mama totems. Hannah, despite visibly shaking now, resisted.

'I think Hannah has been cutting herself,' Alex said. 'I know from my experience with Ricky that physical pain can serve as a distraction from emotional suffering.' He made sure his tone was gentle, soothing. He met Hannah's glare steadily. 'I'm guessing that for you, as a teen, cutting was a source of comfort and control. Grown-up Hannah generally relies on intellect to overpower emotion. Now that strategy is failing, you've regressed to the cutting.' He paused and sighed. 'Is that right, Hannah?'

'Of course it's not,' Margaret objected, but she was clutching at straws. This woman didn't know the children she'd raised let alone the son she'd left behind. She had abandoned one and ruined the others with her indulgence. 'Hannah would never have—'

'Oh, but she did,' Stef interjected and Alex switched his gaze. 'When you share a bathroom, you find out certain things. And you get used to' – Stef made air quotes with her fingers – '"a cry for help" that never actually threatens to even cause a scar.' She paused and breathed in sharply. 'Only enough to leave an indelible impression on a younger sister.'

It was satisfying. Alex was tempted to issue a touché as Hannah tumbled from her pedestal.

'I didn't know that you knew, Stef,' Hannah said in a small voice. 'I'm sorry. But we have to get out of Hughesdale. There's something sick going on here. I want to go home.'

'There's something sick going on *here*?' Stef countered.

Oh, there was the power of the incensed in her voice that, so far, had lain dormant. In contrast, Hannah had nothing left. She hadn't even seized a chance to berate Alex for following her boyfriend. She collapsed onto the other end of the pew.

'And you want to go home to Rex?' Stef continued, still standing. 'Jesus, Hannah. Alex has done you a favour. You should be thanking him. He's giving you a chance to honestly assess what you want before it's too late.'

Just as Alex had anticipated, Stef was right behind him. It was gratifying, for the time being anyway. But it was clear she hadn't finished.

'Even a fool … a greedy fool, can see that,' Stef said.

•

It was easy to join the dots of what preceded the greedy fool comment. Heart-on-her-sleeve Stef hadn't lasted long. Alex suspected she could only keep a secret when her own self-perception was potentially under threat. And really, not divulging that he had paid her mortgage would be a better indicator of her loyalty, but this would work too. And here it was playing right into his hands – Hannah's effort to regroup and his own chance at a rebuttal.

'You followed Rex,' she said. 'You followed – stalked – my partner and took photos. And now, you've gone ahead and paid Stef's mortgage. That's hundreds of thousands of dollars. The question on both counts, Alex, is why?'

It was almost too perfect. Alex had to suppress a smile. 'Let me paraphrase that slightly,' he said. 'Why would I do my level best to expose a possible transgression in your relationship? And why would I help our baby sister through financial stress?' He tapped on the church pew, index finger to little finger and back again. 'Because, Hannah, you and Stef are my sisters. You're my flesh and blood. Because your welfare, your wellbeing, is my concern.'

Hannah shook her head, but Alex could see that she was coming to terms with the fault lines of her questioning.

'You're twisting all this around,' she tried. It was a weak effort with no wind behind the sails. Alex knew when a show of kindness worked best.

'You've had a big shock tonight, Hannah,' he said. 'Please understand that I'm here for you. I promise that despite all the time we've lost, I will always be here for my sisters. Always and forever.'

Margaret blew out a breath. She would never be included in that promise. She didn't deserve to be. But she could help cement the ground he had laid this evening.

'We don't really know what has happened between Rex and that girl, Hannah,' Margaret said. 'But we do know that whatever it is had nothing to do with Alex, other than him being the one to disclose it.' She turned to Alex. 'It's extraordinarily generous of you to pay Stef's mortgage.'

'It is, Mum,' Stef said. 'Alex has changed my life. At least *you* can be happy for me.'

'I need to get out of here,' Hannah said. 'I'm going upstairs to pack. Come with me, Mum.'

'Please, Hannah,' Margaret begged, copying Alex's own tapping fingers. Alex visualised slapping her hand away from the pew. He did not. 'Please stay. For my sake. I owe it to Alex.'

'Maybe you do, Mum,' Hannah said, staring Alex down. 'But I don't owe Alex anything.'

He shook his head. Oh, but Hannah did owe him. At the very least, she owed him retrospective timeshare in her sunny childhood. Her cutting was garden-variety. Had she been the one to land in his adoptive family, Hannah would have gone the same way as Ricky.

Margaret attempted to stand and immediately collapsed back down to the pew as though folding in on herself.

Hannah's brow was furrowed. She had little choice now. Margaret barely had energy to climb the stairs to her room let alone the conviction to uproot herself from Hughesdale. And Hannah wouldn't leave her behind. Not if she truly believed there was something sick going on. They would be staying for the full week, as planned.

But Stef was becoming complacent in expecting Alex's support. There would be no room for complacency in the new family order. Alex needed to inspire adoration and fear in equal parts.

Tomorrow he would be shifting the spotlight onto Stef.

•

It had been such an eventful evening that Alex hadn't found a chance to check his messages. As he cleaned his teeth, he worked through them. The first two were invitations for upcoming functions. The third, a heads-up that a state politician had failed on her commitment to extending the lease on one of the Carpenter family mines. The fourth message was a request for a character reference for a defendant in an unsavoury trial that was slated for early the following year. That one might come in handy. Alex starred it.

The fifth was from Rosie. It was nothing but dribble and gobbledygook. She hadn't even acknowledged his carefully crafted birthday message or the sweet gesture he'd told her he made in resetting all his passwords in her honour. But none of that was the point.

It had been an inspired idea to courier her a brand-new iPhone Pro Max (gold). Already, the small investment was paying dividends. Now Rosie had her old phone to communicate with her parents and a secret one to impress her friends and stay in contact with Alex.

Their rapport was developing beautifully.

CHAPTER THIRTY-FIVE

Stef got downstairs for breakfast just in time to see Hannah opening the side gate in her training gear. Good. She wasn't in a hurry to see her sister after last night, and Hannah definitely needed a run. Hopefully, it would make a difference to her mood.

Cecilia was preparing homemade bruschetta. The waft of frying bacon and basil pervaded the kitchen. As Stef waited for her serve, her stomach rumbled and even Cecilia smiled.

It was the first day the weather was less than perfect. Low, dark clouds filled the sky, moving quickly so that the formations kept changing. The breakfast table today was set up on the covered verandah. It was a bold move, given the elements, but Stef supposed they could shift everything inside quickly should it begin to rain.

'Morning, Stef,' Alex greeted, pulling out the chair beside him.

He was wearing a long-sleeved chocolate ribbed polo and cream pants. He was so casually chic. Despite the dramas of the previous evening, her brother looked well slept. Not so for her mum, who sat opposite. She was taking very small bites of bruschetta as though eating out of politeness rather than hunger. The smile she gave Stef didn't reach her eyes.

Poor Mum. Hannah really had a lot to answer for. The apology she'd offered about her cutting was seriously lame. Stef had dealt with those teenage times alone. She hadn't told anyone except Liam. She'd barely had a sense of what she was dealing with and even less of an idea how to help. And yes, it was hazy now, buried under a ton of memories, but there was something supremely selfish and self-obsessed about cutting. Especially as a middle-aged woman. Who, actually, was the fool?

Stef was glad at least that Alex paying her mortgage was out in the open. Why should she have to hide a spot of good fortune? Alex had been right when he suggested Hannah might feel overshadowed by her. Jealousy had certainly brought out her sister's inner ugliness.

Stef reached out and cupped her mum's coffee mug. As she'd suspected, it was stone cold. She tipped it out on the lawn and refilled it from the freshly made plunger. As Marg nodded acknowledgement of the small act, Stef finally remembered her dad's advice when her mum wouldn't get out of bed. *Just let her be, Steffie. The more we try to bring her out of herself, the longer it will take.*

'Unfortunately, I have to attend to some urgent business in town this afternoon,' Alex said. 'Given that we have inclement weather on the way, Cecilia has volunteered to conduct a cooking lesson. I believe she's thinking of Asian fusion at which, I can personally guarantee, she is a dab hand.'

'That sounds excellent,' Stef enthused. 'There's a lot I could learn from Cecilia.'

'Yes, there is,' Alex said, which was a little odd given that Stef was a pretty good cook herself, but she let it go. Stef was not one to hold on to a small slight that was most likely intended to be humorous. 'Of course, the bonus to this plan is that the fruits of labour from the Fidler women will be our dinner.'

'Good,' Marg said absently. 'That will be good.'

'Especially for Hannah,' Alex added. 'Because being unable to prepare a decent meal is no badge of honour.'

Given that Alex had used the same phrase to describe Hannah's change of heart about having kids, Stef guessed he was making a link. Something about that rankled, but she left the comment alone. Instead, she reached out to serve herself the last of the freshly poached eggs but Alex beat her to it, scooping it up and putting it on his own plate.

Stef laughed it off. Obviously, Alex was feeling playful. She watched as he exaggeratedly rolled up his sleeves to get stuck into his breakfast.

'Alex, that's a nasty rash,' Stef noted. On his inner left arm was a large patch of angry red and bumpy skin.

'It's eczema,' he said. 'It flared up overnight.'

'Oh no,' Stef sympathised. 'Maybe it was triggered by the stress?'

Alex shrugged. 'In the scheme of things, what went down last night wasn't stressful,' he said. 'Anyway, the rash will vanish quickly. I'm well versed in what creams work for me. I've had eczema on and off since I was a baby.' He ran his hand over the inflamed area. 'Gillian told me that the day she picked me up from hospital I had eczema all over my infant body.'

Inside Stef's chest, a flicker of doubt ignited. It took several seconds before she spoke.

'Alex, you already told us that story,' she said, modulating her tone. 'Remember? But the last time, Ricky was the one with eczema. You were wearing a hand-knitted lemon jumpsuit. Your hair was clean and brushed. You smelled of lavender.'

'Did I say that?' Alex asked, but he was looking at Marg rather than Stef. 'Did I indeed?' He brought his hands into prayer position in front of his mouth before lacing his fingers together at his chest. 'Thank you for pointing out the discrepancy, dear Stef,' he continued. 'And what a wonderful memory you have. To pin down the fine details too. The colour of a hand-knitted jumpsuit. The smell of lavender.'

Alex sat back in his chair as if marvelling at Stef's recall. But when he leaned forward, there was a hard glint in his eyes that she couldn't ignore.

'It must be nice to have had a ripple-free childhood from which you can retrieve memories so cleanly.' Again, Alex focused on Marg. She seemed to be vanishing in front of Stef's eyes. 'Which one was I, Margaret?' he asked. 'Was I the clean, adorable bundle? Or was I the festering, sickly mess no one wanted to touch? You'd remember that much, wouldn't you? Did you spend every moment you had studying me, committing me to memory, in the two days we had together? Or did you look away?'

'Alex. Stop,' Stef pleaded. 'Please. You're upsetting Mum.'

'I thought you were perfect.' There seemed a permanent apology planted in Marg's voice during these Hughesdale days.

'The nurses never said otherwise. But they were treating me more as a delinquent teenager than a mother. They limited the time we had together, and I had no idea what questions to ask once they confirmed you were healthy.'

Suddenly, as though prompted by the tears that trickled down Marg's cheeks, the heavens opened. Rain pelted, the drops impossibly large and moving in all directions with the wild wind.

Stef ushered Marg inside. When she came back out, Alex was sitting in exactly the same position, watching the weather as though mesmerised.

'Alex, it's not your fault,' Stef tried, her voice carried into a swirling gust. 'I'm no psychologist, but your childhood was obviously traumatic. I think that could be why your memories are mixed up.'

'You see, Stef?' Alex replied. 'What a great listener you are. You truly want to get to the bottom of things and you're brave enough to do the work.'

There was a crack of thunder. Alex waited for the reverberations to pass.

'Which is why, tonight,' he said, 'we need to talk about Rosie.'

CHAPTER THIRTY-SIX

The Adelaide Foothills were impossibly beautiful under a threatening sky. Hannah used every ounce of inner turmoil to power her stride. She imagined running until she found an escape from all the chaos in her life. Should a ladder miraculously appear, she would climb it without hesitation.

It was the freedom of running without boundaries that was making her feel exhilarated. She had briefly checked in with Alex and Marg as they sat on the verandah in anticipation of breakfast. She'd half-expected Alex to forbid her from exiting the side gate, perhaps finding it locked.

But, of course, no such thing had happened. Alex had been conciliatory in his demeanour. He had been encouraging, admiring even, of Hannah's decision to go for a run. The gate had opened without a hitch.

Hannah wasn't inclined to listen to music. Some of her best thinking was done while she ran and she needed to utilise every brain cell. Yes, there was something primary amiss with Alex. Hannah didn't buy for a moment that exposing the basis of her relationship or showing her the photo of Rex and Bethany were attempts at aiding her personal development. Perhaps Alex didn't even truly understand his own motivation, but it seemed that he wanted to pull Hannah down from whatever pedestal he believed she was propped up on.

But perhaps he was satisfied now. Hannah still wanted to leave Hughesdale, but that might trigger a flare-up and it would be her mum and Stef left to endure the repercussions. It was probably best to tough out the rest of the stay. She'd extract herself from any emotional entanglement with her brother slowly. When she got back to Melbourne, Hannah could quite easily refuse contact. She already had enough of a mess to sort out with Rex. And Hannah couldn't remember a time she and Stef had been so at odds.

There was a buzz in her hip pocket. Hannah tried to ignore it, but she slowed down. She'd always been able to intuit when a text was from Rex. His apparent betrayal hadn't affected that.

I'm at uni. Had some marking and decided to use your office. It's strange looking out your window. Seeing through your eyes. Perhaps I need to acclimatise by doing more of it. Albie called me lovelorn and of course it was a joke, but I have no humour for it. I hope things are going well for you, Marg and Stef. I'll be waiting under the skylight. Arms outstretched. Xx

In the middle of a dirt road, surrounded by lushness, Hannah stopped. Why would Rex send her such a text? Did he think she would stand by him regardless of the circumstances? Because, if what she suspected was true, she wouldn't. Couldn't.

If Rex was going to father a child, it should be hers.

Hannah shut her eyes in search of a version of her child as a baby, a toddler, even an adolescent, but he refused to manifest.

Had he given up on her, this little soul looking for a body?

Hannah really needed to set her mind. If she wanted a child, it would need to be a decision propelled by certainty. Could she honestly tell herself that she wanted a baby regardless of whether it carried Rex's genes? In spite of the fact he would not be involved?

There was quite a hill coming up. Hannah started again with a jog. She would need momentum.

Would Rex, after all his declarations, really have impregnated Bethany? If so, had it been intentional? Had it been so, it would malign the purity of his convictions. Rex was proud of his transparency.

She could call and ask him right now. If he assured her she was mistaken, if he was pissed off that she could even harbour the suspicion, she would be overjoyed. But, if Rex confirmed it, she would have to break up with him. And she would fall apart. It was crucial that she kept it together to cope with the remaining time at Hughesdale. If she was going to crumble, she would do it at home. In private.

Hannah picked up the tempo. Bethany. Fucking Bethany. Rex had a soft spot for shaved hair and tattoos. Perhaps the contrast appealed to him.

She hated him.

His exclusion of Alex in the message was telling. Rex had never had to deal with such a complication in Hannah's life. He'd never had to process the reality of her being with another man. But Alex was a complication. And this text made it clear her brother was not one Rex would dedicate himself to working through.

Hannah re-read the text. She imagined Rex frozen in time under their skylight, waiting for her, arms outstretched.

She was halfway up the hill when the skies opened. Not a gradual build but sudden and alarming. She tucked her phone under the waistband of her leggings and pulled her singlet down. She looked around. There were a few trees to her left that would provide shelter, but she was pretty sure there'd be lightning and thunder soon. Given how things were travelling for her at the moment, Hannah fancied herself as unlucky enough to be struck.

On her right, not far from a low wire fence, was a storage barn. Hannah hurdled the fence and ran towards it. Inside were a dozen or so bales of hay. The sound of the rain was amplified as it pounded on the metal roof, but in the centre, she was mostly protected from the wind.

It was both beautiful and bracing. Hannah sat on a square bale of hay, trying to stay in the moment. Leaves were being whipped around in the wind out there as though choreographed. A mystical thinker might try to follow the pattern and see if it spelled anything out, delivered any earthly answers.

Stef would do that.

There was a dead mouse at her feet. Hannah changed bales. She brought out her phone just to see if it was dry.

The home screen showed a new Facebook message. Although Hannah had created a profile, she rarely used it. As a lecturer at a university, it was better to stay away from social media.

The wind was howling now, competing with the rain for greatest volume. Hannah clicked through to the message, finger poised to press delete on what was most likely to be spam.

It was not.

Dear Hannah, I heard that Alex had found his biological mother and sisters. Your profile pic shows a staggering likeness. I'm his ex-wife. I don't wish to tempt fate by making contact, but I feel obliged to warn you to tread carefully around Alex. Keep your own counsel. Devise an exit strategy. Despite his considerable charisma, despite his outward show of support, the man is capable of great darkness, as were his adoptive mother and grandfather. I count my blessings that I've been able to build a new life, but it's been at the cost of all that I had, all that I was, before my first marriage. Kind Regards, Cara Romano.

Cara's profile photo showed a dark-haired, blue-eyed woman of around her own age. Hannah clicked on it and was taken to her public Facebook page. It was full of happy family shots – a redheaded husband who seemed to be permanently looking lovingly at his wife, and two strawberry-blonde daughters who Hannah guessed were around Rosie's age.

The wind was dying down now, the rain easing as Hannah pressed the phone icon in Messenger.

CHAPTER THIRTY-SEVEN

The dress had hung in Stef's wardrobe for over two months with the swing tag attached. It was past the date she could return it for a refund as she'd reassured herself when she bought it. Oh, but it was gorgeous. The printed floral on white linen was pure class. Stef put it on before purposefully removing the tag.

Zimmermann Ninety-Six Filigree Dress – $950.

If Hannah recognised the brand, she would probably try to guilt Stef about not being financially responsible. But Stef refused to feel guilty.

Not about the dress, anyway. Not when she was about to reveal the worst of herself.

Stef had to trust her brother. Alex had helped ease her financial burden. Perhaps this would ease the emotional one – for herself and for Rosie. Because the last thing she wanted as a mother was for her child to be carrying a private and heavy load throughout her life.

It wasn't going to be easy, but Stef was up to the task. She was capable of the emotional labour if that's what was necessary. She would be honest with herself and the others. Unlike Hannah.

Footsteps sounded in the hall. Stef waited for them to pass and then looked out. Hannah was climbing the last set of stairs. It was odd, since there was nothing on the top level except for a turret that served as Alex's study. Especially odd because Alex was still in town for work. Knowing her sister, she was probably searching for his adoption papers to get absolute proof he was who he said he was. Which would be ridiculous, given they pretty much looked like the same person.

Whatever Hannah was doing up there, it seemed like trespassing. Quite the hypocrite since she'd been so pissed about Alex following Rex.

Stef chose the white sneakers the sales assistant had suggested to go with the dress. It was unusual, since she generally preferred a little heel. But tonight she needed to be comfortable.

She heard a car and walked to the window. Alex's Maserati was pulling up in the circular driveway. Her heart raced. It was pure instinct that propelled her up the last set of stairs to warn Hannah.

•

It was close to 6 pm when Stef started making her way to the drawing room. Despite the suggested five thirty start for cocktail hour, she wasn't rushing. She would do this, but there was no way she could muster enthusiasm.

She could see the fire flickering before she walked in. They were all there. Alex handed her a margarita without commenting on her lateness.

'Margaret, Hannah,' he said, interrupting their conversation, 'Stef has something to share. Something she has kept secret for too long.'

'Well, that would be up to Stef,' Hannah objected.

Stef felt the pinch of her sister's warning. *You'll be next, Stef. I can feel it. I can feel it. I can feel it.* And yes, she was next, but she would not resist. She would embrace the experience.

While the others sank into armchairs, Stef stood in front of the fire. There was no point procrastinating. Alex knew the story. He could tell it himself if he wanted. At least this way, Stef would be able to control the narrative. In her keenness to off-load onto her new brother, she'd blurted it all out to him at once. But Alex was right – it was time her family knew too.

'Mum, Hannah,' Stef began, 'you might remember we had a stringybark tree in our backyard. It wasn't the most beautiful tree. Liam and I had considered cutting it down until it became home to a pair of tawny frogmouths.'

Stef stopped and breathed in a happy memory of her children birdwatching together. Of shared binoculars and smiles.

'The kids loved watching the pair. They googled to find out which was the male and which the female. The male was silver grey with black streaks and the female had reddish brown mottling, which is apparently called rufous. Heath developed a crush on that word, Hannah. He'd use it even when it didn't make sense.' For a moment, the memory of laughing with Liam and Heath over his word crush took hold.

'Those tawny frogmouth lovers would sit side by side on their favourite branch, pointing their beaks in the air,' Stef continued. 'Whenever he saw them move, Heath would shriek with delight. There wasn't any shrieking from Rosie, of course. Even at ten, she'd never indulge in such an open display of excitement. But she was engaged with those birds – especially when Liam climbed a ladder and found three eggs in their nest.'

Stef took a sip of her margarita, noting the serious expressions of her mother and sister. Alex seemed, if anything, a little bored. Perhaps he was waiting for the momentum of the story to pick up, but he had orchestrated this ... confession. The rest, at least, could be on Stef's terms.

'Those birds were practically joined at the hip,' she continued. 'Where one ended, the other began. During the day, the father looked after the eggs. At night, he and the mother shared the responsibility. We were counting down the days until they hatched. There was only a week or so to go.'

Stef paused. She didn't want to continue. It would make it all real.

'Stef and Liam's relationship was disintegrating,' Alex said then. 'It was *dysfunctional*. That seems to be the preferred term in the present company.'

Hannah stood up. 'Stef and Liam were teenagers when they got together,' she said. 'Outgrowing each other is not an example of dysfunction.'

Alex smiled at Hannah, and despite Stef's proximity to the fire, she felt a chill.

'Perhaps Liam wasn't impregnating other women, Hannah,' he said, his tone at odds with the force of the statement. 'But they had developed their own brand of instability. Maybe their relationship was more intense than you gleaned? And maybe, as opposed to the phrase you like to bandy around, living inside Stef's head *isn't* actually the mental equivalent of being on a Caribbean cruise.'

Alex's words had the effect of pushing Hannah back into her chair. Stef would have liked to push her off the planet. She wished she hadn't gone upstairs to warn her of Alex's arrival, wished Hannah had been caught snooping for whatever the fuck she was after.

Stef ploughed on. 'At the time, we were both frustrated. We were disappointed with ourselves and each other,' she continued. 'Despite giving up the interior design course so I could work full-time to support us while he upskilled, Liam hadn't stuck it out. We'd always bantered with each other, but by then, the banter was ugly, fuelled by booze. I was getting really good at insults. I'd think up the nastiest things and aim them right at him.'

Hannah shook her head. It was too late to be sorry.

'One night,' Stef said, wiping a runaway tear, 'one particular night, Heath was on one of his regular sleepovers. We had new neighbours a few doors down with a daughter, Lucy, who was around Rosie's age. Poor Rosie didn't get many invitations, but I'd managed to wrangle a sleepover for her there. We'd planned to go out for dinner, but there wasn't enough money in our account to go anywhere nice. So we cooked at home. And drank. We danced around the kitchen with the boom at full volume. Around midnight, we transferred to the backyard. The talking turned to arguing.'

Marg had her head in her hands now. Perhaps that's what their mother had always done in times of discomfort?

Stef cleared her throat. She tried to still her trembling lips.

'I was yelling at Liam about what a useless father he was,' she continued. 'Telling him that Rosie took after him, that she had all his worst traits. I said that she was moody and spiteful and all-round unlikeable, and the only reason she was at a sleepover that night was because I'd put in the effort to set it up and Lucy didn't know yet how annoying Rosie could be.'

Stef paused and massaged her throat where the next words would be rising.

'Neither of us knew that Rosie had had a fight with Lucy and come home. But there she was, emerging from our garage with a rifle. And our baby, our ten-year-old daughter, pointed that thing at me. Then at Liam.'

The tears flowed freely now.

'She screamed that she hated us both. And she did. She really did. Her face was bright red with rage. She wasn't in control of her emotions, but she seemed to know what to do with that gun.'

Her mum gasped, standing up suddenly. 'But where,' she exclaimed, a hand clapped over her heart, 'where on earth would Rosie have got a gun?'

'And how would she have learned to use it, Stef?' Hannah asked, standing next to their mother, her eyes narrowed in disbelief. 'In suburban Burwood, surely the neighbours would have heard the shots?'

Stef gestured for them both to sit down. It was hard enough

to get through this without her mother and sister standing over her. Marg stumbled backwards into her chair. Hannah's movements were wooden.

'Liam's father stored it in the garage without telling us,' Stef said. 'You both know that Marshall ditched the booze and found the lord in the last years of his life. And even though Liam couldn't really forgive him, we both thought he'd been tamed. But it turns out that when Liam and I were out, the old prick had been teaching Rosie how to handle a rifle. How to hold it, aim it, and shoot it. The gun was never loaded in those practice sessions, so the neighbours wouldn't have heard anything. But Rosie was sharp. She knew just by following where the old prick looked every time he mimed loading the rifle where he'd hidden the bullets.'

Marg folded her arms, pressing them close to her body. Hannah's fists were clenched on her lap.

Stef put her empty glass on the mantelpiece. 'That shitfight of a night, a shot was fired,' she continued. 'Because of the garden lights, I could see the bullet hole it left in the fence. But then there was another. I assumed it went into a bush, but Rosie must have known straightaway because she dropped the gun. I remember her running across the lawn and kneeling down. I can tell you, that sobered me up. Liam went over to her but I couldn't move. He took the gun and put it back in the garage.'

Stef shut her eyes and blocked out her mother, sister and brother.

'Then Rosie wailed,' she said, feeling the tremor it had caused on that very night. 'I've never heard anything like it. It stunned me out of my stupor, and I went to her. I dropped onto my knees next to my baby girl.'

Stef remembered to breathe.

'Rosie was cradling the body of a tawny frogmouth,' she said.

'The mother.'

CHAPTER THIRTY-EIGHT

Hannah barely recognised Stef as she walked through her train wreck of a story.

Alex had induced this. Hannah's objections had been pointless. She had been kidding herself about earlier wins, too. Alex was changing the order of the Fidler family. She was no longer the eldest sibling. If Hannah had ever held sway, it was not the case now. She was stranded in the middle.

'Marshall was never a good man,' Marg said and Stef took a step back with the force of the words.

'We thought – we hoped – that Rosie would enjoy tinkering around in the garage with her grandfather. Like Heath does in the shed with Dad.'

'But Jim is … *Jim*,' Marg moaned. 'Jim can be trusted.'

Stef's hand shook as she refilled her glass from the jug. 'Yes, Mum,' she said, her eyes uncharacteristically hard, 'we should have known.'

'I'm sorry, Stef. I didn't mean …' Marg began.

'Oh, but you did,' Stef said. 'Liam and I were oblivious until after the accident when Rosie admitted Marshall had been teaching her to use a rifle in our own garage. That's got to be negligent, hey? It showed a lack of judgement, at best.' Stef paused, but it was clear her anger was mounting. 'Maybe that's not as bad as getting pregnant on purpose at seventeen though,' she continued. 'Or withdrawing yourself from the children you kept whenever you felt the urge to wallow.'

'Stef. Stop.' It was supposed to be a demand, but Hannah's voice was too small and Stef's fury too large.

Marg was all but gone. A shell.

'The male bird sat alone on that branch for days,' Stef said to no one in particular. 'He didn't eat or drink or incubate the eggs. He just whimpered. Do you know what that sounds like? A tawny frogmouth's whimper?'

Stef flopped into an armchair. 'Rosie does.'

For a while, no one spoke.

'We cut down the tree,' Stef said finally, 'and buried the poor eggs that would never hatch. We let the male bird go in another area and told Rosie it was best to forget. But Liam and I knew we had to end our marriage. Everything had gone too far.' Stef scoffed as she looked at Hannah. 'So, how was that little Caribbean cruise, sis?' she added. 'How does that sound to the only mother-of-the-year who's never had an actual child?'

•

The toxicity came at Hannah in a blast. She could only withstand, not reply.

'You know what Liam told me at the end of that night?' Stef asked, looking up at the roof. 'He said he wished he could be a proper father like Jim. He reckoned that instead, he'd become like his own.'

'Rosie needs guidance and discipline,' Alex said. 'For everyone's sakes, I'm stepping up to the plate. I think you'll all be surprised at the direction I can give her and Heath. Together, we can mitigate Liam's influence.'

Hannah gathered a handful of hair at the nape of her neck and pulled it, hard. She recalled the interminable teen years when the young couple were always in Stef's room, playing music and laughing. Then a specific memory landed. That day Hannah had worked up the courage to ask a fellow student on a date. He'd tried to let her down gently, but she'd seen his horror at the very thought. Hannah didn't recall a thing about the guy now, but she did remember channelling the hurt into fury about the volume of the music coming from Stef's room. She had burst in there. Stef had rolled her eyes, but Liam must have detected her ravaged sense of self because he turned down the volume straightaway, then reached into his pocket and pulled out two little bags of weed. 'My shout, Han,' he'd said as he gave her one. Liam, who at the time had nothing but a downtrodden mother, a cruel and violent father and a home that looked like a tip.

Liam had his faults, but he could never become his father. Hannah wished she could reassure him of that. She should have been kinder.

But Alex was effectively ejecting Liam from their lives. They were all gone, or at least had a foot out the door, because of Alex.

Jim. Rex. Liam.

Hannah reached into her inside breast pocket. It had been surprisingly easy to find the receipt in Alex's study. It was verification of Cara's version of events. Alex might have been different had she not been removed from his life.

Perhaps the information would bring him comfort. Perhaps it would enrage him. Hannah didn't know and she wasn't inclined to find out. Why should Alex even have a chance at comfort while methodically destroying the relationships around him?

This secret would not eat Hannah alive.

CHAPTER THIRTY-NINE

Alex looked around the drawing room at his mother and sisters. Seeing them so reduced did not bring him joy. But finally, all their secrets were out in the open. From now on, he would be the most important person in their lives. Not an adjunct. Not a novelty half-brother, but the pivotal family member who would facilitate and adjudicate the new order. He would yield his power carefully. Strictly, yes, because a true leader had to command respect. But there would be rewards, both financial and emotional, for their compliance.

'Take a good look at your offspring, Margaret,' Alex said, and it wasn't unkind when truth was the driving force behind his words. 'All of us are damaged goods. Not one of us can sustain an adult relationship. Not one of us is capable of bringing up happy, healthy children. But we can be there for each other.'

Margaret's crying was silent, as was Hannah's. Stef's, as could be expected, was noisier. Guttural.

'My theory is that the guilt you felt about throwing me to the wolves seeped into the parenting of your children – the ones you coddled and loved unconditionally. Now, thanks to our time

255

together at Hughesdale, you can begin to see yourselves and each other in the light of truth.'

All three women listened attentively through their tears. They were finally learning how to treat him.

With caution. With devotion. With respect. And with gratitude.

Always with gratitude.

They would do this his way. Alex would never be sideswiped like his clueless brother had been all those years ago.

It was time to press that point home.

'My brother found his birth mother when he was just shy of nineteen,' Alex said. 'William and Gillian were furious at the betrayal. I pretended I would never do such a thing myself, but I was curious. Ricky would be my canary in a coalmine.'

Alex shook his head. Cecilia had left the Asian fusion dinner in the kitchen ready to be reheated, but dinner could wait.

'They were barely through a first coffee when the woman Ricky had pinned so much hope to, the woman he'd drawn with wings since he was six years old, told him he had been a mistake she had no intention of revisiting. His birth mother said she had a proper family – a husband, son and daughter – and there was no way she was going to ruin their lives.' Alex focused on Hannah now. 'Ricky started cutting after that. It was only after he was profiled in the sports pages of the *Adelaide Advertiser* that this woman saw fit to contact him again.'

Alex opened a bottle of shiraz and poured a glass for each of them before continuing.

'The article was titled "What a Catch" and it framed Ricky as a youthful eligible bachelor. Sporty. Handsome. Rich. And, surprise surprise, his birth mother had a rethink. She sent Ricky a photo of his little brother and sister that he immediately framed, though he had to hide it in one of his drawers to avoid questions from Grandfather and Mother. The girl had a halo of red curls. The boy was gap-toothed and holding a soccer ball. In that period, Ricky stopped cutting. He was happier than me. Brighter. More animated and handsome. In our house, when one sibling was a winner, the other was automatically the loser.'

Alex paused, giving them time to digest how that must have felt for him as a teen. How he'd seethed at Ricky's seeming good fortune while he was left to slink in the shadows.

'After a while, Ricky's birth mother sent a request for money. Small amounts at first, that he paid from his own account. Ricky told no one. She kept delaying the dates when he could meet his brother and sister, dangling them in front of him like a carrot. Finally, she sent a request for ten thousand dollars. Ricky didn't have access to that much money. Foolishly, he took the request to William. Oh, and that knocked Ricky right off the pedestal. Grandfather was furious. I heard him tell Ricky that looking for his birth mother was like going through the rubbish and expecting to find a winning lottery ticket. William said that Ricky was a gullible cretin and he was being played like a violin.'

Alex had been lurking outside the kitchen door when it happened. He could practically see himself clambering back onto that empty pedestal.

'William made Ricky dial his birth mother's number on the spot. Grandfather told her there was not, nor would ever be, another cent coming to her from the Carpenters. That even beyond the grave, he would make sure of it. Within a day, Ricky's birth mother's phone was disconnected.'

There was an old painting of Hughesdale hanging in the drawing room. Alex walked over to it. He took it off the hook. On the wall behind, there were two faded crayon pictures – Ricky's stick figure mother with wings and his own version.

'Six weeks after that call, Ricky hanged himself,' he said. 'He never met his brother or sister.' Alex shook his index finger in the air. 'Don't ever try to play me like Ricky's mother did. The results would be disast—'

The intercom in the hallway buzzed. There was a car outside the main gate. But Alex was not expecting anyone and, regardless of who it was, he did not appreciate the interruption.

'Make an appointment,' he said into the receiver. But the car stayed put. The windows were tinted and it was dark, but Alex could see a hand reaching out to the keycode pad.

The gate opened.

But that was impossible. Only he and Ray knew the most recent eight-digit code.

Or, more accurately, he, Ray, and the person whose birthdate he'd used to set it.

CHAPTER FORTY

As soon as she heard the pounding knock, made with the heel of a small hand rather than the knuckles, Stef knew who was at the front door. Clearly annoyed, Alex reached for the knob, but it was Stef who got there first.

Standing on the verandah under the sensor lights was her dad and Rosie.

'Mum!' Rosie charged straight inside, flinging her arms around Stef's waist in a way she hadn't done for years. Her dad remained put.

'I'm sorry for arriving un—' he began but stopped short when Marg and Hannah came into the entrance foyer. He walked inside without an invitation.

'See, Pop?' Rosie said. 'I knew something was wrong. I could feel it in my bones.'

Stef saw the carnage through Rosie's eyes. Standing under the chandeliers, Marg was shrunken and subdued. Hannah, pallid and defeated. And herself – a mess emotionally and physically.

'What are you doing here, Rosie?' Alex asked, his tone inauthentically light.

Rosie pulled away from Stef. She reached into the pocket of her jeans and pulled out a gold phone, holding it up to Alex.

'I needed to give this back to you,' she said.

Stef shook her head. 'Sweetie, what do you mean?' she asked. 'That's not your phone.'

'It is,' Rosie said. 'Alex sent it to me. Didn't you *Uncle* Alex?' Rosie's tone was shrill. Uneven. In the face of it, Alex was calm. In fact, he looked mildly amused, encouraging Rosie to go ahead without providing an answer.

'You know, Mum, that I've wanted a new phone forever. And this is the one I would have chosen. But Alex asked me not to tell you or Dad. I was only supposed to use it with my friends and him. He said it could be our secret. And that's not right, is it? That's why I ended up telling Pop.'

Stef pulled her daughter in close. It was a deception that had the potential to further separate Rosie from both her parents.

A strategy to divide them.

'Did you do that, Alex?' Stef demanded. Adrenaline kicked in. Stef was a mother lioness. 'Did you give Rosie a phone and tell her to keep it a secret from her own parents? Seriously?'

Stef watched as her dad walked, slow motion, over to Marg. Watched her mother collapse into him. His stature. His goodness.

'Whoa, Stef,' Alex said. 'This is an overreaction. The phone was a gift. Nothing more.'

'It was a bribe,' Rosie said, and Stef saw her daughter surpass her in emotional intelligence. Little Rosie may have been born with prickles, but they were there for a reason. Prickles were protection. 'Alex was trying to get me on his side. But I'm not stupid. I won't be used like that.'

'Oh come on,' Alex said, shaking his head. 'You're being silly, Rosie. There are no sides. You must have misunderstood.' His charming smile was plastered on. 'Let's all go into the dining room and have some of the dinner your mother helped to cook this afternoon. We can settle this in comfort.'

Everyone remained still.

'When I told him about the phone, when I told him about the bad feeling in my bones, Pop listened,' Rosie said much more quietly now, and Stef immediately got the implication. She hadn't listened to Rosie's qualms. Not properly. Like she should have.

'Rosie, what did Alex say to you and Heath in the backyard the day he gave you the AirPods?' Stef asked. 'When you told me he was a dickhead and took Heath back to your room.'

Rosie obviously didn't need to search for the memory because she spoke immediately.

'He asked us who we thought would win if we were in *The Hunger Games*,' Rosie said, her eyes narrowing. 'Then he said he'd take a bet that it would be me.'

It was an arrow to the heart. Stef had dismissed Rosie's concern.

'Heath didn't get it because he's too scared to watch the movies. But it was a bad thing to say. I could tell Alex wanted to set us against each other.'

'Stef, this is ridiculous,' Alex protested and now the calm was disappearing from his voice. In its place was a coldness that permeated the entrance foyer. 'You said yourself that everything was too PC these days. Remember? Musical chairs and everyone gets a chair? Pass the parcel and everyone gets a prize. Divvying out the loot from the Piñata.'

Stef shook her head. 'You've been doing it here too, Alex,' she said. 'Pitting us against each other.'

Jim looked with concern at Marg and his daughters before addressing Alex directly. 'I think it's time to leave. We can go to a hotel in town and get a flight back to Melbourne tomorrow.'

'You will not,' Alex said, eyes flashing as he stepped up to Jim. 'You will not let the musings of a disturbed child bring an end to the time I have planned with my mother and sisters. That would be a mistake.'

Jim took a step closer to Alex. 'Can you go and pack your things, Margie? You girls too,' he said.

No one moved. Alex pointed his finger at Marg. Then at Hannah. Then at Stef. 'If you leave, if you abandon me now the way Margaret abandoned me fifty-six years ago, there will be no going back,' he seethed.

Rosie, standing in front of Stef, her back pressed against her, began to cry.

Alex was wild now. The elegance and charisma stripped away. He crouched down in front of Rosie.

'You think you've come to the rescue here, Rosie?' he demanded. 'But you're the opposite of a heroine. You're a destroyer.' The way he spoke was hypnotising. Deliberate. 'What does a tawny frogmouth sound like when it whimpers, Rosie? One whose lifetime partner has been killed. Whose babies will never be born. I believe the sound is like a newborn's cry. Perhaps it's like the noise you're making now?'

Stef didn't even know she was going to do it. She reached out and slapped Alex across the face. Hard.

Then, with Rosie, her mum and dad, she went upstairs to pack her things.

•

Oh, Hannah was eager to escape the dark shadows that were Hughesdale and its history.

But as she looked at her half-brother, at his slumped shoulders, his pained expression, she couldn't leave him just yet. She of all people could identify with his anguish at being unloved. It was, after all, a primary human need. Hannah reached into the pocket of her blazer. She walked over to Alex, sat on the floor next to him and handed him the receipt she'd found in his study among Gillian's medical records.

'Gillian coerced Cara into getting the Mirena,' she said. 'Your adoptive mother told your wife she was only just becoming used to sharing you with her, that she couldn't bear to share you with a child you'd most likely be obsessed with. She threatened to disinherit you and implied that she would hurt herself or worse unless Cara capitulated. She promised that after two years, Cara could start actually trying for a child. She said two years would give her time to wrap her head around the idea.'

Hannah stood up. 'Cara did love you, Alex,' she said. 'She wanted to have children with you, but your marriage was poisoned by your adoptive mother. I guess it's up to you now whether you keep attempting to divide and conquer. Whether you choose to poison.'

She didn't wait to see how Alex took the revelation. It was a parting gift.

Hannah knew she never wanted to see her brother again.

PART THREE

INFILTRATION

CHAPTER FORTY-ONE

In Hannah's dream, she and Rex were fishing off a rock in the moonlight. Not talking – just being. When her phone rang, the moon exploded. Stars were catapulted in all directions. Hannah jolted upright.

'Dad, what is it?'

There was a series of heavy breaths, as though he'd forgotten the need to talk on a phone.

'It's your mother,' he said eventually, pausing again for a hundred years while Hannah's throat closed over. 'She's had a massive stroke, Han. I called an ambulance and came with her. She's in the ICU.'

Hannah reached out to Rex, but he wasn't there. His side of the bed was fully made, her side a tangle of sheets and blankets.

'Dad. Is she ... is Mum going to be okay?'

'They don't know. It's touch and go.'

Hannah could hear the clap of her dad's hand over the receiver. A couple of sobs and some beeps that sounded like hospital equipment before he spoke again.

'Can you tell Steffie? We're at the Epworth. Richmond.'

Hannah was up, tossing on clothes, grabbing her handbag and keys.

'Oh, Rex,' she said, and he didn't answer because he was no longer there, but Hannah went on. 'It's my mum, Rex. It's Marg.'

•

Stef was wearing white trackpants, a black long-sleeved T-shirt and slides. A vest in a half-hearted attempt to cover the fact she was braless. She'd aged since Hughesdale, much more than should have been possible in the six-month interim. She threw her arms around their dad, crying noisily into his shoulder as Hannah stood back.

'Mum will pull through, Dad,' Stef said. 'She's a fighter.'

Stef turned to Hannah for affirmation. She nodded. Was the one to open her arms. She pulled Stef close but there was still some restraint in the response. It was in the tensing of Stef's back. The lightness of her squeeze.

Hannah and Stef were becoming attuned at demonstrating their support for each other only in the obvious ways. Black and white ways, impervious to interpretation. These days, sibling shorthand was an endangered language. On the cusp of extinction.

The agreement to tread carefully with each other was unspoken. But they had officially agreed, for the wellbeing of the extended Fidler family, that Alex was no longer welcome in their lives.

'Where are Rosie and Heath?' their dad asked.

'I called Liam,' Stef replied. 'I left before he arrived though. They would have been by themselves for half an hour or so, but they were asleep anyway.'

Hannah felt an overwhelming desire to call Rex. An overwhelming desire to erase what had happened. Reverse the wheels her brother had set into motion.

'I wish you'd trusted me, Han,' Rex had said. 'But I hope you get to figure out what you actually want.'

It was amicable. Two grown-ups deciding their relationship had run its course. But with his words, Hannah sensed the last vestiges of love being sucked up into their skylight.

She couldn't lose her mum too.

A young doctor, prematurely bald, approached them in full surgical scrubs. He looked like Hannah felt. Strung-out. Exhausted. In need of something that continually eluded him.

'This was a massive haemorrhagic stroke,' he said. 'We've put' – he looked down at his clipboard – 'Margaret into an induced coma. The goal is to reduce the work of the brain cells and protect them from increased pressure inside the skull. Currently she's in a serious but stable condition. I'm afraid it's just wait and see as to the long-term effects.'

'But what does that mean, actually?' Stef asked. 'What can we realistically hope for? What might be the long-term effects you mentioned? Surely there are some guarantees?'

The young doctor barely repressed a sigh. For a moment, Hannah was incensed on Stef's behalf. Would probably have called him out, except that Alex was striding towards them.

•

The acknowledgement of Jim and his half-sisters was cursory. Not much more than a nod. Hannah stared in disbelief as the young doctor repeated the prognosis to Alex. She turned to her dad, lifting an eyebrow, and he shook his head. She repeated the process with Stef. Neither of them had communicated Marg's stroke to Alex, or at least were admitting to it.

'How did you find out?' she tried as the young doctor walked away, but it was obvious that Alex wasn't going to grace the question with a reply.

Instead, he dialled a number on his mobile.

'I want to speak with Professor Gupta,' he said. There was a response on the other end that Hannah couldn't make out, then Alex spoke again. 'Yes, I understand that,' he said evenly. 'But I have reason to believe Indira will make an exception. Tell her it's Alex Carpenter, of the Adelaide Carpenters. Tell her it's urgent.'

It was a command. There was no doubt about that. Alex kept glancing at his phone as though expecting a call back. He addressed Jim, Hannah and Stef all together. 'Professor Gupta is the leading neurologist in Australia for haemorrhagic strokes,' he said. 'We need her on board.'

Her dad sat down on one of the padded vinyl chairs and Stef immediately sat next to him, both silently looking up to Alex.

Hannah recalled a recent attempt to locate Cara Romano's Facebook page. It had been taken down. Of course she didn't know exactly why, but it had been such a wholesome scroll of happy family pics – nothing that seemed to require retraction. She suspected it had to do with Alex finding out she'd made contact.

Hannah had no doubt that Alex could influence the quality of Marg's care.

Alex's phone rang and he took the call from Professor Gupta.

'Thanks for returning my call, Indira,' he said, taking a few steps away from the others. 'It's about my mother.'

●

Arriving within the hour, Professor Gupta oozed authority. It was almost comical to witness staff emerging from relative torpor to peak alertness as she issued instructions. There was no doubt that Marg was in the best of hands.

Also, no doubt that Professor Gupta had been ripped away from other patients to prioritise this one. An ethical dilemma the Fidlers were content to sweep under the carpet with the debris from their time at Hughesdale.

Hannah still didn't know how Alex had found out about Margaret's stroke, but her brother was here now. He was making things happen. In this time of crisis, he was clearly the most effective of all of them.

When Professor Gupta addressed the family, she focused on Alex. She advised that they would soon be bringing Marg out of her coma. The vital signs were there. Professor Gupta was optimistic.

Compared with this, the happenings at Hughesdale paled into insignificance. In every aspect of their body language, her dad and Stef were deferring to him. They all were.

Alex was back.

Hannah wandered away from the ICU. There it was, on the floor below. She had probably taken it in subconsciously from the map at reception. The Carpenter Maternity Wing. No wonder Dr Gupta had been so amenable to treating Marg.

Hannah stopped outside the nursery. Coached by a nurse, a young woman was trying to breastfeed. It looked as though she was having trouble getting the infant to latch on. The baby kept pulling away, screaming.

Hannah rested her head against the glass. She pondered motherhood in its infinite manifestations. Wondered if any of them might fit.

'I thought you'd be here.' Stef was beside Hannah. They both peered into the nursery. This time, the baby latched on to its mother's breast. Settled and sucked. It made Hannah want to howl.

Stef put a hand on Hannah's shoulder. 'Mum's out of the coma,' she said.

CHAPTER FORTY-TWO

'Both carers come with excellent references,' Alex told Stef. 'They're qualified nurses and Margaret will be looked after around the clock.'

Stef's summer garden was looking magnificently lush with purple and pink hydrangeas and fragrant frangipani. She rescued a couple of stems that had snapped. She would complement the flowers with some greenery.

'That's amazing, Alex,' she said. 'I know Mum will need help with lots of things while she's still paralysed on her right side. But it's not fair that you foot the entire bill for her home care.'

Alex shook his head. 'It's more than fair,' he assured her. 'I made some terrible mistakes when you, Hannah and Margaret came to Hughesdale, Stef. I fully acknowledge that. But I've learned from them. This, I can get right. So please let me.' He reached out for the stems. Stef shrugged and handed them over. 'I have just the home for these,' he said, leading the way inside.

As they entered the living room at the front of the house, Stef gasped. Sitting on her own coffee table was a Bacchantes vase. She circled the table, unable to speak as she took in the beauty of the piece. René Lalique's design of young priestesses was divine. She had been to an art auction with her bosses from Furniture Gallery a couple of years back and held her breath as the bidding for one just like this surpassed $20,000. Even from a distance, the piece was striking. Stef could hardly believe there was such a precious item right in front of her.

'Bacchantes,' she managed eventually.

'I saw it on High Street and thought of you instantly,' Alex said.

Stef shook her head in wonderment. 'You did?' She gestured to the vase. 'You saw this and thought of *me*?'

Alex chuckled. 'Would you like to come and take a look, Heath?' he asked, and it was only then that Stef realised her son had been watching the exchange from the doorway.

Over the summer holidays, Heath had grown three centimetres. His grey school pants were too short. Soon, Stef would take them over to her mum's to let down the hem. Marg seemed almost ready to take on small tasks. It would give her a sense of achievement in what was bound to be a slow recovery.

'Is it special?' Heath asked as he approached.

'Absolutely!' Stef said.

'Why?'

Stef was about to answer but her son was focused on Alex.

'Well, for one thing, it's very old,' Alex said. 'It would have been created in the nineteen twenties.'

'That's even before Pop was born,' Heath said, eyes widening.

'It is,' Stef agreed. 'Which is part of the reason why it's so valuable.'

'Valuable means it's worth a lot of money,' Heath declared. 'How much did it cost?'

Alex made a stop sign with his hand, quashing Stef's impulse to check her son.

'Twenty-two thousand dollars,' Alex answered.

Heath's eyes popped. 'And you're giving it to us?' he exclaimed. 'For no reason?'

Alex clasped his hands under his chin. 'Yes, it's a gift for your family. Oh, and there are many reasons why, Heath, not the least of which being that I feel very lucky to have you in my life. I want to celebrate that.'

Alex's motivation was pure and palpable. If the Fidlers had advanced him a second chance, he had already earned it out. Obviously, he had learned a great deal from what went on at Hughesdale. Although it had been painful and there was still scar tissue, they all had. It was time to move forward.

Heath clasped his hands under his chin, modelling Alex. Stef resisted the urge to point it out. The growth spurt had left Heath uncharacteristically self-conscious.

'I feel lucky too,' Heath said. Then, as if testing the words, he quietly added, 'Uncle Alex.'

It was lovely to see the gentle nudge Alex gave Heath. The way Heath returned it.

•

'The Bacchantes would be safe in there,' Stef said, gesturing to a lockable cabinet in the corner of the room.

'I think it belongs on the mantelpiece' Alex countered. 'A vase like this shouldn't be locked away. You should put real flowers in it. It should be enjoyed.'

Stef nodded. The mantelpiece was high enough that an accident was unlikely, and life was full of calculated risks. Though she drew the line at putting water in the collector's item, Stef arranged the stems from her backyard and placed the arrangement in the centre. The vase seemed to overlook … to pervade, the whole room. In contrast, none of her other paintings or decorations seemed to matter.

A key turned in the lock. Rosie barged in. Stef could hardly wrap her head around how her daughter could make the PLC uniform look so … not slovenly, that word was out of date, but messy. Her tie was skewiff. The jumper over her school dress half tucked up and half down. There were bruises on her legs from her new obsession with skateboarding. Her refusal to wear kneepads.

'Jesus,' Rosie said as she noted Alex's presence.

'Alex gave us a valuable vase, Rosie,' Heath said, pointing up at the mantelpiece.

Rosie looked. Made a sour-lemon face.

'It was made even before Pop was born,' Heath tried again.

'Yeah?' Rosie replied. 'Maybe that's why it looks like ancient porn.'

'Rosie. They're priestesses.' Stef tried to keep a scolding tone from her voice. It would only incite. Early days in Year Seven at PLC were not, as Stef had hoped, calming her daughter.

'Whatever,' Rosie said. 'I'm just getting changed and going out again.'

Stef tensed. 'Where?' she asked. 'And who with?'

Rosie rolled her eyes, ignoring both questions as she headed up the stairs to her room.

Stef led the way back to the kitchen, serving up orange and poppyseed cake for afternoon tea. The front door slammed behind her daughter. Heath took his plate to the lounge. As he turned on the PlayStation, his shoulders seemed suddenly slumped. Stef wondered how long he would keep enduring his sister's small rejections before he gave up trying.

'Rosie has a new social group,' Stef told Alex. 'Boys and girls. I don't know where she met them. They're not from her primary school or PLC. I'm glad she's found friends, truly, but I've heard some worrying things about them. I mean, as far as I know they just hang out – in parks, at the shopping centre. But I fear they're a bit ...' She paused. Could hear the twang of judgement in what she was about to say. Said it anyway. 'Rough around the edges.'

Alex took a sip of his coffee. He looked Stef in the eyes.

'I'm not going to pretend I know anything about parenting, Stef,' he said. 'But the first year of high school – the first year of being a teenager – has to be pretty important developmentally.'

'You should see the awesome graphics in this scene,' Heath called out. Given that he knew his mother had zero interest in the graphics of his games, it was clear the invitation was to Alex.

'Coming,' Alex said, standing up and beginning the walk over to Heath.

'So, what do we know about this group, Stef,' he said over his shoulder.

'Only what other parents have told me,' Stef admitted. 'I've seen some of the kids around individually and in pairs, but never as a group. God,' she paused, 'maybe gang is a better word. It's clear that at least some of them are vaping. That's been commented on quite a lot.'

'I think we need to base our opinions on observation,' Alex said. 'Right, Stef?'

Her heartbeat increased. She needed help. Rosie was heading in the wrong direction. In fact, she was *careening* in the wrong direction.

With the nod of her head, Stef understood she was giving permission.

CHAPTER FORTY-THREE

A fresh crop of first years filled the lecture theatre. From the lectern, Hannah could sense myriad fears of their new environment. The hangovers and comedowns. The jostling for status. The broken hearts. The soaring hearts. The shifting of fashion choices to reflect attitude over beauty. The dorms and rentals and embarrassment about still living with parents.

The veil of newness they collectively twitched underneath.

They were beginning with Tim Winton. Hannah had fought hard to get *Breath* on the syllabus. She understood many of the students would try to get away with watching the movie, but she hoped she could convince most of them that interacting with the text was well worth the effort. Out of all the writers Hannah admired, Winton was the best at evoking quintessentially Australian culture.

Rex loved Tim Winton's work too. Upon release of every one of his books, each of them would buy their own copy. Pace themselves so they could sit up in bed, engaging in discussion when mesmerised by a sentence or a scene. Making sure not to deliver spoilers.

Hannah did not know what would happen when another Winton book was published.

'Adolescence. Ambition. Thrillseeking. Passion. Defeat,' Hannah launched. They were an easier audience than they would be later in the year. Manageable. At this stage, most students didn't want to stand out. They were still figuring out how they wanted to project themselves. Deciding which social groups they wished to identify with and how they could make that happen. Eventually, they'd have the confidence to challenge Hannah at every juncture, but for now, they were attentive and malleable.

She was a third of the way through when ... Alex? There he was, in the same seat he'd sat in for her *Godot* lecture the year before, when his arrival into their lives had seemed an unadulterated godsend. Hannah knew it was the same seat because of the proximity to the pole that hid the person Ethan had been kissing.

Ethan was the father of Bethany's baby. Not Rex. Recently, Hannah had run into him on campus, infant son strapped into a sling against his chest. She had been reluctantly gracious in her congratulations. Endured Triple-Threat-Ethan transfer his barking enthusiasm to fatherhood as though he was the world's first.

Hannah knew now that the day Alex took the fateful photos, Ethan's car had broken down in the uni car park. That he'd had to wait for a tow truck, so Rex had offered to take Bethany to the appointment at WUMe.

A simple explanation. A gallant effort.

Rex was who he purported to be. Hannah, a mirage.

There were murmurs as Hannah paused to refer to her notes, abating as she forced herself to return to her body.

For the rest of the lecture, Hannah did not even hazard a glance in Alex's direction.

•

As the students filed out, Alex indicated his intention to meet Hannah at the base of the stage. Hannah shook her head and countered that she would meet him halfway.

Too much terrain had already been surrendered. He hadn't even let her know he was coming! Hannah would fight this new incursion, even if she was simultaneously wondering what Alex thought of her finale.

Alex had just put the strap of his bag across his shoulder when Katrina from the admin office walked through the side entrance and made a beeline for him. Hannah knew from experience that it was unlikely Alex had been able to squeeze a word in by the time she reached them.

'Oh, hello, Hannah. Alex and I were having the most delightful conversation about all sorts, weren't we, Alex?' The widening of his eyes told a different story but Katrina didn't notice. 'I'm sorry to hear that you and Rex have broken up. It's a shame. God help us all if he starts dating someone even younger than you. Seems to happen all the time, especially on a university campus. You'd think a sophisticated man would prefer someone closer to their own age, someone who's able to share in similar experiences.'

Katrina was closer to Rex's age. Alex's too. The message was, very unsubtly, including both men. A maximisation of potential.

'I was just saying … to *Alex*,' Katrina continued, 'that on the upside, it's a wonderful thing when a new brother just waltzes into your life and takes such an interest! My own brother hardly even knows what I do here. If you asked him, he'd probably tell you that I work in admin, not that I'm the head of admin. Which is why I have the power to reserve a seat for Alex should he want to attend any of your lectures. All I'd need is a phone call. Even a text would—'

'Thank you, Katrina,' Alex said but she didn't take the hint.

'Alex, this is not okay,' Hannah said. 'It's invasive. I don't want to be wondering if you're in the audience every time I give a lecture.'

'Oh, it's not just the lectures,' Katrina declared. 'Your brother will have access to your tutorials too. Just think, he's only picked the one subject and it's *yours* Hannah. That's very special.'

'Alex, I sure as hell don't want you turning up at my tutorials,' Hannah said, her heart beating fast. 'It's just – not right.'

Alex shook his head. 'I would like to attend a few of your lectures, Hannah,' he said. 'I find them highly elucidating. I'm happy to give you notice, though. The last thing I want to do is to interrupt your flow. But I have no intention of crashing your tutorials. I have no intention of slaving over essays and trying to blend in with a bunch of twenty-year-olds.'

'Oh, they're not all twenty-somethings,' Katrina said. 'We have quite a few mature-age students. In fact—'

'In fact,' Alex took over, focusing entirely on Hannah, 'Katrina here has not delivered information about my enrolment in the spirit in which it was intended. Clearly, it's beyond the scope of her admin capabilities.'

Katrina crossed her arms, nostrils flaring. 'Well, excuse me, Mr Carpenter,' she said, 'for going above and beyond to expedite your paperwork. I'll have you know that my job is very complex. Many people rely on me. I have been essential in making this university function for fifteen years. Without me—'

Alex made a circular gesture with his hand, an instruction for Katrina to wind up her rant. Hannah grimaced to witness her eyes glisten with unshed tears.

'Katrina, I'm sure there was no offence intended,' Hannah said, but Katrina's eyes were on Alex.

'I do hope you understand, Mr Carpenter, that everything I've done for you can be undone,' she said. She turned sharply on her heel and one foot came out of her navy court shoe. She shoved it back in and stormed through the exit.

'Goodness me,' Alex said with a wry smile. 'Looks like I hit a nerve there.'

'Yes, you did,' Hannah said with a sigh. 'Maybe you could send her flowers or something?'

'I'll send something,' Alex agreed. 'But Hannah, I do hope we've cleared that little mess up?' He lifted his right hand. 'I, Alex Carpenter, do solemnly swear that I will never show up at a Hannah Fidler lecture without prior approval. And that tutorials are completely off limits.'

Hannah smiled, pushing his hand back down.

As they passed through the exit door, it was as though Katrina had left a wisp of indignance behind. Like a spray of cheap perfume that Hannah had no choice but to walk through.

CHAPTER FORTY-FOUR

It was the reprisal of a role that Gillian would have thought beneath him the first time. She would be turning in her grave. Her rule of thumb was to employ private investigators for the dull, dirty stuff. The collection of information took time. Endless hours in a car waiting for something to happen. Going through bins. Following leads that mostly went down a rabbit hole.

Those jobs were not considered appropriate for the Carpenters. What they were good at was targeting information for maximum impact, directing outcomes that suited their agenda. That was a skill set above and beyond anything a private investigator could provide.

Yet, had she tried it, Gillian may actually have enjoyed aspects of information collection. There was something satisfying about doing it oneself.

The grey Adidas trackpants and oversized bottle-green logo tee were about as unrelated to anything else in Alex's wardrobe as possible. The bulk belied his slim frame and the peak cap covered most of his silvery hair. He was a Generic Older Man. Still, he wouldn't risk being spotted. There was a line of trees circling the skate park. Alex could easily see Rosie and her new friends from this vantage point. There were a few parents watching, taking photos. Alex was just one of them.

They were a fluid group, disbanding often for a skate on the ramp, occasionally interacting with others. But Alex was patient enough to let the core reveal itself.

In total, there were seven – four boys and three girls, including his niece. Two of the boys and one of the girls looked at least a year older than Rosie. It was hard to tell who owned the vape pens, but Alex identified a ceremony around the passing and receiving. After handing it over, the giver would place their right hand over their hearts. This was a club of sorts.

The boy who dragged on the vape pen now was one of the older ones. Wildly curly blond hair and a sleeper nose-piercing. He wore ripped jeans and cheap underwear that showed above his waistband. No Calvin Klein for this kid. This was the one Rosie most often looked to. Skateboard tucked under her arm, she sidled up to him.

A few metres away, a blue-haired girl passed a small foil package to a boy with a mullet. He put it into his pocket, went straight on his phone and gave the girl a thumbs-up. Alex's best bet was that this was a money transfer.

Alex's eyes swung back to his niece. It seemed she was experimenting with some flirting, Rosie-style. Flirting with disdain. The way the little cow conducted most of her interactions.

Despite all he'd done for her and her family, Rosie's attitude towards Alex dripped with that disdain. She was ungrateful.

Rude. The situation was becoming untenable. And Stef, with her lack of discipline, was pathetic.

There was only so much fury Alex could quash down. But he would keep delaying gratification in favour of the long game. The ability to do so was buoyed by seeing his influence rubbing off on Heath. His nephew's rapt attention was an antidote to Rosie's dismissiveness. Alex hoped – no, expected, that Heath's burgeoning respect would be further expanded with this afternoon's surprise.

Rosie said something to the curly, blond-haired boy and he responded by holding the vape pen high in the air. She did not grace his actions with a response. No demeaning jump and grab for Rosie.

She thought she was in control.

The blond boy acquiesced. Rosie held the vape to her mouth. Alex took more photos.

For the library, Gillian, he thought. As Alex walked away from the skate park, he sensed, despite the DIY nature of this task, his adoptive mother's approval.

•

'What do you mean?' Heath asked as Alex led him and Stef across the road from their house. 'You mean you brought the *whole* building?'

The elevator was dated. Alex could hear the mechanics as it chugged from floor to floor, but that didn't put a dent in Heath's enthusiasm. Nor did the brown shag-pile carpets and seventies wood-panelled walls in the empty apartments.

'I *bought* the whole building, Heath,' Alex corrected with a smile. 'The plan is to fix it up and resell. Currently, it's a "Renovator's Delight", but we know it's a great location, right? And I have plenty of ideas on how to bring it up to scratch. Modernise the façade. Knock out internal walls so the apartments become open plan. Add some big balconies to the lower levels. And imagine a rooftop garden.'

'This block has been for sale for a long time,' Stef said, clearly concerned. 'I thought the previous owners submitted plans, but they were rejected by council. In fact, I'm sure of it – half the neighbours objected. People around here are resistant to change.'

'I wouldn't worry about that, Stef,' Alex told her, and it was a wonder, really, that she could doubt his due diligence. 'The last owner probably just hadn't done a proper feasibility study ...'

Before Alex could continue, Stef's phone rang. 'It's work,' she mouthed, walking into the foyer and leaving Alex and Heath alone in another musty kitchen. Heath's brow was furrowed.

'What if council doesn't let you do the fixing up?' he asked.

'They will,' Alex assured his nephew, but he could tell it wasn't enough.

'How do you *know* that?' Heath asked.

Alex paused. An image of himself around Heath's age sprung to mind. Sitting in a giant armchair in the drawing room at Hughesdale, Alex's legs hadn't reached the ground. Grandfather William lit his pipe. He was in unusually good spirits.

'I seized an opportunity today, young man,' he had told Alex. Alex couldn't recall the venture, it was the execution that William focused on. The greased palms. The strategic wielding of influence. Therein lay success. Alex hadn't understood all of it, but he had listened intently, determined to earn the confidence his grandfather was sharing with him, alone. Not Ricky. Alex. The rightful heir to William's legacy.

Now, Alex crouched down to his nephew's level. 'If I tell you how I know my plans will get through council, do you think you could keep it a secret? Just between us?'

From the foyer, the sounds of Stef's work call continued. Heath's nod was both vehement and sombre.

'There's one particular councillor who holds sway in determining which plans are given a green light,' Alex told his nephew. In Heath's demeanour, Alex could see himself. The concentration, the gravity of being chosen to receive this business confidence was writ large on his face. 'His name is Serge Artemis. When the renovations are complete, Councillor Artemis will be the owner of the very apartment we are standing in.'

Heath leaned on the kitchen bench, hand under his chin. Alex waited for the penny to drop.

'It's like a gift?' Heath replied eventually. 'But a *top*-secret gift. Sort of paying back a favour.'

'That's exactly what it is,' Alex confirmed, and Heath took a giant leap towards becoming an adult. 'If you don't want to be ordinary in this world ... if you're not happy with mediocre, you have to be enterprising. Make your own luck. If success is what you're after, Heath, you've got to create opportunities then grab them with both hands.'

'Success is what I'm after, Uncle Alex,' Heath said, dead serious.

'As it should be,' Alex replied. 'And I think you have the knack, so I'm going to share one more bit of advice with you, if you're ready for it. Just between us.'

'I'm ready,' Heath said.

'Secrets are key to building success. I worked hard to find out what Serge Artemis doesn't want the public to know about. Having secrets in my library is like insurance. Serge has double the motivation to ensure that this renovation and several other projects I'm involved in around Melbourne get the green light. Heath, gather secrets about everyone in your life whenever you can. You never know when they'll come in handy. And, if you do it well, it should feel almost like a hobby.'

It was a special moment as Alex watched Heath trying to process the advice. His obvious appreciation for being trusted with the confidences. His respect, or perhaps even awe, was deeply rewarding.

From the foyer, Stef's phone call was ending. 'Okay. I'll get that order off right away. Bye.' Before she re-entered the apartment, Alex took the opportunity to put his finger to his lips.

Heath responded with a hand on his heart.

•

'The best news,' Alex said as the elevator stopped at level five, 'is that I'll be keeping this penthouse for myself. That way, when I'm in Melbourne I can be close to you guys. And to Margaret.'

Heath raced out into the expanse first. He spun around in the lounge and kept spinning as he made his way onto the terrace. A child again.

'I can see our whole house from here,' he yelled. 'It's so cool!'

Stef put her hand on Alex's arm. 'I don't know what to say,' she told him. 'I just … I know you're trying to stay close and help with Rosie.'

The photos of Rosie and her gang of fools lingered between them. Stef still hadn't acted. Claimed she didn't know how to broach the subject of Rosie vaping without implicating Alex for gathering the evidence, which was just an excuse. Alex didn't care whether Rosie knew he had her number. The sad, ridiculous truth was that Stef had no backbone. Rosie was running rings around them all.

'I based the decision on many factors,' Alex assured her. 'One of which is to help you with the kids. But, Stef, I saw an opportunity. Not just for me, but for you too.'

Stef gave him a quizzical look.

'I'm going to need an interior designer on board,' Alex said. 'Getting all the apartments ready for sale will be a huge job. I want you to do it, Stef. Work with an architect on all the spaces – for my own place, this penthouse, I want you to do it all. Fixtures, fittings, furnishings. No budget. I just want it to be beautiful. But that's just for starters. I have my eye on other properties too. I'm getting some excellent industry intel here in Melbourne. There are many opportunities out there. And, Stef,' Alex paused before bringing the offer home, 'your skills, your talent, are wasted at the Furniture Gallery.'

Alex could read Stef like a book. He could see that she was impatient to rip out the fluorescent lights in the kitchen. She'd most likely want to replace them with some expensive pendants. She walked around the island bench in the kitchen and ran a hand over the cheap chipboard.

Alex smiled. 'Marble?' he prompted.

'Gold calacatta,' Stef said dreamily. 'And the rooftop garden could have Dedon furniture. A yoga pavilion. A hibachi barbeque. But, Alex—'

She should be leaping at the opportunity. Yet, here she was, looking her gift horse in the mouth. Forcing Alex to do the hard sell on offering her a better life. Pathetic.

'I can double your salary,' he said evenly. 'Or we can profit-share. And you'll have autonomy, Stef. No more nine to five. You'll be able to choose your own hours, spend more quality time with the kids.'

Stef blew out a breath.

'When I zoom in on mum's phone,' Heath called from the balcony, 'I can even see the special vase on the mantelpiece.'

Stef shook her head. 'I appreciate the offer. And I'm flattered. But I do actually love my job,' she added. 'And my bosses. So, I'll think on it, okay?'

It was bitterly disappointing, but Alex nodded as congenially as he could manage.

'Hey, Rosie. Look up here!' Heath waved with both arms. 'Uncle Alex *bought* this whole building. And this is going to be his own penthouse!'

Alex stepped forward. From street level, Rosie gave him the finger.

As soon as she went inside, into the house Alex had paid off for them, the little cow pulled down the blinds in the front living area.

CHAPTER FORTY-FIVE

The Year Five classroom at Burwood Heights Primary was testament to a teacher who truly cared. Bunting hung from the rafters, celebrating the language of simple maths equations. Class readers of various levels were lovingly colour-coded in a way that discouraged students (and parents) from obsessing about their reading level.

Self-portraits lined the walls, each with a caption that bellowed something positive about the featured student.

I'm Cindy and I'm very good at making new friends!
I'm Waleed and I am a very fast runner!
I'm Penelope and I'm excited to become a big sister!

Liam was wearing a business shirt that looked as though it belonged to a white-collar worker – an attempt to disguise his tradie status and his own troubled schooldays.

He pulled a small chair out from under the table in front of Ms Porritt's desk. His eyes wandered to Heath's self-portrait.

I'm Heath and I love playing basketball!

'Heath was rapt to have made it onto the team,' Liam told Ms Porritt.

'He was,' Stef agreed.

Ms Porritt nodded. Stef supposed she was only a few years out of uni. She was wearing a conservative navy pencil skirt and an awful appliqued T-shirt (butterflies). But there seemed to be an enthusiasm that, in Stef's experience – especially from the teachers she had encountered during Rosie's primary years – seemed to wane over time.

'Heath *was* thrilled to make the basketball team,' she said. 'But actually, that's what I need to discuss with you.'

Stef frowned. A montage of the times she and Liam had been summoned to the school to discuss Rosie's behaviour flashed through her mind. Never had they been bidden to talk about Heath. At parent–teacher interviews, phrases like 'it's a pleasure to have Heath in my class' were the norm. Whatever this was about was most likely a mistake.

'I don't want to place undue emphasis on the incident,' Ms Porritt said and the monarch butterfly on her chest fluttered its wings. Stef shifted in her seat. 'But I have noticed some changes in Heath lately. He has been ... a little less inclined to co-operate with his peers. Have you noticed any changes at home?'

'No.' Stef's lie was knee jerk. She had noticed some changes in Heath. For one, he was less inclined to sidle up for a hug. He also seemed to have grown out of the longstanding habit of mollifying his sister. But such changes were a natural part of growing up. And God knows, Rosie had pushed him away so many times it was inevitable Heath would eventually stop trying.

'I have,' Liam said, and Stef could have kicked him. 'He seems, I don't know, a bit distant.'

'Is there anything going on at home that could have precipitated the change, Liam?' Ms Porritt asked.

Stef looked sideways and Liam shrugged. Sweat stains were appearing under his armpits.

'It's all pretty run-of-the-mill when he comes to our place,' he said pointedly. Stef gritted her teeth.

'Okay,' Ms Porritt said, and when was she going to get to the point?

'We talk about determination a great deal in this class,' she said, uncrossing and re-crossing her legs. 'We encourage each other to strive for our goals. But we also emphasise that we must do it in a way that's fair and equitable.'

Der, Stef thought, channelling her inner Rosie.

'Heath is the poster-boy for fair,' Liam said.

'The PE teacher, Mr Salmon, seconds that,' Ms Porritt said. 'Which is why Heath's behaviour is something we should nip in the bud.'

'What *behaviour*?' Stef asked.

'Mr Salmon is in charge of selecting the basketball team,' Ms Porritt said. 'Unfortunately, we have too few players to make two teams and too many for just one.' She paused. 'He held trials. Heath didn't make the cut, so Mr Salmon gave him his second choice – handball.'

'But Heath *did* make the team,' Stef protested.

Ms Porritt leaned forward. 'The problem is that Heath made the team because Chiara changed her mind and decided to play soccer.'

'There's nothing wrong with that,' Liam said. 'Kids change their minds all the time.'

'Yes,' Ms Porritt said. She reached into her drawer, pulled out some PlayStation games and put them on the desk. Stef counted five. 'But when Chiara's parents saw she had acquired these without their knowledge, they pressed her.'

Ms Porritt's T-shirt should never have been worn by an adult. Stef gulped down an urge to tell her so. And maybe all that bunting, all the children's work that was displayed on every centimetre of wall could be a distraction for the students. Yet another woke indication that they were all special.

Musical chairs and everyone gets a chair.

Pass the parcel and everyone gets a prize.

'Heath gave these to Chiara,' she said, handing the games over to Stef, 'in exchange for her pulling out of the basketball team.'

•

It was dusk by the time they got outside, the sky painted in dazzling shades of pink. The school gate creaked as Liam closed it behind him. Parked in the street, a few spots up from Stef's new red Mini Cooper, Liam's ute looked shabbier than ever.

'Well, Ms Porritt certainly knows how to make a mountain out of a molehill,' Stef joked. 'God, what kid doesn't do a trade here and there.'

Liam stopped and turned to her. 'Maybe, Stef,' he said. 'But there has been a lot of change in Heath's life lately. Marg's stroke, of course.' He started walking again. 'But also ...' Stef waited for him to spit it out. Wondered how she had ever tolerated his snail pace. 'Alex seems to have become a big influence on Heath.'

'And?' Stef urged, but Liam seemed to have used up all his words. 'Listen,' she said, 'Alex has taken a lot of stress away from our household. He's eased my financial burden. He's taken full responsibility for Mum's at-home care so that she can be with Dad and not in some soulless rehab hospital.' Stef unlocked the driver door and tossed her Fendi handbag onto the passenger seat. 'It's only natural that Heath would respect his uncle.'

Liam moved in front of the driver door now, blocking Stef's entry. A ghost of the old husband.

'Is it?' he asked. 'The PlayStation thing isn't right, Stef. And yes, of course I did trades as a kid. A Sunny Boy for a Wagon Wheel, but not expensive games, and not for a spot on the basketball team. That's different.'

Stef bristled. She motioned for Liam to move away from her car door. 'The main difference,' she said, 'is that Heath has something to trade these days.' She sat in the driver's seat. 'Because of Alex.'

Stef saw the comment land. Satisfying in part, but sad too.

'We can both talk to Heath about this basketball thing,' she said. 'But it's a blip. Rosie, on the other hand ...' Stef shook her head. 'She's the one we should be worrying about. And I can guarantee that Alex has zero influence on her.'

Had she been able to explain how she got the photos of Rosie and her crew, Stef would have shown Liam. Instead she told him, again, that Rosie was hanging out with the wrong kids. Vaping.

'Rosie is going feral,' she said.

'Like I did?' Liam replied, and now Stef had to repress a smile in memory of the rebel teen she had loved.

'Exactly like that,' she told him.

•

By the time Stef arrived home, it was pitch black. The lights were on in Alex's apartment opposite.

On the porch was an exquisite bunch of flowers. She picked them up and headed inside.

Reading the attached note, Stef's heart seesawed.

CHAPTER FORTY-SIX

Hannah planned her movements around the campus to minimise running into Rex. But there he was. Waiting for coffee at the uni cafe was a solitary exercise for Hannah, not so for Rex. A tall young woman in a hijab clapped her hands in response to something he'd said. Two men laughed appreciatively at the exchange.

At a corner table, a former student gave Hannah an almost imperceptible nod.

There was a machine in the staff kitchen. The coffee it produced was God-awful, but at least Hannah wouldn't have to endure more of this. She was already in the courtyard when Rex caught up with her. He looked well, despite having gained a few kilos, but that was inevitable given he was staying with Albie. The glasses clipped to the front of his shirt were frameless, the same ones he'd tried on when they went shopping together before the split. Hannah hadn't approved them.

'Leaning into the new year?' he asked. 'All those idealistic new students really lift the atmosphere, right?'

'Yes,' Hannah replied, but she was definitely not going to indulge his desire to wax lyrical about idealistic new students.

It had been a yearly event she was ready to opt out of. 'I'm just … getting on with it.'

'Okay,' Rex said. 'So, are we nearly ready to set the date? Do you need a hand getting the house prepared?'

She shook her head, trying to keep it casual, though each time she thought about the finality of auctioning their townhouse made the pit in her gut explode.

'I have a small get-well gift for Marg,' Rex said. 'Maybe you can swing by my office and collect it some time?'

No doubt it would be nuanced and thoughtful. Wild horses couldn't drag Hannah to his office. There was enough of Rex at home.

'Can you leave it at the front desk?' she countered.

Rex blew out a breath. Thankfully, he didn't reiterate that they could still be friends.

'I'll do that right away,' he said. 'But did you know there's a temp there now? He makes you show ID every time you pick up something. Katrina has gone on stress leave – indefinitely.'

Hannah's jaw dropped. Katrina lived for her job. She would proudly inform anyone who'd listen that she could count her sick days over fifteen years on two hands. She openly and vehemently argued that employees exploited leave for mental health issues.

'Do you know what happened?' Hannah asked.

'Apparently there was an official complaint made about her. It was anonymous and the higher-ups weren't inclined to pay it much mind, but poor Katrina was distraught at the blight on her perfect record. Hey, Han, are you okay?'

Hannah collected herself. From the air. The pavement. Squashed the pieces together randomly.

'Excuse me.'

The student speaking wore a waistcoat and trackpants. His eyebrows were plucked into thin semicircles and his feet were bare. If there was a theme there, Hannah couldn't pick it.

'A few of us are heading over to the pub. I believe, since your extra help led to my latest dazzling mark, I owe you a beer.'

'You most certainly do,' Rex replied.

The student looked to Hannah. Quite obviously he decided not to extend the invitation.

•

'May I help you?'

Seeing an attractive, grey-haired man – someone Katrina would have made a beeline for – behind her desk was disconcerting. The signed picture of Dame Edna and Madge had disappeared from the back wall as had the money plant on her desk. There was no jar of snakes. The only remnant of Katrina's reign was a tile stuck in the centre panel of the desk.

The answer is no. Now, what do you want?

'You should have a parcel for me,' Hannah said. 'From Professor Rex Carlisle.'

'Please have your ID ready,' the man said. As he walked into the back storage area, Hannah fished around for the lanyard she kept in her bag.

The parcel was small but heavy. A statue? Paperweight? Hannah showed her ID and signed for it.

As she walked to her office, Hannah couldn't shake the strangeness. Katrina's presence in that office had been all but erased. It made her think of Cara's wholesome family Facebook page disappearing just days after she contacted Hannah with the warning.

She wondered how many others Alex had, effectively, erased.

•

She hadn't cooked a real meal since Rex left. Dinner tonight was a couple of boiled eggs. Hannah switched on the TV and channel-surfed. God, they had ... *she* had a million streaming services and there was still nothing to watch. She left the TV on for company, poured herself a pinot grigio and walked through the glass doors into the twilight courtyard.

Tomorrow was Friday. The first of their bi-weekly dinners at her parents' since her mother's stroke. In the past, Hannah never really contemplated whether she enjoyed the ritual. It had just been a given.

Now though, Hannah grasped at the positivity of Marg's recovery. She drew comfort from the prospect of her dad's kiss landing on the top of her head. Oh, and she was going to make a big effort with Stef. Try to break down a layer or two of the barrier that still lay between them.

Hannah missed her sister. She missed the intimacy, the way they used to laugh at things no one else got. Stef was having more problems with Rosie. Hannah would listen. Empathise. She would be supportive and non-judgemental.

A dose of the ever-delightful Heath could be the perfect antidote to Hannah's maudlin mood, too.

All of this was true. But the main reason Hannah was looking forward to the occasion – one she'd admit only to herself – was that due to a business commitment, Alex wouldn't be there.

Perhaps if she found the right moment with Stef, she might confide her misgivings about Alex enrolling in her course, ask if there was anything he was doing that was making her similarly uncomfortable. A private talk with Stef might help lighten the weight of the giant stone that seemed to lie permanently on her heart.

Unfair perhaps, especially since Alex's assistance in providing home care had been instrumental in speeding up Marg's recovery. But Hannah was nostalgic for an evening with the original, unadulterated Fidler clan.

CHAPTER FORTY-SEVEN

Stef saved her tears until after she'd hung up. Under the circumstances, Tonia and Bruce had been more than gracious. Jesus, they'd even sent her those divine flowers with a Furniture Gallery card wishing her all the best in her future endeavours.

But Stef had heard the bewilderment in their voices. The weight of their disappointment.

Yes, she had been almost there in deciding to accept Alex's job offer. But for him to hand in her resignation on her behalf, effective immediately? For Tonia and Bruce to get that news from a stranger?

They deserved way more.

Stef paced the living room. From the mantelpiece, the Bacchantes vase stared down at her. Through the window at the other end of the room – the building Alex owned. The penthouse he would keep for himself.

She was penned in. Her breath was too shallow, coming in fits and starts.

'What time are we leaving?'

Stef breathed in for four counts. Held her breath for four counts. Breathed out for four counts.

'Mum?' Rosie demanded from the kitchen.

'Fifteen minutes,' Stef managed.

Rosie was at the door now. 'Promise the weirdo isn't going to be at Gran and Pop's?' she asked.

Stef wiped her eyes. She felt a sudden and overwhelming urge to blurt out all her mixed-up feelings to her sister. Despite their differences of late, Hannah was the only one who could possibly understand. And with Alex out of the state for work, tonight would be her chance.

Stef missed Hannah. Found herself, guiltily, sharing her daughter's sentiment.

'I promise,' she said.

•

The wrought-iron gates at her mum and dad's place were open. The porch lights on in readiness for guests as usual. But the half-dozen stairs Stef had traipsed up and down for all her thirty-nine years were gone, replaced by a concrete ramp with new siderails.

Could she have forgotten that was happening?

Stef had never seen her dad in trackpants. Marg had always regarded them as evidence of 'giving up'. But there he was in grey marle.

'It's good to see you, honey,' he said, and Stef wished she could bottle the kiss that landed on her forehead. The timelessness of it. The reassuring consistency while everything else around her kept changing.

'How's our big high school girl?' Jim was asking. 'And Heath, matey, you must fill me in on your latest PlayStation escapades.'

'I hardly even play anymore, Pop,' Heath said. 'So, are we coming in?'

Suddenly aware he was blocking the door, Jim stepped aside. In the hallway gallery, among the regular fare, were two new framed photos. One was of Alex and Marg, taken at the hospital just days after her stroke. The other, the one Heath now stopped to study, was a sepia shot of Alex at around Heath's age, holding up a giant trophy. Stef resisted comment. She wouldn't actually know what to say anyway, especially about the old photo. It felt like a misplaced attempt to recreate history.

'When did you get the ramp done, Dad?' Stef asked instead.

'About a week ago,' he answered. 'I told Alex we were managing. I mean, given it's only temporary that Marg will need a wheelchair, I didn't feel like it was too hard to wheel her out the back door and down through the side gate. And I know this might sound silly, but that staircase hosted the pitter patter of you and your sister's little feet.' He shrugged. 'Alex sent a crew over anyway. And he was right, Steffie. It does make it easier to take your mum out.'

Her dad's wink seemed forced. He lowered his voice. 'I think it's best to take the path of least resistance where your brother is concerned,' he said.

Was it, though? In the long run?

Marg was set up on the sofa, all dressed up in a pink blouse and cream pants. Her hair had been recently set. Her lipstick was a darker shade of pink, applied too heavily, as though by another hand. Stef sat beside her.

'How are you, Mum?' she asked.

With her left hand, Marg indicated the right side of her body. As she spoke the right side of her face lagged. 'I've still got some paralysis,' she said. 'But things are gradually improving. And Jurgen here has been an angel.'

The nurse who entered from the kitchen was tall and broad. He handed Marg some pills and waited until she put them in her mouth before giving her a glass of water.

'Mind my halo,' he said to Stef with a German accent and a grin. 'And you're very welcome, Margaret. It's my job. I'll just freshen your bedding.'

Her mum patted Stef's arm. 'I'm lucky,' she said. 'Alex insists that Jurgen and Fiona will stay until I don't need them anymore.'

Thankfully, Hannah's arrival steered the conversation away from what a godsend Alex had been. Her dad had his arm around Hannah's shoulders as they came in from the hallway. As Stef got up, he released her.

'A get-well present from Rex,' Hannah said, handing over a parcel. Marg rested her right hand on top to keep it steady as her left did the slow work of opening it. The scented candle she passed around was personalised. In rose gold, under her name, the inscription read, *You're braver than you believe.*

'Pooh Bear,' Marg said, tearing up a little. 'That's very sweet of Rex, Hannah. Especially since you're not together anymore.'

The comment hung in the air for a moment before Rosie cut through it. 'Those sneakers are sick.' Rosie had helped herself to the sweet biscuit jar, but Stef knew better than to criticise the small things. Instead, she marvelled that there was (almost) enthusiasm in her daughter's voice.

'Why thank you, Rosie,' Hannah said. 'And how are things with you, Heath? Have you been making any more toys with Pop?'

'No,' Heath answered, and maybe Stef misheard, but he seemed to exhale the word 'lame'. At least her dad didn't seem to pick up on it. Inwardly, Stef urged her son to default back to the kid he'd always been. The factory settings version.

'Hannah Banana,' Stef said, and fuck it, fuck the judgement and superiority, this was still her sister and Stef needed her. The hug she gave was returned in full strength. An extra squeeze at the end.

'I miss you, Steffie,' Hannah whispered.

'The beef stroganoff looks ready, Margaret,' Jurgen said, returning to the lounge. 'Your bed is made up. Fiona will be here first thing in the morning. So, I'll leave you to your lovely family now.'

Jurgen was sweet. But as the front door clicked closed, Stef felt relieved to be alone with her lovely family. The unadulterated version.

•

'The old handrails had our initials carved in the paintwork,' Hannah said once she and Stef were alone in the kitchen. 'It's seriously selfish that Alex forged ahead to replace them just because Mum needs to get around.'

'It's beyond the pale,' Stef agreed with a smile. 'Those handrails should have been heritage-protected.'

As Hannah scooped cups of rice into the cooker, Stef got the feeling her sister was weighing up whether to say something. It was in the way she paused before tipping rice from the cup. Stef made a conscious decision not to break the silence.

'Alex enrolled in my course,' Hannah said eventually. 'It's just … too much. On one level it's a gesture of support but, Steffie, it's like I see him everywhere on campus.' She paused. Cleared her throat. 'I mean, even when he's not there,' she added.

Stef picked up a serving spoon and sighed. 'It makes you feel both penned in and exposed?' she suggested.

Hannah's nod was immediate and emphatic. From the lounge room, a rare peal of Rosie-flavoured laughter.

'There's something else,' Hannah continued. 'I don't even know how to describe it, whether I'm off target. But it was a woman from admin who told me about his enrolment while I was in the lecture theatre with Alex. When I objected …' Hannah blew out a breath. 'Alex tore strips off her. And now she's on stress leave. I don't know whether it's fair to connect the two.' Hannah stopped speaking. She stirred the rice. 'I'm sorry, Steffie,' she said. 'I shouldn't be putting this on you. Especially when things are going so well between you and Alex.'

Stef leaned against the kitchen bench. She shrugged and shook her head.

'I have so much to tell you, Han,' she said. 'So I'll just blurt it out. But we're not going to be able to dissect everything now. How about you come and stay at my place after dinner?'

'I'd love that,' Hannah said. 'Now, blurt.'

'Alex resigned on my behalf.' And even though no one else could hear from the lounge room, Stef felt compelled to whisper. 'I was going to do it anyway because he offered me my dream job in interior design. But, Han, he rang Tonia and Bruce, and ... oh my God, he didn't even give them notice.'

'Jesus,' Hannah said. 'You've been there for years. That's ... well, it's outrageous. It's beyond overstepping. How did you find out he'd done it?'

Stef threw up her hands. 'Tonia and Bruce sent me flowers and a card wishing me all the best.'

Hannah shook her head, her hand covering her mouth.

'But wait, Han, there's more – Alex bought the apartment block directly opposite our place.' Stef struggled to get the words out. She knew how it would sound. 'That's where I'll be starting my interior design work.'

She could see the weirdness of it registering on Hannah's face. As their dad and Heath entered the kitchen together, Stef reset her expression.

'Just wondering if we have five minutes before dinner?' her dad asked. 'I want to show Heath my new woodwork tools.' He put a hand on Heath's shoulder. 'I'm taking requests, matey,' he said. 'I can make you anything your heart desires. As long as it's made of wood.'

'Sure, Dad,' Stef told him.

Heath stepped sideways and her dad's hand dropped to his side. As they exited the kitchen, Heath looked back. The eye roll was unmistakeable.

'Wasn't it just months ago that Dad taking Heath into the shed would have thrilled him?' Stef asked.

'Yeah, that's a fair call,' Hannah answered. 'But I guess everyone has their off days. Even Heath.'

'There's so much going on that I can hardly focus on Heath,' Stef told Hannah. 'I mean, it pales into insignificance compared with his sister. Rosie is mixing with troubled kids, Han. They vape. Probably smoke dope. I don't know what to do about it.'

Hannah rested her head on Stef's shoulder. 'You know, I was just thinking that Rosie seems less ... prickly. Maybe she's found her tribe? A joint here and there doesn't constitute high crime – even if that's the gossip around Burwood. And Rosie was never going to be an average private-school teen.'

Hannah lifted her head. 'I think you should give her some freedom, Steffie,' she said. 'Rosie will find her own way.' She turned towards the rice cooker, but not before Stef saw a glistening in her eyes. 'Because she has two very loving, very available parents. Like we did. Like we do.'

It was so heartfelt that it slammed Stef in the chest. She'd never really considered it in this light before because Rosie and Hannah were very different, but Hannah definitely hadn't been a run-of-the-mill teen either. Maybe it gave her more insight at this point. And she was spot-on about Rosie's mood tonight.

'Thank you,' Stef said. In a ritual from their youth she reached out and pinched her sister's arm and was rewarded with a flick of the tea towel.

'Also, I'm looking for a sperm donor. I want to start IVF.'

The way Hannah tacked on that enormous revelation so casually struck Stef as hilarious. Her laughter set Hannah off too, and it was a while before either of them could speak.

'Can I help pick the donor?' Stef finally managed. 'Because I'm thinking Sven from Iceland. Who happens to be a brain surgeon and a philanthropist.'

'I guess I would consider Sven.' Hannah smiled. 'Stef, I'm so glad we ...'

Suddenly, Rosie stomped into the kitchen. Any trace of her previous calm and contented demeanour had completely evaporated. Her face was ablaze with fury.

'You promised, Mum!' she spat.

CHAPTER FORTY-EIGHT

Alex had only moved a few pieces of furniture into the penthouse. He hadn't intended on spending time there until the renovations were complete. But here he was, armchair pulled onto the balcony, Scotch in hand. In this pivotal moment, it felt important to stay close.

There never was a business meeting in Canberra. Or, more accurately, his discussion with the Minister for Finance had taken place on Zoom. Alex would never miss a ritual dinner with his new family, especially not the first one since Margaret's stroke.

But he had believed that arriving late and unexpectedly would give the Fidlers a moment to collectively appreciate what he had done for them. The upgrades he had introduced into each of their lives. It had given him pleasure to think of Hannah, Stef and the children walking up the ramp he had organised for Margaret, satisfaction to imagine them recognising the changed photo gallery as a reflection of the new order. At the time of their arrival, one of the top-notch nurses he'd employed would still have been there.

There had been little doubt that conversation would spring from the seeds Alex had sown. That their gratitude would be lifted higher when Stef shared the news she'd be working for him. Celebrated further when Hannah let them know he had enrolled in her course. Alex had dared to expect he would be entering the house on a cloud of accolades.

But.

The disgrace that was Rosie Simmons ruined it. Swiftly. Immediately.

'What are you doing here?' the ungrateful little bitch had demanded. 'Can't we have a single night together without you, weirdo? Can't you just stay away?'

Oh, and they all tried to shut her up, but the girl was on a roll. Issued forth with the clincher Alex would not forget. Nor forgive.

'You. Will. Never. Be. Part. Of. This. Family.'

'Stop, Rosie!' Heath had screamed and gone to stand at Alex's side. The solidarity was duly noted, but it couldn't remedy the evening's catastrophe. Less than half an hour after his arrival, Alex had left. Down the ramp he'd commissioned for Margaret's welfare and into his hire car, leaving the debris behind.

He'd seen Stef's car pull into the street at nine fifteen, then this sleepy suburb momentarily rocked by the ugly fight between her and Rosie. It was interesting that Heath turned and looked up. Given that it was dark and his lights were off, the boy couldn't have known that Alex was there, on the balcony.

But perhaps, like himself, Heath had intuition.

Alex took a sip of Scotch. There were several missed calls on his phone. From Margaret. From Hannah. From Stef. Now, though, most likely the Fidlers would be hoping for a good night's sleep and some resolution in the light of day.

Alex scrolled through the photos on his phone, coming to the pictures of Rosie and her gang of fools. He'd had time to deeply consider how best to employ the resources in his library. He zoomed in on the curly-haired boy his niece clearly had a crush on and took a screenshot.

Rosie was resolutely blocking access to the role Alex deserved in the Fidler family. Casting shadows on the veneration he had earned.

Alex could not sit back and tolerate the dissension anymore.

It was time to act.

CHAPTER FORTY-NINE

When her sister called, Hannah was drafting essay questions on *Breath*. It was very Stef to assume because she had two weeks' holiday before she started working for Alex, that Hannah also had time to pick up during business hours. Hannah didn't call her out on it though, because it felt good to be connected with Stef again.

'Have you heard from Alex?' Hannah asked.

'We've texted,' Stef replied, 'but I haven't seen him in person since the apocalypse. Have you?'

'Not in person either,' she said. 'But you know how I went to that Monash IVF information evening last night?'

'Oh my God, I'd forgotten. How was it?'

'Fine,' Hannah answered. 'Really just preliminary stuff I mostly knew. But, Stef, afterwards a nurse told me that should I wish to go ahead, they had been supplied credit card details for as many rounds of treatment as might be needed. By someone called Anonymous.'

'Wow,' Stef said. 'So even though he probably thinks Rosie is devil's spawn at the moment, Alex is up for helping another niece or nephew come into the family. Does that influence whether you'll go ahead with IVF?'

'It actually does, Stef,' Hannah admitted. 'It means that I may be able to afford to hold on to the house. I could pay Rex out and take extended maternity leave. But I do wonder about the strings attached.'

'Fuck the strings attached,' Stef said. 'However it might look, it'll be worth it when you hold your baby.'

Oh God, it was ridiculous, as though the hormones were already flowing, because Hannah had to blink back a tear.

'How's Rosie?' she managed.

Hannah could hear Stef opening the sliding doors. She could visualise her walking out into the jungle of her backyard where Rosie had shot that poor tawny frogmouth.

'She's been okay, actually,' Stef said. 'It's probably just a temporary ceasefire, but the episode at Mum and Dad's seems to have cleared her out. I hope Alex can move past it. I will tell you this though, after what she did I'm definitely not going to broach the subject of him resigning on my behalf.

'I think you're right about Rosie finally finding her tribe, Han,' Stef continued. 'It's always been such a battle for her to fit in. So, I'm taking your advice and giving her some freedom. Weirdly though, it's Heath who's got me more puzzled now. He seems to have ditched the friendship group he's been part of for years, which is fine – I know it happens all the time in primary school. But the kid he's started hanging with, Luca, is the same kid he used to say was a bully ... Han? Are you there?'

Rex was at the open door to her office, mi[...]

'I have to go, Stef,' Hannah said.

'Your sister,' he said, after Hannah hung up. 'I always [...] Stef. She has a lot of heart.'

Hannah scratched her forehead. Rex would never apply such a description to her.

'When you lose a partner, you lose their family,' he continued, and there he was, pulling the chair out from Professor Darbandi's desk next to hers. 'I know that's no major revelation, but I want you to understand it's a sadness I carry.'

Hannah didn't much care about the sadness Rex carried. Especially since it was so well camouflaged when any of his plethora of admirers was around.

'How are things with your new brother?' he asked.

'Well, he's hardly new. And he's fitting in seamlessly,' Hannah lied. 'He's added an extra dimension to all our lives.'

Rex picked up Professor Darbandi's coveted fountain pen and twirled it.

'Do you ever wonder who sent that anonymous complaint about Katrina?' he asked. 'It's just that there was a rumour going around that she was venting about Alex being rude a couple of days before it was lodged.'

Hannah suspected that the link Rex was making was solid. But she shook her head. Because he was also right about not being part of their family anymore. 'Rex, why are you here?' she countered, and he actually had the cheek to look hurt.

'We need to agree on a date for the auction, Han,' he said.

'I'm having second thoughts about that,' she replied.

'Are you thinking private sale?'

'I'm thinking I might buy you out,' Hannah said.

Rex leaned back in the office chair. 'I'm surprised you'd want to live there without me,' he said, and Hannah widened her eyes at the arrogance. 'I wouldn't want to live there without you,' he concluded.

And there was the sucker punch.

Silence.

'If you want to get three valuations, we can talk about it,' Rex said finally. 'I know your financial situation, Han, so I have to assume you'll be borrowing a fair slug of money to make this happen. And maybe it's not my business, but I'm going to say it anyway – if that fair slug of money is from your brother, don't take it.'

'I agree,' Hannah said, standing up now, 'that it's none of your business.'

Looking at Rex's back, his slumped shoulders, Hannah could see a trace of the sadness he carried. Perhaps there was a genuine residue of concern there too. But there was no love anymore. Not even from her end.

Hannah got back to work.

CHAPTER FIFTY

'Luca Demarte is a total dick, Heath,' Rosie said. As soon as Stef entered the kitchen she wanted to turn around and walk back out.

'He's a bully. Just like his sister was in my year. Why would you want to hang out with a kid like that?'

Heath poured himself an afternoon bowl of cereal with a studied nonchalance Stef had never witnessed on him.

'Why do you care?' he replied.

'Because it's stupid,' Rosie insisted. 'I mean, that kid stole lunch money from a preppie.'

'You don't know that,' Heath said. 'It's just something Luca was accused of. No one ever proved it.' He picked up his bowl and made a move down the hallway.

'Don't walk away!' Rosie demanded. 'Mum, make him listen.'

'Okay, guys,' Stef said, 'let's be calm about this. What is the point you're trying to make, Rosie?'

'The point?' she echoed, looking at Stef as though she was a complete fool. 'The point is that Heath wants to be a bully. He thinks it's cool. And it's probably because he's learning the ropes from your horrible brother.'

Stef blanched. 'What do you mean by that, Rosie?' she demanded.

'Oh yeah,' she said. 'Heath just *forgot* to mention that Alex has been picking him up from school pretty much every day lately. Isn't that right, Heath?'

He shrugged. 'Why *should* I mention it? Relax. It's no big deal.' He paused and milk slopped over the sides of the bowl. 'And I don't care what you think, because you're a loser, Rosie.'

Stef ran a dishcloth under hot water. By the time she got to the splash of milk on the floorboards, Heath was heading upstairs to his room. She took a deep breath. It was a little disturbing that he hadn't mentioned getting rides home from school with Alex. Just months ago, her son would have given her a blow-by-blow account of everything that happened in his day.

'Are you seriously going to let that little shit call me a loser?' Rosie demanded, hands on hips, hovering above Stef as she crouched to wipe the spill.

'Rosie,' Stef said, standing up, 'I seem to recall you flinging that word at your brother many times. You might not like it, but Heath is allowed to choose his friends. And to have a relationship with his uncle. There's no need to get so riled.'

'There's no need to get so riled,' Rosie mimicked. 'Well, guess what? I *am* riled. You're so stupid, Mum. Your whole family are like … jellyfish. Blobbing around, never taking a stand while a shark just swims in, ready to take you all. I hate it here. I hate you.'

The cloth was too saturated. A stinkier version of spilt milk dripped back onto the floorboards.

Rosie hated her.

It felt true.

'I'm going to live with Dad and Prue,' Rosie finished.

●

'So, how do you feel about gold calacatta in all the bathrooms?' Stef asked, showing Alex images on her iPad. 'I have a quote.'

'I feel great about gold calacatta, if you do,' Alex said, glancing at the quote without seeming to register, or care about, the price.

'And I think the Christopher Boots Prometheus decorative pendants would be divine in the lounge,' Stef said. 'But there are heaps of other options on the website. And, of course, they are expensive.'

'They're perfect,' Alex said.

Stef walked from the kitchen to the lounge. 'We could mix it up here,' she said. 'Have most of the lighting emanate from recesses and pelmets. Or would you prefer a chandelier to remind you of Hughesdale? Maybe a modern version?'

Alex tapped his heart. 'I don't need a reminder of Hughesdale,' he said. 'I'll still be there at least half the time after these renovations are complete. So let's ditch the copy chandelier idea and go with some original Stef Fidler.'

'Well, that's a relief, cos I don't think Burwood has seen chandeliers for some time,' Stef quipped to draw his attention away from the warmth that rose in her cheeks.

Alex's return smile was rewarding. There was no doubt he'd been hurt by Rosie's comment at her mum and dad's dinner a couple of weeks back. But things were slowly returning to an equilibrium. After Stef's initial apology, Alex hadn't referred to the incident and she wasn't about to reopen old wounds.

'An automated system might be the way to go to control the lighting and other electrical devices. I think we may be able to extend it onto the rooftop garden too. You could operate the spa and night lights up there remotely.'

'That would work.'

Again, Alex didn't flinch at the price tag. Stef was going to be able to perform wonders. This truly was her dream job. And though she wouldn't say it aloud, she'd been glad to begin it without Rosie's presence in her house. As usual, her daughter was doing a fabulous job at maintaining the rage. She'd been with Liam and Prue for over a week. When Stef rang, Rosie didn't pick up. When she texted, no response. Eventually Stef would have to find a way to bridge the gap between them, but for now, she was appreciating the respite.

Back in the kitchen, Stef opened a small Perrier for Alex and then one for herself.

'I feel the need to pinch myself,' she told her brother. 'Thanks for this opportunity. I just ...'

In the pocket of her Ginger and Smart dress, Stef's phone buzzed.

'Is Rosie with you?' Liam asked straight up when she answered.

'No,' Stef said. 'Why?'

'Prue just got a call from PLC thanking her for leaving a message on the absentee line this morning. The woman said she was checking in to see if Rosie was feeling better and was likely to be in tomorrow for her class excursion to the museum.'

An involuntary shudder ran down Stef's spine as she stepped onto the balcony.

'The thing is,' Liam continued, and for Liam, it was almost a rant, 'Prue didn't call the absentee line this morning. Rosie wasn't sick. I'm guessing she just wagged for the day, but, Stef ...' He cleared his throat. 'There was a row last night. Rosie insisted she wanted to live here permanently. I told her no. I said we couldn't break the custody agreement. I was worried about your brother sicking lawyers onto us. Cos the prick threatened me. Did you know that, Stef?'

'I'll call you back.'

She walked briskly through the penthouse to the elevator, shadowed by her brother. As she crossed the street to her house, she almost broke into a run. Heath said he hadn't seen Rosie. Stef looked in every room. There was no trace of her daughter having been there recently. And Rosie always left a trace.

Stef's heart raced as she opened the sliding doors to the backyard, Alex still right by her side. Rosie must have been furious. Hurt. She must have felt so rejected. She would have stewed on it all night. Stef could sense the danger of those feelings pulsing in her own veins.

Above her, the sky was darkening.

Her daughter, her baby, was thirteen years old.

Stef picked up her phone. 'Rosie isn't here. She isn't at my place,' she told Liam.

'Steffie,' he said in a choked voice. 'Rosie's phone is switched off.'

CHAPTER FIFTY-ONE

A couple of hours ago, the fraught gathering at Stef's had seemed an overreaction. If Rosie wanted to punish her parents, disappearing was the way to do it. But as the clock ticked past 11 pm, Hannah's discomfort started to rise in sharp increments.

Alex was pacing the hallway making call after call with no opportunity for interruption, so Hannah chose English Breakfast for him. Earl Grey for her parents. She handed the chamomile to Stef, accompanied with cliches she seemed powerless to stop.

'Rosie will be okay.'

'Any moment, she'll walk through that door. Or she'll go back to Liam and Prue's.'

'Maybe her phone ran out of battery and she's just with a friend.'

The supposed calming effects of chamomile weren't working because Stef slammed down her mug.

'Rosie would *never* let her phone run out of battery,' she snapped. 'She's thirteen years old. It's her lifeline. She has a portable charger! And if she is with a friend, well that's not much comfort, Hannah. I know almost nothing about her friends since, stupidly, I decided to follow your advice to give her "freedom".' Stef made air quotes with her fingers.

Hannah had to work hard to withstand the blow. She wobbled backwards as Stef answered her phone and put Liam on speaker.

'The police have been here,' he said. 'Prue and I have filed a missing person's report. They're going to send you a list of questions too. Fill out the answers as soon as you can.'

Liam paused and Hannah could feel the ravages of his flood of emotions even over the phone. 'Tell your brother,' he said, but no one would need to tell Alex anything because he was emerging from the hallway, 'that this is on him. I would never have told my baby ...' Liam had to stop and collect himself before continuing. 'I would never have told my baby she couldn't live with us if he hadn't threatened to mount a custody battle if we mixed up the routine.'

Hannah suddenly felt nauseous. Liam had his shortcomings, but he didn't deserve that. She looked at Alex askance, but there was no reply in his expression, only undivided attention to the situation at hand. Her phone ticked over to 11.21 pm. She hadn't noticed that Heath had slipped out of the lounge, but now he was shadowing Alex as his uncle took the phone from her.

When Alex spoke, it was for all of them to hear.

'It may give you relief, Liam, to deflect blame. So I'm factoring that in, given the circumstances. But make no mistake, mate.'

Hannah had never heard Alex use the familiar Aussie word. From his lips, it was anything but endearing.

'I make no apologies for helping Stef impose a little order on the chaos you engender.' There was no emotion in Alex's voice. It was even. Reasonable. 'And a gentle reminder, Liam, that Rosie was in your custody when she disappeared.' There was nothing gentle about that reminder.

Marg leaned into Jim and he hugged her.

'Now, you go and see if you can fill out any more questionnaires for the police. I will employ my own resources to find your daughter.'

There was no reply from Liam.

'I've been speaking with a friend,' he said, not missing a beat. Addressing Stef but encompassing everyone with the scan of his eyes. 'Minh Nguyen is an excellent private investigator. The best of the best. She tells me that Rosie's phone was last switched off in Berwick just after six this evening.'

'But why would she be in Berwick?' Stef's voice was shaky. 'That's ages away from here. And it was over five hours ago.'

For a moment Hannah thought her sister was going to collapse. She moved towards her but Alex got there first. He half-carried her to a free armchair.

'I've sent Minh some pictures of the kids Rosie has been associating with,' he said, and his proactiveness made Hannah feel completely incompetent. 'She has the name and address of a boy in Rosie's group.'

Alex's keys were on the hook in the kitchen. He retrieved them and took his coat off the stand.

'Kid's name is Jordon Stokes. He's been in the foster system for three years. He's currently placed with a family in Burwood

East. Minh was able to get his mobile number. We're going to meet with him now,' Alex said. 'See if we can find any leads.'

'I'll come,' Hannah said at the same time as Stef. Jinx.

Alex shook his head. 'Stef,' he said sternly, 'you need to be here in case Rosie turns up.' He looked at Hannah. 'And you must be here for Stef, Margaret and Jim.'

He said it as though it was a no-brainer. As though all other options were off the table. But something in Hannah wanted to resist. She had been a rebel teen herself – yes, it was a long time ago, but perhaps she was the most well-equipped to extract leads from this Jordon boy.

'I will let you all know what's happening every step of the way until we find her,' Alex said.

He seemed to emanate assurance that he and his private investigator would find Rosie. And, perhaps unfairly, Hannah wondered whether he already knew something they didn't. Alex seemed to read her thoughts. When he looked at her again, his eyes were hard.

'Look after your family, Hannah,' he said.

CHAPTER FIFTY-TWO

Jordon's foster mother looked like a full night's sleep had long since been a realistic expectation. When Alex made the mistake of resting an elbow on the Laminex table, the sleeve of his jacket came away sticky.

The kid was as thick as a brick. Alex would have liked to fast-forward, but everything needed to be done meticulously.

'Has Rosie ever mentioned a favourite place? Somewhere she might go when feeling troubled?' Minh asked Jordon.

'Nah.' Jordon shrugged. 'Well, Rosie likes the skate park, but not, like, at midnight. There's no lights on there now.'

'Right,' Alex said. 'Good point.'

The kid was clearly unused to positive reinforcement. He sat a little straighter.

'Has anyone different come around your group lately? Perhaps a new friend?' Minh asked.

'Nah,' Jordon said, a blond curl obscuring one eye. 'Rosie's the newest in our gang. We don't just let anyone in.'

Alex had to suppress a smile.

'Okay. But has there been anyone you guys don't normally communicate with making contact?' Minh asked.

'Nah,' Jordon said. Then, finally, a flash of possibility in his eyes. 'Well, there was one chick, actually. About a week ago.'

'And how did this woman make contact?' Minh prompted.

'She just come up to us and gave us a card. Said stuff about there always being somewhere to go if you've got problems at home. A safe house for teenagers. She was some kind of do-gooder, like, a social worker or something.'

'What did she look like?' Minh asked.

'I dunno. Just like a normal lady I s'pose. I remember she had grey hair even though she didn't seem that old. But she had a hat and big sunglasses on so I couldn't see her face, really.'

'Jordon, there would never be a business card for a real safe house,' Minh said. 'The whole idea is that the location remains secret. You understand that, right?'

It was clear that until that moment, Jordon hadn't given it a thought.

'It's okay, love, you weren't to know,' said the foster mother.

'Then what? Why? Shit. Was it a trap? Is Rosie going to be okay?'

'She will be,' Alex said soothingly. And honestly, Jordon's care factor was touching. Alex would make sure the kid escaped any implication of wrongdoing.

'Who took a card from the woman?' Minh asked.

'Just Rosie and me,' Jordon said.

Bingo.

'Do you happen to have kept that card?'

'Nah, I binned it.'

Alex's heart dropped.

'I'm not that good with faces,' Jordon said after a few beats. 'But I got a photographic memory.'

•

Jordon hadn't been able to recall a phone number, but he had trotted out the address with ease.

'This one,' Alex told Minh as they arrived in her car. It was a large white stucco house in a leafy Berwick street. Properties spaced for privacy. Front yards well-tended.

'There's no lights on,' Minh observed. 'I've tried to do a search on the title, but the house is listed under a shelf company. If you can wait another fifteen minutes, I might be able to find out who the silent directors are. Perhaps even why they're silent.'

'No, Minh,' Alex insisted. 'That's of no use to me. If my niece is in there, if my darling Rosie is being held against her will, there's no time to waste. I'm going in.'

'We have no evidence that Rosie is being held hostage,' Minh said. She pointed to the boards covering the front windows. 'And it looks like it's locked up tight. How do you plan to get inside?'

In response, Alex retrieved the tyre iron from Minh's boot. 'Like this,' he said urgently, holding it up outside the open driver's window.

Minh placed her hands in prayer position. 'I would advise strongly against that, Alex,' she said. 'If you're right about Rosie being held in there, breaking in could be dangerous. I suggest we call the police.'

Alex resisted an eye roll. He wished he could just cut to the chase, but of course, she was only doing her job.

'This could be a matter of life or death, Minh,' he said. 'I'm not waiting for the police and your help would be greatly appreciated. So, are you in or out?'

•

The stairs were wide. Generous. Alex ascended them first.

The double doors were mahogany, flanked by frosted sidelights. The brass knocker, a lion with a magnificent mane. King of the jungle. As he banged it against the door, Alex felt the adrenaline kick in. Flight was for cowards. Always fight.

'Rosie!' he yelled loudly enough for neighbours to hear. 'Rosie, sweetie, are you in there?'

There was no answer. Alex repeated the action. The words.

'Listen,' Minh said.

Perhaps his thumping heart had drowned it out. It was faint, almost other-worldly, but it was a cry for help.

Given that he had a perfectly good key, it was a shame to smash one of those lovely frosted panels. But he needed to make sure this unfolded correctly.

Upon the first strike, a large crack appeared.

Alex could not wait to stride into the chaos of Stef's house with Rosie in tow. Into the atmosphere of pent-up emotion and crippling inactivity. Into Stef's guilt and Hannah's residual, hurtful distrust. Into the collective self-disgust of having been part of the problem that propelled Rosie to an uncertain fate.

From that moment, Alex would forever be the solution.

Upon the second strike, the glass shattered. They could hear Rosie more clearly now, though what she was saying made no sense. Just a repeated plea for something to 'stay away'.

It was poetic that the third strike made it possible for Alex to climb through into the house. He immediately opened the door for Minh. It was imperative that she witness it all. When they reported back, Minh was to be the voice of the chorus.

There was a desk and a couple of chairs at the front of the house, but otherwise it was empty of furniture. Rosie wasn't in sight, but it was easy now to follow the sounds.

And there she was. Crouched in the enclave at the back of the desk. Agitated. Batting away some unseen ghouls. Spiders, perhaps? Alex had heard of that happening on a bad trip. If it had been within his power, he would have planted pockets of pleasantness in her hallucinations. He really would have.

Alex squatted in front and Minh stood behind.

'Rosie,' he said. 'Honey, you're safe now.'

•

'Of course it's a great relief that we found Rosie,' Minh said. 'The reunion, as you can imagine, was quite an emotional scene. It could definitely have been a worse outcome without Mr Carpenter's bravery and determination.'

Minh kept speaking but all eyes were on Alex. The welling of tears. Hearts swollen with pure gratitude. Doubts annihilated. He was the saviour. The conquering hero. Lauded by all. Respected. Admired.

From now on, he would be untouchable. Inescapable.

Finally, Alex was The Brother he deserved to be.

EPILOGUE

Three Years Later

Compared with his uncle's, Heath's house seemed kind of pathetic. Embarrassing. If he had friends over, he preferred to bring them here. Just over a week ago, in the spa on the rooftop garden, he'd got to second base with Brigid Zimmer. Heath was the first boy in Year Eight to achieve what all the others dreamed of, but he wasn't going to crow about it. Unless she'd told girlfriends, only he and Brigid knew.

Heath opened one of the Cokes Alex had left for him. His uncle was going to be in Adelaide on business for another week. As usual, he'd locked his study, but Heath had found that key ages ago. It had been disappointingly easy. The underside of one of the marble basins in the ensuite was a pretty basic spot.

The desktop password, though, had eluded him for several months. Heath turned on the Mac. Since his last attempt, Alex had changed the screensaver. Gone was the whole family photo from last Christmas at Hughesdale, replaced with an image of Alex at the Botanic Gardens, Raphael riding on his shoulders, his little hands clasping his uncle's neck.

Heath's toddler cousin, with his always messy ginger hair, green eyes and just the right number of freckles, sucked attention from everyone in the family. But Alex was obsessed. The kid only needed to open his mouth to score a round of applause.

Heath had a sudden urge to shut the computer down again. Actually, to smash it would be more satisfying. But he did neither. Because being impetuous might feel good in the short term, but he had to stay disciplined to pursue the big picture.

It wasn't for Rosie's sake that Heath was driven to find the missing puzzle pieces from the day she disappeared. She was easier to live with than she used to be. Her meds made her calm and way less bitchy, though he stayed away from her when she got those weird flashbacks.

Over time, though, while everyone else's curiosity had faded, Heath's had ramped up. Instinct told him that Alex knew more about that day than he'd fessed up to. Since the rescue, his top status in the family had been cemented. Unquestioned. No one made the smallest of decisions without consulting him. And even though Alex's over-the-top adoration of Raphael seemed an indication that he was losing his edge, Heath still had great respect for his uncle.

But, if there was evidence, it was possible Heath could find it on Alex's computer.

Raphael's initials and date of birth. Backwards. 12025071FJR. Bingo.

•

A week before Rosie disappeared, when she'd run away to their dad's, a stranger had randomly given her a card with the address of a supposed safe house. Heath would have suspected something was off, but clueless Rosie had swallowed the bait. And nobody had ever found out who'd set it.

The number of business files on Alex's Mac was beyond impressive. Heath wished they'd teach actual life skills at Scotch College instead of the useless bullshit they fed the students. Alex's investments were diverse – stuff Heath's loser father in his rental house knew nothing about. Mines. Share portfolios. What interested Heath most though were the properties. This penthouse was just a tiny drop in Alex's ocean.

His sister had regurgitated the story many times. Rosie had taken two trains from Burwood to Berwick and the supposed safe house. A middle-aged woman with greyish hair and brown eyes had welcomed her. She'd poured Rosie a glass of orange Powerade from a jug and enquired kindly about her circumstances. They'd sat in the foyer while Rosie spewed out her list of petty grievances.

Half an hour or so later, Rosie began to feel woozy. She started to question why stalactites were hanging from the ceiling. Why a monkey was clambering over the desk. Every time she'd told that bit, Heath had to suppress a grin. God, his sister had been such a sucker. He would have known straightaway that he'd been drugged. Anyway, the way she told it, the monkey stole her phone and disappeared. Rosie searched for the woman who'd greeted her, but she was gone too. Every door and window was locked. Impenetrable.

Over the next few hours, Rosie's hallucinations ramped up. The foyer became a jungle. Wild animals roamed, more stalactites dropped from the ceiling piercing anything in their path. One went through the beak of a pelican and out the other side. Blah, blah, blah. Unable to discern what was real, Rosie had taken refuge under the desk, where she was found and rescued by Alex and Minh. Tests had confirmed there was LSD in her system. Cops had checked the Berwick house but there was no trace of the woman she'd mentioned, not even a fingerprint. Maybe she'd been wearing gloves? Or maybe Rosie had imagined her. They'd checked the deed to the Berwick house, but it was owned by a shelf company and the directors were silent.

Heath knew that Alex was a silent director of several shelf companies. He understood that transparency was not always the best way to do business. Alex wasn't one to crow about his achievements either.

With a bit more effort, the cops could have got to the bottom of who owned the house, but they'd lost interest when Rosie was found.

A folder called 'Library'! Heath recalled the advice his uncle had given him just after he'd bought the building. *Having secrets in my library is like insurance*, Alex had told him and he'd felt so special that he still remembered it word for word. He hovered his mouse over the folder, enjoying the anticipation.

There were so many subfolders. In time, Heath would explore each thoroughly. It would be a thrill to go through the one labelled H. J. S. – Heath Justin Simmons. But for now, he would remain on task. He clicked on the folder labelled R. G. S. – Rosie Grace Simmons. The first file, 'Profile', was dull. Rosie's birthdate, report cards, medical history.

The next – labelled 'Life Lessons' – struck Heath as way more interesting. There were a few photos of Rosie hanging out at the skate park with a bunch of losers. An enlarged picture of Jordon, the kid Alex and Minh had interviewed who supposedly tipped them off about the address of the safe house. Heath flicked through to the next shot and gasped.

The card that had supposedly never been seen by anyone but Jordon and Rosie was right there, onscreen.

Safe House for teens with domestic issues.

You will be welcome any time, 24 hours.

36 Henley Street

Berwick, Vic. 3806

But wait, there was more.

The next picture was of a young woman with prematurely grey hair and brown eyes. Underneath was the name *Natasha Vronsky*.

Alongside the photo, dated on the morning of the day Rosie disappeared, was a screenshot of an email.

It's time to go to the house. If the girl turns up, you know what to do. All going to plan, a glowing character reference from Carpenter Enterprises will be in your inbox tomorrow. Best of luck with your upcoming trial. Alex Carpenter.

It was already more than enough.

He rose from the office chair and walked around the penthouse, appreciating it with new eyes. Alex could, theoretically, transfer the title. Heath would be happy to be a silent director. He wasn't after external validation. This was about personal satisfaction.

Secrets truly were the key to building success. Now he had the juiciest one in his own library. The big decision was how best to utilise collected information. That was what required the skill.

The question was: What would Alex do?

ACKNOWLEDGEMENTS

I started this story several years ago, spurred on by my long-term collaborator in children's and YA fiction, Meredith Badger. Nan McNab and Andrea Mayes also gave their time and expertise generously.

Hilary Rogers helped whip the first part of the manuscript into shape for submission, creating a pitch that made me want to read the book immediately.

In 2019, I shared excerpts of *The Half Brother* with Antoni Jach's Novel Writing Workshop Masterclass XXV, receiving invaluable feedback from a talented and focused group.

In later drafts, Jacinta Halloran, Thalia Kalkipsakis and Melissa Thurgood gave me the almost unquantifiable gift of seeing the manuscript from angles that hadn't occurred to me. I hope I didn't bore you to tears, but if I did, it was worth it.

Sandy Grant, a wonderful supporter of Australian books and authors, saw fit to pass the manuscript to Alex Craig. It's been a luxury and a learning curve to work with such a skilled and generous publisher on my first novel for adults. I've enjoyed every minute and already want to go again.

Meticulous editing by Dianne Blacklock and Alisa Ahmed opened my eyes to many shortcomings in my work, sparing the reader from finding out for themselves. I'm so grateful to all at

Ultimo Press and feel privileged to join such a professional team and an amazing stable of authors.

Many thanks to Maryrose Cuskelly, Vikki Wakefield and Jacinta Halloran, whose own books I admire so much, for the thoughtful endorsements.

Mum and Dad, my champions always, thank you for introducing me to a life-long passion for reading and writing.

To Jack, Billie and Hugo, I love you more. No returns.

Marty, husband extraordinaire, I could never have written this book without your support. Thanks for letting me lean on you when I couldn't be strong.

Christine Keighery (who also writes as Chrissie Perry) is the author of more than thirty-five novels for children and Young Adults. Chrissie wrote thirteen books in the hugely successful *Go Girl!* series. Her young adult title, *Whisper*, won a White Raven and IBBY award and was shortlisted for the CBCA and the WA Premier's Awards. Her work has been published in ten countries, including the US, the UK, Spain, Brazil, Slovenia and Korea.

Christine divides her time between coastal Fairhaven and Southbank, Victoria.

The Half Brother is her first novel for adults.